SAVAGE

AN ASH PARK NOVEL

MEGHAN O'FLYNN

PYGMALION
PUBLISHING

SAVAGE

Copyright 2020

Distributed by Pygmalion Publishing, LLC

For the lost. The broken. The grieving. The healing.

Want more from Meghan?
https://meghanoflynn.com

"WE ARE ALL READY TO BE SAVAGE IN SOME CAUSE. THE DIFFERENCE BETWEEN A GOOD MAN AND A BAD ONE IS THE CHOICE OF THE CAUSE."
~WILLIAM JAMES

1

THE COBBLESTONES in the alleyway were sharp as tacks beneath the soles of her boots, not that Regina Jackson was particularly bothered by that little bit of discomfort. Everything hurt lately, her eyes aching from the moment she awoke—her bones felt sore like they were straining to burst from their tendon prison but were just too damn exhausted to follow through. That was how Petrosky felt every damn day if you believed his bellyaching, but she didn't have time to feel bad; she'd spent yesterday trying to get her son set up with a new caregiver. He'd headbutted the last one. She loved him, loved him with all her heart and soul, but people didn't like to talk about the hardship that went along with special needs. The pain. The abject terror of what might happen when you were gone. And in her line of work, that possibility was always a little closer than she liked.

A breeze hissed up the alley, bringing with it the subtle tang of rot, sweet and bitter, the fragrance like grass clippings and cut tulips tossed into a pile of long-stagnant water. It was possible that was exactly what the stink was—she couldn't see much past the enormous set of dumpsters that blocked half the alley, and the bricks on either side of the crumbling cobblestone walkway seemed to be grappling with the clouds. But though she couldn't see the police cars, she knew they were there; red and blue lights flashed maniacally against the dumpsters, the reflection turning the metal sides into pulsing strobes—no grass on the breeze now. Just the stench of decaying flowers, like someone had dumped perfume into a sewer. She sidestepped a particularly large puddle of black water, the top shiny, reds and blues dancing on the top like fireworks on a dark lake. She was still squinting at it when her feet splashed into another puddle, sending a spray of gray water over the tops of her boots and the cuffs of her navy suit pants. *Just great.* She stomped a little extra hard past the strobing dumpsters. *Click-thunk. Click-thunk-squish.*

The far end of the alley came into focus first—a line of cruisers and crime tape and barrel-chested officers just itching to get the first glance at whatever mess waited for her on the other side of the trash bins. She paused. A car? The little green Fusion sat tucked behind the dumpsters, unassuming like a wart on a toad. A bumper sticker that said "Life is Better with a Beard" adorned the back window, a sign Petrosky would surely take to mean whatever hipster lay inside had deserved to die slowly. But it didn't look as if this was the case. The victim lay prone beside the back door on a piece of thick plastic sheeting, his shirt soaked in ruby, his blue eyes wide to the clouds. Bloody hands grasped at nothing, crimson nails facing upward as if prepared to accept some offering that would never be enough to repair the gash that bisected his throat—his neck had been slashed open like a gaping secondary smile. Beneath the neat lines of his close-cropped facial hair, both the carotid and the jugular appeared to have been severed; even the pale tube of esophageal tissue was slashed. The hair along his jaw was stained with gore. It wouldn't have taken long to bleed out from a wound like that; unconsciousness would have claimed him within a minute, probably much less. Efficiency was the name of this killer's game.

She sidestepped the body and peered through the open back door into the car's interior—a fast-food bag on the floorboards, a few slips that looked like receipts. But no blood. She drew back and frowned at the body, at the plastic sheeting beneath the man where wide swaths of red marred the opaque material—smears, but nothing that resembled spray. She scanned the walls of brick, the dumpster, the cobblestones, but she saw no signs of struggle, no splatters of red. The victim hadn't been killed here. Premeditated, probably, a bloody mess, absolutely, but Decantor had sounded strange on the phone, too tense for this to be a standard homicide. What was she missing?

"Thanks for coming."

She looked over. Decantor was approaching from behind the crime tape at the far end of the alley, breaking from the pack of uniforms for the twenty feet of vacant cobbles between them. No one with him to jostle the cup of coffee he held in one hand, no one to knock the manila folder he carried in the other. But...that was strange too, wasn't it? Why weren't there techs here scrambling for evidence? Maybe he'd been waiting for her—it was always good to get a peek at the scene before the techs started picking things up. Helped you get into the mind of your suspect. She stepped around the body and met Decantor by the car's front bumper.

He passed her the coffee cup. "For your trouble." His voice was tight, lower than usual, as if apologizing for giving her coffee.

She nodded her thanks. "Is Petrosky on his way?"

Decantor sniffed, his eyes easing to the brick wall off to their right before coming to rest on her face. "I didn't call him."

No wonder he sounded strange. Was he trying to keep

Petrosky from getting in on this case? Did he know how far her partner had fallen? It wasn't exactly a secret. Sure, Petrosky never smelled of liquor, and he still showed up and did his job—some might argue more professionally when he had whiskey running through his veins. He even wore suit jackets these days. But it was in the eyes. In the way he talked. You had to know him well, but the signs were there. If she saw him drinking, she could justify getting him fired, could rationalize taking him away from her son. Petrosky was the only person Lance had never been violent with; her son had punched her more times than she could count, but he'd never so much as raised his voice to Petrosky.

She sipped at the coffee, trying to refocus. Decantor's gaze was tight, hard, his eyes deep pools of onyx that suddenly resembled the muddy water she'd walked through to get here. Unlike her, unlike Shannon, unlike the girls next door to Petrosky—street girls he'd adopted and put up, who seemed to look at him as a father—it appeared Decantor was done with Petrosky's bullshit. Maybe he'd already gone to the chief.

Her phone buzzed, and she dropped her eyes to the screen: her partner. *Speak of the devil.* Maybe he already knew; maybe the chief had already talked to him. But she wanted to know for certain before she called him back. "So, does Petrosky know you're boxing him out, or what?"

"I just wanted to make sure there was something to tell before we brought him in," Decantor said, too slowly. And it wasn't just his eyes or his voice; his face was drawn, his dark skin shiny with sweat. His lips, usually so easy to smile even when greeting her at a crime scene, remained downturned— anxious. There was more on his mind than not wanting to upset Petrosky, more than thinking her partner was unstable.

She frowned. "What the hell is going on, Decantor?"

He was no longer looking at her—his gaze dragged along the brick wall, then the car, and stopped on the body. The silence stretched. "You know the serial I've been working on?"

Yeah, she did. Her boyfriend—well, ex-boyfriend now—had been considering doing a book on him. Everyone loved a good serial-killer story, he'd said, but she thought it was exploitative. That it encouraged more bad guys to go out and act in the hopes that the media would write about them too. Fame was as good a motivator as any. "Didn't he go underground? It's been a year since he killed anyone, right?"

Decantor nodded. "Yeah."

She waited. So what was new? What was the problem all of a sudden? Why was she here? He had Sloan, his own partner—he didn't need her.

He sighed and shook his head. "I just can't believe no one saw it before."

"For fuck's sake, spit it out, Decantor!" She sounded like Petrosky—the old man was rubbing off on her.

Voices floated over them, the murmuring of the flatfoots beyond the crime tape…or maybe the techs were finally here. Decantor extended the manila folder, his eyes grave. "I'll let you take a look. Call it a case consultation."

She leaned closer, narrowing her eyes at the tag—the name. The world around her froze, her lungs useless and icy in her chest. *Oh fuck.*

Her phone buzzed again, the world around her started spinning once more, and she snatched the cell from her pocket. "You're too late, Decantor. I've got my own case." Was her voice shaking?

His eyes widened, the file still held aloft like a little boy with a flower for an indifferent girl. "But—"

"But nothing. You call me when you have something concrete."

No way she was playing messenger on this one.

No way in hell.

2

THREE WEEKS LATER

THE BUZZING CAME AGAIN, a persistent brainfuck that would not quit. A bee...was it a bee? A goddamn wasp, surely, here to shoot a stinger into his eye, a needle that would pierce through his gray matter. Would his brain leak onto the bed? Would he care?

Bzzzt. Bzzzt. Bzzzt.

Duke grumbled, thick lips flapping—too close. The dog's breath was warm against his neck. The side of Petrosky's face was wet. "Aw, fuck." He pushed himself to seated, wiping the slime from his grizzled jowls. "What are you doing up here anyway? You're not supposed to be on the bed."

Duke licked Petrosky's elbow, then collapsed back onto the pillow as if he hadn't heard a word of it. The phone buzzed again.

Fuck, fuck, fuck. Petrosky squinted at the night table, the vibrating phone, the half-full bottle of Jack. The digital clock read eight thirty. Yeah, on the later side, but they'd just solved a case yesterday. Another rapist in jail, getting his three hots and a cot. That bastard would be locked up for far too short a time, counting down the days until he could abuse another unsuspecting victim. Castration...that'd be better.

Bzzzzt. Bzzzzt. Bzzzzt.

Fine, asshole, fine. He reached for the nightstand, paused briefly when his fingers grazed the bottle, and then fumbled the cell to his ear. "Yeah."

"You're not just waking up, are you, you cantankerous bastard?" Jackson's voice was clear and alert. She'd probably woken up at five, worked out, eaten a sensible breakfast, taken care of her kid, and done god knew what else while he and Duke were snoring. Damn overachiever.

Petrosky tucked the cell against his shoulder and grabbed the bottle of Jack. The top made a high-pitched *zzzz* sound as it unscrewed, far more pleasant than the incessant buzzing of the phone. "Are you kidding? I've been up for hours; gotta get my pedometer steps in." The amber liquid sloshed in the bottom of the bottle—lower than he'd thought, though he didn't recall drinking it. Didn't recall much of anything last night after Shannon and the kids had left. At least he'd managed to hold it together until he was alone; fucked up though he was, he still had something worth holding on to, and things had been good, hadn't they? Great, really, having Shannon and the kids around.

The phone had gone silent. Had she hung up? "Fine, I lied about the pedomete—"

"I need you at Rita's."

He heaved himself to standing, clinging to the neck of the bottle for dear life. "I already ate."

Again, the silence stretched. The Jack sloshed. And then… clanking, like silverware against dishes, the low beeping of a walkie, and the uneasy din that could only be described as the drone of a crime scene. *Shit.* He drew the bottle to his lips and let the liquor burn down his gullet and into his belly, the warmth spreading, calming the too-fast throb of his heart. He hadn't even noticed his heart going haywire, but now the thudding broke into his temples. The world around him pulsed. "What happened?"

"Kidnapping."

Not homicide—not yet.

"If you're at Rita's...is the vic someone we know?"

A loud noise blared through the phone, the bright clang of shattering glass. "Just get your ass down here, would you?"

He opened his mouth to reply, but the phone had gone silent—Jackson was gone. He tilted the bottle back and drained it dry.

———

THE RIDE to Rita's Diner was punctuated by the stink of a breakfast burrito—Shannon had made him stop smoking "for the kids," but it was nicotine or grease, and damn if his waistline wasn't pissed at him. His heart doc would have been pissed, too, if Petrosky'd managed to make it to any of his appointments.

Black-and-whites were already parked in the nearest four spaces, Evan Scott's used Caddy wedged among them. The forensics guy was a genius, and his father, George, was Petrosky's only real friend—at least he used to be. It turned out the man had far less tolerance for bullshit than was necessary to deal with Petrosky's dumb ass. Petrosky still wasn't sure what he'd done to get the guy to finally stop calling. Not that it mattered anymore.

He grabbed his suit jacket off the passenger seat and shrugged it over his gray T-shirt as he headed across the lot, the buttons too tight to attach. Hot already. The temperate late-summer air that had kept sweat off his brow during yesterday's evening walk with Billie had vanished, replaced by the sticky ball-sweat mugginess of August. Then again, maybe the stickiness was easier to ignore when you were three shots deep as he'd been last night—he'd had only one, maybe two shots this morning. Petrosky cleared his throat, tasting the mint on his breath. Two unmarked cars in the lot besides Scott's ride: an old gray Buick and a burgundy Kia. Did one belong to the victim? Through the glass doors, he could see three, no four, other cops, positioned around the perimeter of the restaurant as if to ward off any incoming diners. One officer sat at the table near the window, a black-haired woman in a pink shirt across from him, her apron clutched absentmindedly in her hand.

He spotted Jackson just inside the glass front doors, her navy pantsuit neatly buttoned, the white of her blouse peeking between the lapels. The fluorescents blared like spotlights against her dark skin, her shorn black hair, the sharp angles of her cheekbones, her narrowed eyes. Her nostrils flared like an angry bull—agitated as hell. *Fuck.* The victim was definitely someone they knew. A cop? One of the waitresses? He tried to prepare himself, tried to guess by examining the tight contours of his partner's lips, but Jackson wasn't looking at him; her attention was focused on a spindly man wearing plastic booties. Not Scott. Must be the new guy. Petrosky had heard that Scott had managed to snag an assistant, but he had yet to meet the man, and he didn't see a reason to change that track record now.

The air smelled of charred caraway laced with the bitterness of burned garlic. Jackson glanced over as he entered, and now he could see that her eyes weren't just narrowed, weren't just agitated; they were sad. His chest constricted, but not near as much as it should have. The booze was good for that—for taking the edge off.

Jackson stepped around the plastic-footsied man to stand beside Petrosky. "Victim's name is Wilona Hyde."

His shoulders relaxed. He knew all the waitresses in this joint, and the names of most of the cops who worked at the precinct, those who might have been regulars at this place—he'd remember a name like Wilona Hyde. *Thank god.* He'd had far too many cases where the vic was someone he knew, and those investigations drove a fucking spike into his heart; it was always harder to work when you couldn't breathe.

"What was the victim doing here? Was she making early deliveries or what?"

Jackson shook her head. "Waitress, working the morning shift."

Petrosky frowned. Must be a new girl. Had she moved to town and started working here because she was running from something else—someone else? Maybe a violent ex had caught up with her. He'd seen that more times than he wanted to admit.

Jackson hooked a thumb at the long front counter, where trays of pastries beckoned from beneath glass cases. On the shelves behind the counter, a coffeepot sat dark and empty— off. "Looks like she came in at five thirty, opened the place up, put in the bagels. When help came in at seven for the breakfast rush, they found the bagels burning in the oven. And no Wilona."

That explained the burned caraway. "Was the front door locked?" Petrosky asked.

Jackson nodded. "Yup. But the other waitress said they usually open the front door for coffee and day-old scones within half an hour of arriving. The place should have been unlocked by six."

Petrosky scanned the register, the gleaming counter, the dark coffeepot. Acrid smoke tingled in his nostrils. The unmade coffee meant the kidnapper had gotten to her after she put the bagels in, but before she had time to scoop the grounds—before they were supposed to open, maybe around five forty-five. If that were true, she'd have had to unlock the door for her kidnapper. Did she know the perp?

"How does she get to work?" Petrosky asked.

"Drives. Her car's still in the lot."

Made sense, most kidnappers had their own rides, but he'd been hoping the guy had made her drive—at least then they'd know what kind of car to look for, put out an APB. He should have figured this asshole was smarter than that—the bastard had abducted her and made her relock the door behind them, thereby ensuring that no customers showed up to report the woman missing before he had a chance to get away. Petrosky glanced at the wall clock behind the counter. The kidnapper was already three hours ahead of them.

"Any sign of a struggle?" He drew his gaze away from the clock in time to see Jackson shake her head.

"Nothing, and no signs of blood or anything else that might indicate he knocked her out. So he was probably armed."

Right. When faced with a gun, most people did as they were asked—no mess. He turned back to the front door and frowned. The tall, slim forensics guy was crouched on the floor near the doorjamb, thin fingers busy with his little bags, his skinny little tweezers. Even his brown hair was thin. *This is some* Nightmare Before Christmas *shit.* "Where's Scott?"

"Out back. That's where Wilona's car is parked." Her gaze darted from the front door to the counter where the register was, and back to Petrosky. "I've got her picture out already. The story goes live next press cycle."

He gaped at her—they didn't yet know if they were dealing with a ransom situation, and some kidnappers went ballistic if the victim's face was splashed all over television.

Jackson raised a hand. "I know what you're thinking, but we can't risk it; she's nine months pregnant, due any day. And if she goes into labor, we have two victims to worry about. Hell, the kid might even be the reason he took her."

"Lots of sick fucks out there." But his voice rang hollow in his ears. *A pregnant waitress.* His guts tightened as a face leaped into his mind—red hair. Chipped front tooth. Red lipstick. *Fucking hell, not her.* He scanned the restaurant as if the woman would materialize out of nowhere, but all he saw were the flatfoots, the slim forensics guy, and the black-haired pink-shirted woman who had come in expecting to wait tables for tips and not to talk to cops for free. "Her friends call her Ruby," he said.

Jackson met his eyes and nodded, though it wasn't really a question.

Fuck, fuck, fuck. Ruby had been the one spiking his coffee on days he couldn't find a bottle. Ruby had added a little edge to his lemonade, sometimes even when Petrosky was with Jackson—not enough to stink, but enough to help. And he tipped her well for it. Hell, he'd driven her to her last doctor's appointment when her car broke down. Paid the mechanic's bill too.

He'd been trying to help her get back on her feet.

And someone had stolen her away.

3

THE WOMAN in the pink T-shirt was glassy-eyed by the time Petrosky and Jackson approached—Mary, right? *Mary Ellen.* She'd abandoned her apron; it lay in a crumpled heap in the booth beside her, the material more wrinkled than the fine lines around her mouth. Her long black hair lay over her shoulders, and he tried not to think about how much it looked like Chief Carroll's hair. He hadn't talked to the chief in...how long had it been? She hated him just as much as George did.

"Tell us about Ruby," Jackson was saying. He followed her lead and slid into the booth across from Mary Ellen, and when the woman raised her head, her eyes hooded with grief or stress or sleep, she looked less like a Mary Ellen and more like the picture of the Virgin Mary that his grandmother used to have over her fireplace. Unlike the way Mary was portrayed in other paintings, her thin lips in a peaceful smile while the child suckled at her breast, Mary had never looked serene in his grandmother's picture. She'd look haunted. And terrified. A far more realistic expression for a mother who knew their kid was going to die.

Mary Ellen's lip quivered, but she hissed a snot-laden

breath in through her nose and sighed it back out. "Ruby was…amazing. Kindest woman I know."

Petrosky nodded; it might have been true, but people always said nice things once you were gone. Platitudes. Bullshit. Except when it was about Morrison. His old partner, Shannon's late husband…he was as close to a saint as Petrosky had ever seen. He raised his hand and rubbed at an achy spot on his chest, just above his breastbone—feeling a little sharp today, stabby. Maybe too much caffeine.

"We only knew each other from work," Mary Ellen said— Jackson had asked her a question, but he hadn't heard it. "I like to think we were friends. She was really excited about the baby. I think…she never really had a close family, you know? So this was her chance to turn it all around." Her eyes filled again, but no tears fell; salty drops clung to her lower lashes like drowning men scrabbling for a rowboat. And her gaze…was that guilt? *What do you know?* And why would she hold anything back?

"She was wonderful," he said slowly. "We all know that." When Mary Ellen offered them a wan smile, he continued, "But I'm willing to bet that something wasn't right." Petrosky kept his voice low and thick with understanding. The last thing he needed was to push this woman into self-protection mode—guilt spurned denial, and it was painful to know you could have prevented harm. "Maybe you suspected something was off, even if you weren't sure?"

Mary Ellen sniffed again, but her eyes cleared. "Lately, she's been kinda…well…" A single tear finally let go of its hold and slipped down her cheek. "I thought she was being paranoid; I even made fun of her about it. But she was right." She shook her head. "I should have listened."

Jackson leaned closer, a little notepad in her hand. She hadn't been using it lately; she said she didn't need it with a memory as sharp as hers, but now… She must be stressed. Something else on her mind? He frowned at the tip of the pen, the fluid lines of thin black ink like rivers of dirty water on the page. "So what was she paranoid about?" he asked, turning back to Mary Ellen.

"She said someone was following her." Her voice came out strangled.

"Did she know who?" The most common culprits were ex-boyfriends. Or current ones. Ruby's burgeoning belly swelled in his brain then vanished once more.

"No, she had no idea—at least I don't think she did. She just said she kept seeing this truck, but she thought she was being silly, figured it was someone who lived nearby, or whatever. And she's been through a lot, getting ready to raise the baby alone." Her voice cracked on the last word.

"We don't want that baby losing its mom, either." Jackson set the pen aside, her eyes on Mary Ellen's face. "If you can tell us anything about the truck, it might help. Make, model?" Jackson laced her fingers on the table. "Color?"

The woman shook her head. "I never saw it, and she just said it was a truck. I'm sorry, I have no idea beyond that." Her nostrils flared as she sucked a fresh batch of snot into her sinuses. "Do you think she's dead? With kidnappings and stuff... I mean, with the baby..." She shuddered, gaze dropping to the table as if her lids were suddenly too heavy to hold up.

"We're going to do everything we can," Petrosky said. But there was no way to know whether she was even alive—whether the asshole who took her had cut the kid out of her guts, left her hollowed-out body in a ditch. He shoved that thought aside. No, they had a chance—still a chance. If the kidnapping was related to the baby, the most likely culprit was—

"What about the baby's father?" Jackson asked. That was the great thing about partners: they could read your mind. Even if sometimes that was a curse.

Mary Ellen's brow furrowed, her lips pursed as if she

were trying like hell to dredge up a long-ago memory. "Name's…Doyle, I think? Not positive. But they haven't talked in a long time. I don't even think he knew she was pregnant—I know she didn't tell him."

Maybe not, but social media made your business pretty clear. And by the time people realized they were being stalked, it was usually too late. A breeze tickled the back of his neck, and he turned in time to see the diner's front door swing closed behind Scott's assistant, Slim. Going out front now. Scouring the parking lot with his little light in his little plastic booties. "What about online?" Petrosky asked, addressing Mary Ellen once more. "Does she ever post pictures, talk about the baby?"

"Oh, god no. She doesn't bother with any of that."

Huh. Now that seemed strange, especially for a girl her age—twenties, early thirties tops. Most people in that age range were intimately connected with each other online. It seemed more common to meet a friend on social media than in a bar. "Why the aversion? Did she have a bad experience?" *Maybe some asshole stalking her?* While the internet connected people, it also opened up the world for douchebag keyboard-warrior crazies who spent their days harassing people so they didn't have to look at their own tiny peckers. But if the kidnapper was one of them, it'd be convenient because they'd be traceable.

"A bad experience?" Mary Ellen was saying. Repeating the question—not a good sign. "Not really, at least not lately."

Here we go. "But in the past?" He leaned forward, elbows on the tabletop.

Mary Ellen's eyes had clouded. "She did have some family trouble. Her dad's an alcoholic. She took care of him for a long time, dropped out of high school to try to support them both. But by the time she was of age…he was asking for more than she could give him." Her shoulders slumped in an almost guilty way as though she were betraying the woman's confidence. Maybe she was, but for some reason, the admission helped ease the ache in his guts. As much of an asshole as he was, he had always been able to take care of his family. *Nah, Julie just died before you got that bad.* He rubbed harder at his chest.

Mary Ellen cleared her throat, her shoulders still slumped, but the gaze she had aimed at the table was now one of realization. "When she stopped calling him back a year or so ago, he found her online, started asking her for money in private messages. When she blocked him, he just opened a new profile. That's why she closed her social media accounts; changed her phone number." The woman straightened and met his gaze. "If anyone has a reason to be pissed, it's him."

4

"WELL, there's a plot twist for you," Petrosky muttered, squinting at his phone where the address of their next stop was lit up in white.

Jackson snorted, her fingers choking the steering wheel like it owed her money. "It's messed up is what it is."

Wilona's father's last known address was a bungalow less than eight miles from Rita's Diner. Chuck Hyde's residence was currently owned by a junkie ex-con who came into the property after his own father died. The owner's name? Doyle Fanning: Ruby's ex-boyfriend. From the phone records, it looked like Mary Ellen had been correct about the timeline—Ruby had cut off all contact with her father last year, and she hadn't spoken to Doyle since the fall, right around the time she would have found out she was pregnant. Nothing made you reevaluate your life choices like another life.

But Chuck Hyde moving in with Fanning...that was strange. Hyde had been spotted at a series of halfway houses and shelters in the months after Ruby cut off contact, but her father had taken up residence with her ex-boyfriend soon after she'd stopped speaking to Fanning too—early December. Had Doyle tried to win her back by letting her daddy move in? "I bet ol' Doyle was pissed when he realized she wasn't talking to either one of them—that he was paying Hyde's way for nothing."

Jackson nodded. "Probably so, but Daddy might have been just as angry at her. And you don't cut your family off for no reason."

He blinked through the window at the stark shadows on the asphalt—telephone poles, electrical lines, a little bird one wrong step from being fried. Yeah, two angry men under the same roof with lots of time to ruminate about how she'd slighted them didn't bode well for Ruby—maybe they'd taken her together. Would she have let them into the diner? Then again, he had seen Ruby let even strangers in for their morning fix; she'd opened the doors early for Petrosky on more than one occasion.

He sighed, rubbing his temples. What were the other likely options? A stranger looking for ransom? The other motivations for abducting a pregnant woman… Well, he didn't want to think about those.

The weeds in the front flower beds were remarkably few, not nearly enough to compete with the hostas that were now sending purple and white buds toward the sky. Maybe that shouldn't have been shocking since Doyle Fanning's current place of employment was the garden department at a home improvement store, but the manicured beds were deeply at odds with the mess on the front lawn. Petrosky and Jackson trudged through a prickly tangle of tall grass long since gone to seed. No cars in the driveway, but neither Fanning nor Hyde had one in their name—resident number three, one Samuel Brenner, had an old Cutlass, which seemed to be the singular mode of transportation for the house. No trucks in sight.

The rapping of Jackson's knuckles against the metal screen door clanged through the early afternoon, the sun speckling the aluminum siding with jaundiced bits of glare.

No porch, just a rectangle of chipped concrete between the beds of hostas. Hyde answered the door rubbing sleep from his eyes, orange and white hair like a goddamn Creamsicle on top of his head. Still sleeping? *Lazy bastard.* Maybe Petrosky was a drunk, fine, but at least he was a productive one.

"Yeah?" Hyde had pale bits of something caught in his red beard, and the crumbs moved when he spoke. Hopefully, bread or crackers and not leftover vomit. Or something worse.

"Mr. Hyde?" Jackson flashed her badge. "Ash Park PD. We're here about your daughter."

Hyde blinked, sleep clearing in an instant. "Wil?" He shook his head. "There must be some mistake. No way she did somethin' wrong."

Jackson tucked her badge away. "Why would you assume we're here because she's done something wrong, Mr. Hyde?"

Petrosky watched Hyde's face, the way his eyes narrowed ever so slightly. Confusion? If Wilona was into something shifty, that might have given someone a reason to go after her, but Petrosky couldn't see it. And it didn't appear Hyde could either.

"I wasn't assumin'." He frowned. "Why'd you say you were here again?"

"Your daughter's missing," Jackson said. "May we come in?"

Hyde's eyes widened, but he did not shove open the main door, nor did he step inside so they could enter. Instead, he pushed the screen toward them and stepped onto the front walk, forcing Petrosky and Jackson back onto the tangled lawn. The summer sun scratched against the back of Petrosky's bare neck as the main door clicked shut. The sweet stink of marijuana wafted over them and dissipated on the breeze. "Missin'? I don't understand." His gaze darted from Jackson to Petrosky and back again. "What happened?"

Petrosky cleared his throat and waited for the man to look his way before he said: "This morning, your daughter disappeared from her place of employment. Have you ever gone to see her there?" Petrosky kept his gaze on the man's face. Ruby had started at Rita's Diner in January after she'd cut off both Hyde and Fanning. Did he know where she worked? With the diner so close to the house, they might have crossed paths accidentally.

Hyde's eyes narrowed further still; he was worried, but the feral kind of worry you see in a cornered raccoon. *Hiding something?* "I wish I could help you, but I haven't spoken to my daughter in a long time."

Petrosky kept his voice low as he had with Mary Ellen—conversational. "Why not? It seems strange that a father wouldn't talk to his child."

Hyde huffed out a breath so hard that scraps of food fell from his beard and sprinkled his shirt with crumbs, but his eyes had softened. "It was my fault. I got greedy, asked her for things I had no business askin' for." He crossed his arms, not quite confrontational—more like he was cold. Or scared. "So, what are you doin' to find my daughter?"

"You're looking at it," Petrosky said.

Hyde's brow furrowed. "I don't see—"

"Her ex-boyfriend lives here, doesn't he?" Petrosky let his gaze wander to the front door, then to the window—had the curtain twitched, just a bit?

Hyde had stopped moving as if his feet had grown roots. "Yeah, he's inside, but I still don't know why—"

"Where were you this morning?" Jackson cut in.

"I…here. Asleep."

"And Doyle?" she said.

"He was here too. With me."

Petrosky cleared his throat in a way he hoped was a little threatening—a warning growl. "How'd you come to live with your daughter's ex anyway?"

Hyde's face pinkened, twin spots of crimson blooming high on his cheekbones. Petrosky wasn't trying to embarrass the man, but it was a weird situation, Hyde had to see that. "We met when he and Wil were together, and then I saw him out in front of the hardware store one day. He offered me a place, I took it." He sniffed. "You think...Doyle had somethin' to do with her going missin'?"

Yes. "She isn't just missing, Mr. Hyde. She was abducted. By someone who knew her routine." They weren't positive on that, not yet, but if he could get a reaction out of the guy... Petrosky rubbed at the back of his neck. His skin already felt burned, like he'd been licked by the devil.

Jackson stepped closer, earning a raised eyebrow from Hyde. "Was she the type of girl who jumped from one relationship to another?" If they asked directly whether she was dating someone new, Hyde would claim ignorance, surely—but maybe he could give them insight if they went at it from another angle.

Hyde shook his head, but his eyes were like ping-pong balls getting ready to pop from his skull. "She hasn't talked to me in...almost a year now. And Doyle in there, he hasn't talked to her either, and Doyle wouldn't hurt her anyway." But he no longer sounded so certain. His voice was too high as if someone had his balls in a vise.

"Why don't you call him out here," Jackson said. "Let us decide."

Hyde hesitated, blinking, but finally, he nodded and rapped his knuckles against the screen as Jackson had done. Somewhere in the distance, a bird squalled. A car door slammed.

The door creaked open.

The man who stepped out onto the porch was nothing like what Petrosky had anticipated. In torn jeans and a green T-shirt, he was five-four at best, bald on top, prematurely gray on the close-cropped sides of his head, his eyes the clear green of an emerald. No wrinkles at the corners. Early thirties, no more, one arm covered in what looked like military tats.

Doyle Fanning ran a hand over his clean-shaven face and nodded first to Hyde, then to Jackson, but stopped when his gaze rested on Petrosky. Familiar, but Petrosky couldn't place him.

"We know each other, hoss?"

Doyle Fanning scowled and crossed his arms over his chest. Yeah, they definitely knew each other for the man to hate him that much. "I guess not," Fanning snapped.

Huh. The bird screamed again, but this time, the silence didn't stretch—Hyde's voice burst through the warm morning air: "Someone took Wil."

Fanning's jaw dropped. He stepped off the concrete slab of a porch to join them on the lawn, his eyes as wide as his mouth. Genuine surprise. Fanning didn't seem to think Ruby should be in danger any more than her father did; he didn't appear to be the one who'd snatched her. So who had?

"Do either of you know someone with a pickup truck?" Jackson said.

Hyde and Fanning exchanged a glance, but this was not the tightrope anxiety of men trying to keep their stories straight. Just confusion. Maybe even worry. "A pickup?" Fanning said. "I guess a few people at work have trucks, but they don't know Wil if that's why you're asking."

"Have you seen Wilona"—*Ruby*—"at all since she dropped you?" Petrosky asked Fanning. "Maybe you missed her, took a little drive past her place, or over to her job?"

The tattoos on Fanning's forearm rippled. "I don't know where she works, and I definitely didn't go to her apartment. She told me not to, said she'd call the cops."

Her apartment—that was telling. Ruby's current address was a little house on East Paddock. She hadn't lived in an apartment for six months. They'd checked. Neither man had mentioned the pregnancy either, and Petrosky wasn't about to ask them—she clearly had reason to keep that baby to herself.

"Call the cops, huh?" Jackson cut in. "Just for visiting the woman you love?"

"I'm on probation," Fanning snapped, and the hairs between Petrosky's shoulders prickled. "It wouldn't take much of anything to get me locked away again." But he wasn't looking at Jackson—he stared daggers at Petrosky. And now Petrosky knew where he'd seen the man: he'd dragged him in once. Cocaine, if he recalled. No…horse—heroin. No wonder he was on probation, and more critically here, no wonder Ruby hadn't wanted to deal with him. That addiction didn't stop; it just went to sleep sometimes. If you were lucky.

"Why would I go see her anyway?" Fanning went on. "*She* dumped *me*." He shook his head as if in disbelief, then raised his tattooed arm and gestured to the house at his back. "I had this place, told her she could move in here, but no matter what I did, it wasn't good enough. So fuck her, that's what I say."

Wilona's father stiffened, his eyes blazing fire, and then his hand flashed out toward Fanning so suddenly that Petrosky startled, momentarily confused. But there was nothing confusing about Hyde lowering his hand once more, palm open and probably stinging after slapping the boy—and that's what Fanning was: a boy. "You watch your goddamn mouth, Doyle, talkin' about my daughter like that. She's better than you'll ever be!"

Fanning squared off with Hyde, bristling, his fists clenched at his sides. "You watch *your* mouth, old man!"

Jackson raised her hands as if she might try to stop them, but Petrosky backed up to give them their space. Both men deserved a punch to the jaw, and if he didn't have to do it himself, all the better.

But Hyde did not lash out again, and Fanning suddenly paused as if recalling that he was on probation and in the presence of two police officers who might look down on assault. He glanced at Jackson and Petrosky and backed up onto the porch slab until his shoulder rested against the screen. When he spoke again, his voice was soft. "I swear I haven't seen her, not for a long time." He drew his gaze to Hyde. "If I knew where your daughter was, I'd tell them. I swear to god."

Hyde met Fanning's eyes. His shoulders relaxed. "I believe him," he said softly, his voice shaking, and it made Petrosky's ribs tighten; he knew that look. Desperation. No matter what Wilona had done, no matter how angry Hyde might have been that she'd cut him off financially, he wouldn't have kidnapped her. And there was no way he'd have let Fanning harm her either.

Hyde's lip trembled. "I'll do whatever you need," he said. "Please find whoever took my baby girl."

5

"AMBER ALERT'S OUT," Jackson said, tossing her cell into the cupholder.

"I fucking hate that Hyde and Fanning are going to find out about Ruby's baby." Petrosky knew he should call her Wilona, but he couldn't get there—she'd always be Ruby to him. He glared out the window. The day had eased into orange faster than he would have thought possible. Outside, jaundiced light danced on every inch of sidewalk that he could see and painted the tops of the buildings gold.

"Nothing we can do about that, and I doubt Fanning will go after custody anyway—no judge would grant it. I'm more upset that we don't have enough on the truck Mary Ellen mentioned to actually look for it."

Yeah, that had been a real kick in the nuts. They'd searched for a nearby street camera, but those set up to surveil the traffic lights had been out for years. The nearest working camera was in the precinct lot. They'd scanned that tape from the time Ruby would have arrived at five thirty to the time Mary Ellen showed up at seven, but no pickup trucks had passed. Hardly any traffic at all on that stretch that time of morning.

He dragged his gaze to the windshield as Jackson parked at the curb. Ruby's house was better cared for than Fanning's place: cosmos and phlox bloomed in brilliant yellows and pinks and purples and greens, creating a wave of color that undulated in the breeze like a shuddering rainbow. The weed-free lawn was clipped to the quick, patches of brown dirt visible just beneath like a balding man with a buzz cut.

The front door popped open easily—not even a deadbolt to keep the crazies at bay, not that he believed the kidnapper had ever intended to take Ruby here. The suspect would have been able to walk into the diner, no questions asked, a task harder to do at a private residence, where neighbors looked out for one another and would certainly notice a strange man lurking around, not to mention the possibility of doorbell cams. And Petrosky was almost certain that their suspect was a man; while a weapon meant that a woman was a distinct possibility, statistics said the person who took her was a male around her age, probably someone she'd had a relationship with. And while their suspect might have been happy taking any woman from the diner this morning, that didn't ring true deep in his belly.

"I'll take the kitchen," Jackson said. He muttered something unintelligible even to himself and closed the door behind them.

The living room was simply furnished: a gray futon, a blue shag rug laid over the top of scarred hardwood, a TV tray instead of a coffee table. By far, the most compelling piece in the room was the giant totem in the corner—honeyed wood carved with the faces of bird-like creatures, all glowering at Petrosky as he made his way farther into the house.

The bathroom in the hall held nothing near as interesting as the carved bird totem. A single red toothbrush in the holder, a single damp washcloth hanging over the bathroom faucet. One towel. He peered into the lower cabinet—no shaving cream or hair gel or razors, nothing to indicate the presence of a man, at least not one close enough to spend the night. The bedroom was the same. Baby books on the nightstand, a purple vibrator on the bed pillow; if someone else had a key, she'd probably have stuck that in a drawer.

The sound of the back door slamming made him pause until he heard Jackson cough; his partner was checking the back locks, seeing if anything had been jimmied, probably searching the mud outside for evidence that a stalker had stood there, peering in at their victim. He glanced back up the hall. The second bedroom at the far end glowed with sunshine, and a tree just beyond the windowpane cast dappled shadows from the center of the room to the hallway floor. He headed that way, his sneakers making a hollow squeak against the wood.

Walls the color of butter, a white crib beneath the far window, a pastel duck mobile hanging over one painted rail. To his right, a little changing table sat beneath a white shelf lined with stuffed animals and a blue piggy bank. A flowered rug adorned the floor. He stepped closer, running his fingers along the padded changing station, the already stocked container of wipes, two packages of newborn diapers. A mason jar glittered from the shelf beside the piggy bank, already full of bills: ones, fives, tens. It looked like the tip jar the waitresses sometimes kept beside the diner register.

He sighed and turned away, his brain throbbing. She'd been so ready for this child. Excited. And this room would be any baby's dream.

Hopefully, the kid would get to see it.

FOUR HOURS. Four fucking hours of pounding the pavement, one house after another after another. None of the neighbors had seen anyone at Ruby's, not since she moved in—"a loner," they said. Mary Ellen seemed to be her closest friend, and they hadn't gone out together once. Ruby had broken cleanly with everything in her old life—no muss, no fuss, no worry that someone might tell her ex about the baby—and there was no sign that she had started up a new social life, no sign that she'd even been on a single date. But she clearly hadn't needed a man. She had her health, a steady job, and a vibrator. Life was probably simpler that way.

So why had she been kidnapped?

By the time he got home, the sun had long since set, and the buzzing ache in his brain had swelled to a dull roar. At least the neighbors' lawn was soft under his feet, the earth easy on his smarting joints, the grass gilded in the glow from the porch light.

Duke's low bellow echoed through the house before he had a chance to knock, and the door suddenly crashed inward—Evie grinned up at him, her blue eyes sparkling. Just like her daddy's used to. His head pulsed harder. "Papa Ed!"

He blinked, trying to force the pain away, but the throbbing remained, a wicked rhythm that shot daggers into his teeth with every heartbeat. He bent and scooped her into his arms anyway, and her little hands around his neck eased some of the tension in his temples. Not to be outdone, Duke nudged his hip with his giant head, and Petrosky shifted Evie to his right arm so he could scratch the dog's ears; his arm muscles hurt more than he wanted to admit, though he didn't remember injuring himself. Aging—it was a bitch. "How are you, little lady?"

"Mommy made us walk all the way here!"

He chuckled, though it made the ache in his brain sharpen once more. "Exercise is good for you," he said, inhaling deeply. The air smelled of garlic and carbs. Pasta?

"Yeah." She frowned. "Why don't you exercise more?"

Shannon's laugh burst from the dining room. "You tell him, Evie!"

Evie nodded knowingly and shifted, wiggling until Petrosky set her down. He followed her into the dining room where Shannon's voice had come from—the girls always saved him the seat at the head of the table, though he told them not to. Shannon sat on the far side, where a low bench made it possible to squeeze the kids in more easily. Henry's booster had been abandoned on the floor behind her, the towheaded boy in her lap instead, her arm around his waist, the other hand gripping a fork like her life depended on it. She nodded to Petrosky, smiling. Billie grinned, too, from her position at the foot of the table and gestured to his seat with the salad tongs. He smiled back. Billie's silver hair gleamed in the light from the chandelier—he'd never understand this generation and their desire to look old well before their time, but he wasn't about to argue. The girl had been through enough. One night she was on the street, the next she was here, and she hadn't looked back so far as he knew. Jane was the newcomer to the group. She sat with her back to him, her curly hair pulled into a low ponytail, but she turned and waved as he approached, still chewing…garlic bread? *Hell yes.* Family dinner night had been one of the first things Shannon had instituted on her return to Michigan, and she'd gladly included the neighbor girls—they'd been his family for years while Shannon had been off in Atlanta.

He slid into his seat as Evie scampered onto the bench beside her mother. "Sorry I'm late."

"We waited for you," Shannon said. "I figured you'd be a little behind with your new case."

He reached for the bread and said around a mouthful of garlic butter: "How'd you know about that?"

Shannon shrugged, and Henry waved his arms from her lap. His round face was slowly losing its pudge—before they knew it, he'd be borrowing the car and telling Petrosky to go fuck himself. "I've got friends in low places," Shannon said.

Fucking Decantor—had to be. The detective had been friends with Shannon and Morrison before Petrosky himself had taken a liking to the guy, and even now, he wanted to slap the burly detective half the time. He helped himself to the pasta—*ravioli*—and stabbed a piece, cheese oozing around the fork's tines like snot, reminding him of Mary Ellen's sniffling. His stomach rolled. "Is Candace still at work?"

Candace worked for a shrink, a gig she'd chosen to help her decide whether she wanted to go into psychology herself. But the doc kept odd hours. Dr. McCallum—the precinct's shrink—was the only other psychiatrist Petrosky knew, but odd hours seemed to be a common occurrence. Nothing to worry about, right? But he'd have felt more comfortable with Candace sitting across from Shannon. Especially tonight.

Billie nodded. "Yup, someone's gotta bring home the bacon. I spent all day studying."

Petrosky paused, fork halfway to his lips. Between college and their jobs, these girls worked harder than he did, and that was the god's honest truth. Billie was in the social work program at the university—said she wanted to spend her life helping people the way she thought Petrosky did. If she only knew what a fuckup he was, maybe she'd change her mind.

Poor Ruby. Out there all alone. And even before she'd vanished, she hadn't had a soul in the world to care about her…except him, as little as he'd managed. A ride to the doc and help with a mechanic's bill? Come on.

Petrosky met Evie's eyes—brilliant blue, the color of the summer sky. Morrison's eyes. If days like today did anything, they reminded him that he had more than most: wonderful people around him, tolerance from those he cared about, and far more love than he deserved. Which also made him recall all the ways he'd failed.

He forced his lips into what he hoped was a passable smile and laid his napkin in his lap, trying to hide the tremor that had crept into his hands. Another hour and he'd be in bed with whiskey warm in his belly, and Duke at his feet acting like he had no intention of sneaking up to drool on Petrosky's pillow. Another hour and he'd be alone.

6

PETROSKY EXHALED a plume of smoke and squinted through the haze at the dawn beyond the windshield. He hadn't had a cigarette in months—okay, weeks—but today's phone call had made him dig his emergency pack out from behind the detergent in the laundry room. Not even seven o'clock, and for the last hour he'd been praying, or as close as he got to that, for the caller to be wrong.

River Rock Road was less than three blocks from the precinct, a neighborhood very similar to the one Wilona "Ruby" Hyde lived in. Well-maintained bungalows with trimmed lawns and neat flower beds and the occasional crooked mailbox. The house Petrosky'd parked in front of was of the crooked-mailbox variety, half the house numbers missing, the yard more dirt than grass. Patchy—that felt appropriate. Thin, like his soul.

Jackson met him on the driveway, the breeze flipping the collar of her gray suit jacket against her cheek. She tugged it back down. "Neighbor says she saw a dark-colored pickup out here around four a.m. Didn't think to call us until she saw the alert on the news, and then suddenly she was *sure* it was the guy who took Hyde even though she didn't see a single person—not Wilona, not the driver."

Fucking figured. But hopefully the caller could narrow their search…if this was connected. "She give specifics on the color?"

"Maybe green or gray or black. Said it was too dark to see clearly." Jackson shrugged and gestured to the lights above the garage, then those hanging from the eaves near the porch. "None of these work, so she really just saw a silhouette in the moonlight."

Well, that's just fucking perfect. They couldn't catch a goddamn break. He followed Jackson to the front door and watched while she tried the handle, trying to ignore the way the breeze ran its ghostly fingers through his hair. Something was off. No one should have been at this house at all; preliminary research said the place had been vacant since the owner foreclosed in April, and the owner himself had been a homicide victim not long after—one of Decantor's cases.

The hinges creaked inward.

The main living room was dim and quiet, insulated from the summer breeze by walls of brick. The air smelled stale. No tracks on the carpet, no bottles or garbage, so the teenagers were staying away too. Yet the gray carpet was plush like it had been replaced just before the owners moved out, and despite the stale air, the place didn't *feel* abandoned. It felt as if the owner might return any minute.

"Whoever was here last night, they didn't bother locking up. They didn't care if someone else wandered in," Jackson said. But she held her hand tight against her hip, just above her gun—ready. In case they weren't alone. *She feels it too.*

"Maybe they weren't doing anything worth investigating." The caller had said the only reason she noticed the vehicle was the truck's horn—honking, and more than once. But their kidnapper wouldn't be so stupid as to knock the horn, even accidentally. Again, he found himself hoping the caller had been mistaken, that this was unconnected to their case. Because of all the reasons for a kidnapper to break into an abandoned property, none of them would be good for Ruby or her baby.

The kitchen had mouse droppings scattered over the linoleum counter like oblong peppercorns, but the room was otherwise devoid of life. The family room was more of the same, the unshuttered windows casting white light against more of that plush carpet—squares of heat in a fuzzy gray cloud. Empty. Suffocatingly still, the kind of quiet that plugged your ears. But they had to be sure.

"Did you hear that?" Jackson had paused in the hall, brow furrowed.

He frowned, shaking his head, but stopped just as suddenly because now he *did* hear something. A barely there sound, high-pitched. Squeaking. He released his grip on his gun, still in the holster—he hadn't even realized he'd been clutching it. His fingers ached. *Fucking mice.* He hated mice. Their beady little eyes, their sharp teeth... The sound was coming from behind him.

He whirled around, suddenly certain that he'd find one of the little bastards on the floor behind his heel, skittering across the tiles on razor-sharp disease-infested claws, but the only thing at his back was a door—no rats. No mice.

The squeaking came again.

He tried to force his heart to steady. All that over a fucking mouse? But his feet refused to move closer to the door. The flesh along his spine lit up with electricity. *Something's wrong. Something's very, very wrong.*

Jackson seemed to have no such reservations. She strode past him as if he wasn't even there, paused with her hand on the knob, and then eased it open slowly. Listening.

The sound stopped.

She glanced over her shoulder. "You ready?"

I'd rather get stabbed in the balls with an ice pick. But at least his feet were obeying him now. He followed her down into the dark.

The stairs were edged with gritty treads that made the soles of their shoes grind like sandpaper. Super inconspicuous. But there were no answering steps from the gloom below, and he could see straight to the bottom landing, the light from the windows making the basement nearly as bright as the upper floors, though the air felt heavier down here, stuffier. Basementier. Their breath hissed in Petrosky's ears. He pressed his back against the wall.

Jackson stopped on the bottom stair and peeked around the corner, muscles coiled. Her shoulders relaxed a little, but her back remained rigid as she edged out into the cellar.

Something's wrong, something's wrong, something's wrong. His heart throbbed against his temples and echoed in the deep recesses of his chest. He swallowed over the lump in his throat. And followed his partner.

The basement was small, a rectangle that would barely fit the couch and totem from Ruby's living room, but the lack of furnishings made it feel more spacious. The only things in the concrete room were three stacks of cardboard boxes, each three high, probably leftovers from the previous owners —discarded books, maybe, pants that had once fit perfectly, now reduced to rags by cookies and too much whiskey. A music box from someone they had once loved. A night-light belonging to their dead daughter. He'd hidden Julie's in the closet—he didn't have a basement.

Petrosky watched Jackson venture deeper into the basement, watched the shadows swallow her as she passed the first window and stepped into the space between them where the bricks blocked the sun. Colder here, he realized, and not just because they were in a cellar—breezy. He squinted. The middle window was unobstructed by the grime that marred the others, but jagged shards of broken glass hung dangerously from the top lip of the frame like the teeth of an angry jack-o'-lantern.

And then the tiniest noise—a squeak. He grimaced, bracing—*fucking mice*—but the sound went on, another squeak and then a squeal, a mewl, again, again until it was a high-pitched wail. For a split second, he imagined it was Jackson, maybe even him, crying, but the noise was nearer to the glass. Somewhere beyond the stacked cardboard boxes.

Jackson was already there, her hands on the top box, bracing to lift, but she staggered back as if the box weighed nothing at all. She frowned and tossed it over her shoulder. It landed with a hollow thunk.

"Jackson?" He tried to peer past her as she grabbed another box, but he couldn't see anything beyond her hunched shoulders, and then she was kicking the stacks aside, all of them toppling—empty, definitely empty. Why the fuck would anyone stack empty boxes? And...

Jackson hit her knees, and now he could see behind her.

Oh god.

On the floor behind the stacks of boxes lay a child—nude, no more than a day or so old, his umbilical cord clamped and scabbed with dark blood, his skinny legs kicking the air. But outside of the scab on his belly, his skin was pink, unmarred by blood or mucus; someone had bathed him. Thank good-ness it was warm in there. Still, he scoured the room for a blanket, for anything that might have come in with the child, a towel, *a washcloth*, but the concrete floor was bare—just the boxes, all those empty goddamn boxes, each folded and taped. Sealed, as if the owner had never intended to use them.

A wave of déjà vu hit him so hard the world went fuzzy. He staggered, blinked—*don't faint, you're going to fucking fall on the kid*—but the world solidified once more when the infant whined again, so weak and desperate it made pain blossom in his own chest like his heart was cracking in two.

Jackson touched the child's forehead with the backs of her fingers as if looking for fever, then rested her palm on his chest. The baby squalled once more, a pitiful high-pitched keening, and Petrosky shrugged out of his jacket and knelt beside Jackson, laying the garment on the cold concrete. Carefully, carefully, he eased the boy's tiny body onto it—tugged the edges around his frail shoulders, avoiding the stump of the umbilical cord, the end tied with...dental floss? *Fuck.* Was Ruby at a hospital somewhere? Was she alive, or were they going to find her body somewhere in this house? Had the kidnapper cut this child out of her?

He forced a breath into his lungs, but the air felt sharp, like inhaling needles. The baby whined, kicking at the jacket, hands scrabbling at the cloth—light, he was so light. Petrosky held the kid against his aching chest. "Shh. It's okay, son. It's okay." He forced himself to breathe, but it was next to impossible, and it wasn't because of the child, he realized, not even because of Ruby, though that was part of it. *Something's wrong, wrong, wrong.*

Jackson whipped out her phone, barking orders for a bus, but he wasn't really listening—his mind raced. All of this, from the basement to the broken window, to the boxes, to the baby...

This has happened before. And that horn, that honking truck horn...

Their suspect had wanted to draw attention to this place. He wanted them here—the kidnapper had left the child *for them.*

He held the boy tighter, the child's downy head against Petrosky's neck, tiny panted breaths soft on his skin. "This has happened before." He didn't realize he'd said it aloud until the words echoed back to him from the concrete walls. He shook his head, careful not to jostle the baby. It couldn't be the same. The last time he'd been in this position, the last time someone had tossed a naked newborn into a basement… No, that guy was dead. Petrosky had watched his head explode. And god, if anyone had deserved it—

"Petrosky?"

He looked over. Jackson's eyes were wide—watchful. But he didn't feel watched. He suddenly felt terrified.

"What's happened before?" she asked.

Sirens wailed in the distance. The child answered, squalling against Petrosky's throat.

"All…this. The boxes. This…baby." He took a deep breath to steady himself, but the air was too thin, like the grass, like his soul, and instead, he wheezed, "I'm sorry."

Jackson's face was grave and laced with a knowledge he was not privy to—deeply distressed. Nervous. But not shocked.

He frowned. "Jackson?"

She met his eyes. "I have to tell you something."

7

THEY WENT TO RITA'S, which seemed appropriate. What was happening here? That basement had been all too familiar, but the case it reminded him of...no way. It made no sense. He felt hollow like someone had snatched his soul straight out of his chest the same way someone had snatched Ruby from this diner.

They'd already put calls in to the local hospitals, but no one matching Ruby's description had been admitted. No body had been found yet either, and it had been at least six hours since the kid's birth—since the truck had dropped him there and vanished. Hopefully, that was a good sign. The suspect would have dumped Ruby's body, too, if he had no more use for her, and it was possible she'd delivered the baby on her own. Unless the press release had simply moved up his timeline and made him more wary of being discovered. Maybe he'd bathed and abandoned the kid since the baby couldn't identify him, but had murdered Ruby and left her body in a place where forensic evidence might deteriorate—Michigan was full of lakes. And ditches.

Petrosky blinked and saw Ruby's face behind his eyelids, her smile as she handed him his morning coffee, one chipped front tooth, bright red lipstick. The secret but joyful glitter in her gaze when she rested her hand on her burgeoning belly. *Maybe it's not Ruby's baby at all. Maybe she's on her way home.*

"I think our case is connected to the Norton case," Jackson announced. She raised her coffee mug to her lips but stopped short of drinking it. The tips of her fingers were pale against the ceramic. "And that both are connected to a case of Decantor's—the murder of the homeowner. I know this is going to be hard to accept, but—"

"Norton is dead," he said softly.

She lowered the cup to the table with a hollow clunk. "I'm not saying it *is* Norton, Petrosky. I'm saying the suspect might have followed the case in the news, that he knows about Norton's crimes. A fan."

Rage blistered his insides. Norton. Adam fucking Norton. Norton's first partner—a pedophile—had abused children, then watched while Norton killed them. And when that guy had become a liability, Norton had killed his pedophile ass too—no great loss there.

Then there was Janice, the woman Norton had been involved with when he kidnapped Shannon and baby Evie— he'd locked Petrosky's granddaughter in a dog crate and sewn Shannon's lips shut. Bile rose in his gullet, and he swallowed it back down. Norton hadn't killed Janice, though; he'd left her behind while he escaped. Norton always had a fall guy, at least at first.

Until he'd gone off on his own. Norton had started his solo career by kidnapping teenage girls and locking them like animals in his basement. Impregnating them. Killing them when they didn't serve his purposes. One night, a girl named Lisa Walsh had escaped Norton's prison with her newborn daughter; she'd smashed a nearby basement window and tossed the baby through. The infant had landed, nude, behind a slew of cardboard boxes—far too close to the scene they'd just left. Norton had caught Walsh again after he'd slaughtered the homeowner, impaled the poor girl on a pike and watched her die slowly, and—

Petrosky's chest spasmed. *Morrison—Norton killed your partner; he killed your son.*

He couldn't breathe. His heart stabbed at the muscles around his rib cage with every frantic pulse. He grabbed his full coffee mug, trying to keep his hands from shaking. "So you think this case is connected to Decantor's homicide? Just because of the location, or what?" Hopefully she was wrong because if Ruby wasn't with a kidnapper, a stalker, someone who might have feelings for her, she was with a murderer.

"I'll let him show you when he gets here. But we can't ignore the fact that Decantor's latest victim once owned the house where we just found an abandoned child—Hyde's child."

"If he is Ruby's baby," he muttered, but he knew that was a long shot. Though they didn't have DNA proof back yet, people didn't routinely leave infants in basements, and the truck was too much of a coincidence. Jackson, thankfully, did not bother responding. She sipped her coffee. *Is Ruby dead? Is she?* He stared at his own mug, untouched on the table, his stomach sour, his brain twisting, spinning, making him dizzy. He tried to imagine that she was here, just another day, and then he *could* hear her behind him, shoes tapping against the tiles with that light, careful gait; soon, she'd be at the table, offering him spiked coffee with that big chipped-tooth smile, a tendril or two of red hair wisping against her cheekbone, and—

A bell dinged. Decantor strode into the diner, a case file under his arm, his face tight. He slid into the booth beside Jackson and laid the file on the table in front of Petrosky without a word. No preamble. No bullshit. Good.

"I hear you have a homicide related to our kidnapping," Petrosky said.

"Yup." Decantor nodded. "Evan Webb moved out of that

house around four months back, right before he died. The place was tied up for a bit with the foreclosure, but it's getting ready to go up for auction."

Auction... Petrosky's shoulders relaxed just a little. That was it—the simplest explanation. "Maybe our kidnapper peeked at the auction sheets looking for a warm place to dump the kid. Maybe the cases aren't related." And then he'd honked to make sure someone found the baby while it was still dark enough to hide his face. Less chance of getting caught that way than if he'd dropped the kid at a fire station or a hospital—too many cameras, too many lights, too many prying eyes.

Decantor's brow furrowed. "What?"

Did he have something in his ears? "I'm just saying, all our kidnapper needed was a place to dump the kid. That doesn't necessarily mean he's connected to your killer."

Decantor had stilled. Jackson, too, was unmoving, her back against the bench seat, hands in her lap.

Finally, Decantor cleared his throat. "It's not about the house. Doyle Fanning wasn't the baby's father. This guy was." He reached across the table and opened the file to a brilliant color photo.

Petrosky's guts clenched, acid hot and thick in his esophagus. *Morrison, oh god, Morrison.* But it wasn't. The man was thirty, maybe forty from the subtle lines around his eyes and mouth. Dark hair, not like Morrison's blond locks, eyes brown, not blue. But the scene around him—the plastic sheeting speckled with crimson, the blood on his lips. The gaping chasm across his throat.

He hid his shaking hands under the table and willed his voice to stay even. "If Evan Webb was the kid's father, Ruby was likely with him before she and Fanning officially split. Cheating might be motive, both for the homicide and for the kidnapping." Ruby's father be damned. And Fanning wouldn't want another man's baby—of course he'd get rid of it. "Doyle Fanning looks better for this all the time." But his voice came out strangled. Too high. He dropped his head, trying to avoid the images, trying not to remember, but when he caught sight of his fingers, like claws against his thighs, all he could see was blood—Morrison's blood—crimson under his fingernails, streaks of scarlet over the flesh of his wrists. He blinked. His hands were clean again.

"Did Doyle Fanning kill five additional men over the last four-and-a-half years?" Decantor's voice remained steady, unwavering.

Petrosky raised his head. "What?"

Decantor blinked at Jackson. "You didn't tell him?"

She reached for her coffee, staring at the cup like there were tiny fucking elves synchronized swimming in the caramel liquid. *Look at me, tell me, Jesus Christ.* "I figured I'd let you have the honor."

Petrosky's fists tightened, no longer shaking. Jackson had been hiding something from him, from her goddamn partner, and it sure sounded like it had been going on a while. "If one of you doesn't fill me in, I swear to god—"

"Oh, my word." They all looked over to see Mary Ellen, her eyes saucers, her shoulders ramrod straight. A small brown stain marred her pink shirt just above her left breast.

Decantor snapped the file shut and nodded to her. "I'll take a coffee whenever you get a chance," he said. Mary Ellen met Petrosky's eyes. Her lip trembled. Then she was gone.

Petrosky turned back to Decantor, who laced his fingers on the table and squared his shoulders. No trace of his usual smile—no hint of amusement in those dark eyes. "Two separate rashes of killings," Decantor said. "Sprees with a break in between. All with the same MO as the one I just showed you. Victims were all killed somewhere else, often in their own homes, and then the killer wrapped their bodies in plastic, put them in the back seats of their own cars, and abandoned the vehicles in some alley or another. The medical examiner says it's the same method each time, no variation: throats slit, right-handed, one quick slash ear to ear, and it's over."

"So, he's a pro."

"He's got practice, but pro might be a strong word; this wouldn't require medical or combat training. We do know it's the same guy, though. Got a set of striations on the edge of the throat wounds that show he's using the same knife—set in his pattern and his weapon. But despite the crime scene similarities, those striations don't match Morrison's wound." Decantor's voice had softened on the last line. *Morrison—Decantor was Morrison's friend too. He was there when I found his body.* Petrosky rubbed at his chest, his sternum on fire, waiting for Decantor to go on, but the bigger man turned away as Mary Ellen sidled up to the table, casting sideways glances at the file, maybe making sure she wouldn't accidentally see something worse. She set a coffee mug in front of Decantor. It rattled.

Petrosky reached for her arm, brushing her elbow with his fingertips. "We're going to find her."

Mary Ellen blinked and offered a wan smile. "Thanks for that." Her lip trembled again, harder this time. "I know she really liked you. She said you reminded her of her dad."

His chest burned hotter. *Her alcoholic deadbeat of a father with crumbs in his beard; no wonder she knew how to add just enough booze to take the edge off.* And the fact that Mary Ellen was talking about her in the past tense... *Fuck.* Mary Ellen had given up already, no matter how desperately she was trying to hope.

"I have witnesses who saw a dark pickup at the scene of one of the earlier murders," Decantor went on as Mary Ellen retreated. His big hands were wrapped tightly around his coffee mug, but they did not shake as he brought it to his lips and took a deep swallow. "And he's gotten more careful; no witnesses for any of the later crimes. And there's nothing to prepare once he arrives at the dump site; the body's already wrapped. It'd only take seconds for him to park the car and run off." His coffee mug thunked back onto the table—loud, harder than necessary. "As for the dry spells, I'm thinking he was locked up, but we have yet to find a registration on a pickup that matches someone who was released during that time from any of the jails in the state. Either the truck is registered to someone else, someone keeping up the bills while our perp goes back and forth inside, or the dry spells are for another reason. And I can't fucking go to the press with no physical description, not with the serial killer bit— people will panic. We're more likely to get someone beaten to death just for driving a pickup than we are to catch a killer."

Dry spells. Murder sprees. Was this the same guy, *really* the same guy who had Ruby? But that truck—that fucking truck. Of course it was. And he was using pieces from Norton's crimes. The throat slashing, the plastic, the back seats, the alleys, and now abandoning a newborn in a basement—maybe that was why he'd taken Ruby in the first place.

Petrosky reached for the file and flipped it open once more. The first image was the man he'd already seen: thirties, throat slit, plastic. The next: male, thirties, throat slit, plastic. The third was the same. And the next. Petrosky shook his head. The MOs on these cases were identical, and if the killer's pattern held, Mr. Webb's death three months ago was likely the beginning of a third spree. But Ruby's kidnapping… No, this wasn't right. "You have a serial killer going after men in their thirties—picky enough in his MO to use the same blade, to keep all other elements the same from the car to the plastic to the method. But there are no female vics in this file." He slapped it shut. "Any evidence that your suspect has ever hurt another woman? Kidnapped anyone else?"

Decantor frowned. Which was answer enough.

Petrosky leaned back against the seat, his muscles finally loose enough to allow it. "Any connections between the other victims?"

"No."

"So why change his process here? Why take a woman connected to another victim?" If she'd been a witness, he'd have slit her throat like the others. He wouldn't have delivered her baby and hidden it in a basement—wouldn't have called attention to it. And he certainly wouldn't have waited three months to snatch her up. Petrosky glared, but it felt like triumph. Maybe they'd find her after all. Maybe she'd be okay, get to bring her baby boy home to the yellow bedroom she'd worked so hard on.

But Jackson did not look triumphant...or convinced. She abandoned her coffee and stared back at him, her nostrils flaring. "You're acting like this is just a coincidence," Jackson snapped. "But there's no way in hell. The connection between the victims, the truck..." She shook her head.

Petrosky addressed Decantor. "Did you talk to Ruby after Webb's death?"

Decantor nodded. "I did. But she didn't report anything out of the ordinary."

Didn't report anything...but she'd told Mary Ellen she was being followed recently, even if she'd believed herself paranoid. "Did you tell her about the truck?"

"The witness saw the truck four years ago—we weren't sure he was still driving the same vehicle. Plus, it was part of an ongoing investigation." Decantor's face clouded. "So no, we didn't tell her."

Ruby hadn't known to be worried.

And now she was gone.

8

———

TOO MANY TRUCKS. No fucking leads. And a postpartum woman running out of time. *If she's still alive.*

Petrosky shoved the case file aside and glanced at the bullpen window, the only hint that the real world even existed outside the large L-shaped space. The brilliance had leaked out of the sky at some point over the last two hours, the hot white of afternoon now a sickly gray like dirty dishwater. But that was better—he couldn't keep his shit together if the world outside shone blue like Morrison's eyes watching him pore over information that might or might not save Ruby.

But where else to start? Whatever had made this guy change his MO, the similarities to Norton's crimes could not be ignored, nor could the use of a common vehicle. They'd all agreed: find the killer and they'd find the kidnapper, and Decantor had more information after months of chasing this asshole. But the thought that a serial killer had Ruby, had maybe ripped her kid out of her guts… Sweat trickled down his back like oil, but it felt distant as if it was happening to someone else. As if his skin was not his own.

He knocked his Styrofoam coffee cup into the trash,

splattering grounds up the side of the can. Scott had already called from forensics and told Petrosky in clipped, professional tones that the infant was undeniably Wilona—*Ruby*—Hyde's child. The newborn had no broken bones, no other injuries, so the kidnapper had placed him down there instead of tossing him through that broken window. That seemed promising—a display of kindness, even if it was like patting a dog's head after you'd kicked it. But the boxes, using a basement at all...those details were stolen right from Norton's case files. This killer had been obsessing over Norton for some time, killing those men the way Norton had killed Morrison, choosing a pregnant woman to mirror Norton's other crimes, staging that basement so precisely. But how far did he intend to take it? And what had prompted this shift in MO from throat-slashing to include significantly different crimes from Norton's savage backlist? He wanted to tell himself that Ruby was fine, that she'd make it out safely, but that would only be true if they could find her—their suspect wasn't going to let her walk away. And that meant they needed more clues than a dark-colored fuck-all truck.

Where are you, Ruby? He let his eyes graze the desk phone as if it might ring, as if Scott might have good news this time, but the phone remained silent, the air punctuated by the staccato clacking of Jackson's fingers on her keyboard. Beyond the phone, beyond the pillar that cut the L-shaped bullpen in two, Decantor's desk stood empty. Sloan's, too, was vacant—Decantor's stocky Irish partner. It seemed Petrosky and Jackson were the only ones crazy enough to be here with a killer-kidnapper running around out there. But at least they were all looking for the same dickbag. If Petrosky missed something, there were three other detectives to catch it, and right now, he didn't trust himself.

He glowered at the file and leaned back in his chair. Anyone could have enough information on Norton's crimes to copy him. The infant found in the basement during the

Norton case had been big news. And the exterminator who'd been present when the baby was discovered had been more than happy to grant interviews—he'd described, in detail, everything from the broken window to the stacks of boxes, talked to every goddamn news anchor who would listen. And if it bleeds, it leads. Even Morrison's plastic-wrapped body had been splashed across the internet in the weeks following his death—journalists on the motherfucking rooftops, snapping pictures like it was a circus. Like his boy was a sideshow. Petrosky rubbed at his chest with a hand that felt oddly numb. Jackson's keyboard got louder, then faded away again. *Clack-click-clicky-clack.*

He sighed. No matter how similar the methods, how obsessed this killer might be with Norton, they couldn't ignore the differences—and these were significant. This killer was efficient, quick; Norton had loved long-term savagery, years' worth of messy torture. This killer had one blade of choice, while Norton had used everything from medieval weapons to a pike where he'd impaled one of his victims, to the chains and cages he'd kept in his very own chamber of horrors.

The clack-clack-clacking of Jackson's keyboard suddenly ceased.

His partner slid into the other chair at his desk with a huff and tossed a stack of pages on top of his folder. His rib cage heated—stinging. Painful. Jackson's neutral expression seemed out of place. "The witness angle doesn't make sense; no way our guy went after Ruby because she saw him. Decantor has a list of witnesses, people who saw the truck, people who signed statements—look at this guy." She tapped the top page so hard he winced on her behalf. "He was *outside*. Shouted at the killer's truck from his front lawn. If the suspect was going after witnesses, this man would have been first on the list."

Petrosky nodded; the muscles in his neck felt loose, one

snapped tendon away from wobbling like a bobblehead. "You're right. I knew it was a long shot, I just…" *Hoped.* For what exactly, he wasn't sure. Hoped that Ruby had been abducted so the perp could find out whether she was a witness? Yeah right. He'd have killed her. So what the fuck did the guy want with her?

Jackson was staring at him. "I know this will be hard for you. And I know you care about Ruby."

Oh, do you now? But he didn't say it—that wasn't why the heat in his chest had flared the minute she sat down beside him. Lies of omission were still lies. "Why didn't you tell me before?" he asked and finally met her gaze. "About the case? Morrison was my partner. If there was a copycat out there—"

"Decantor didn't catch the case until a few months ago when the guy dropped Evan Webb within our city limits. And even then, he wasn't positive it was related. Slitting a throat isn't that uncommon, not enough for him to believe it was directly tied to Morrison. Well, until now." But Petrosky didn't believe that, and from the way her jaw had tightened, neither did she. Decantor had been at Morrison's crime scene—he'd been there when Petrosky had found his partner, he'd pulled Petrosky out of that car, held him back, Petrosky's hands wet with Morrison's blood. The moment Decantor walked onto that crime scene, he'd have known, the same way Petrosky had just from looking at the photos.

"Petrosky?" Jackson was still talking, but he couldn't speak. His throat had closed, the pads of his fingers damp—if he looked down, would they be stained with crimson? Luckily, she didn't wait for him to respond. "I think he just didn't want to involve you unless he had to, especially when it'd be…sticky. Having you on the case with that history there."

Sticky. *Like blood, like my boy's blood.* He shook the thought off, but she wasn't wrong about the complication of being too close. He didn't even know how he'd make it through the day without his spiked morning coffee; preparing it at home would be tempting fate to drag him back into the hole where he'd lived after Morrison's death, where the only thing tethering him to reality was the hard steel of the gun at his temple.

He frowned at the stack of pages on the desk. "And now?"

"Now we're all after the same guy."

"The same guy or the same *pair*." Petrosky crossed his arms. "Norton had a partner for most of his homicidal career, so if our killer has a hard-on for Norton's crimes, he might be working with someone else."

Jackson raised an eyebrow. "Someone who drives a truck?"

"Maybe. It's possible only one of them keeps getting locked up, and the other has the truck registration, which is why we can't find overlap with the jail records. Plus, the crimes themselves are labor-intensive. It takes a lot to roll a man in plastic and heave him into the car without spilling a drop of blood on the back seat." And they'd gone over the forensics, combed those cars top to bottom, looking for any evidence of the man who'd done it. And found nothing. The bastard probably lined the driver's seat itself with the plastic; one car did have a bit of tacky residue on the back of the headrest. Probably tape.

Jackson's gaze was on the window, thoughtful. "This might explain the change in MO. Maybe two Norton fans met up and realized that one of them likes to kill men, one of them prefers...kidnapping pregnant women."

Kidnapping, not killing. He wasn't sure she was sold on the idea, nor was he, but he appreciated it all the same. And despite knowing that Ruby's body hadn't been found, that the kidnapper had let the child live, they both knew they were running out of time. Eventually, the kidnapper would tire of her, or his fantasy would run its course. Their best-case scenario was probably a man who fancied himself a Norton incarnate: It meant he'd keep Ruby alive. He'd torture her, yes, but she'd live long enough for them to find her.

So how could they do that? What did they have? *Fucking hell.* He glanced once more at the pages on the desk, then abandoned them and stared at the ceiling—dirty, stained, but brighter than the haze outside. "Let's assume we have one homicidal copycat or two spree killers working together who suddenly got a taste for kidnapping. We'll have to expand the search for other crimes related to Ruby's abduction. But every homicide victim we know about was a male in his thirties—no connections between them outside of the physical description. All big men; burly victims, hard to subdue."

Jackson's fingers drummed on the desktop, a steady rhythm of bone on wood. "So our guy is probably strong. Like Norton was."

Or he has a way to distract them while he slits their throats. And if he had a partner, that would be far easier. He lowered his gaze.

Jackson was frowning. "Is there…"

He waited, watching the hesitation play across her face—tense lips. Furrowed brow. "Spit it out, Jackson."

She swallowed hard and continued: "Any way Morrison was killed by this guy instead? I know the neck wound didn't match, so not the same blade, but if he's smart, he'd have ditched the original weapon to avoid us connecting the cases sooner—Morrison's murder was huge, public, no way our guy would keep a weapon every cop and his mother were looking for. And the MO is just so perfect. Plus, Norton never did anything else like his; Morrison's murder was an anomaly, a deviation in pattern."

Petrosky shook his head. "No, Norton admitted killing Morrison." Hadn't he? God help him, he couldn't recall, and just the thought of diving back into Morrison's murder, the thought of *remembering*, made bile rise in his gullet. *Turn it off, you old fuck. Be logical. You can do that.* He coughed to clear his throat—it stung. "Besides, Morrison was killed the night he found Norton's hideout. It would be a hell of a coincidence."

"Yeah, yeah, and there's no such thing as coincidence. I'm just saying…Norton liked having partners. That's all." She ran a hand over her shiny skin—was she sweating? The growing darkness outside the bullpen window felt heavier than it had just a moment ago; even the ceiling felt lower as if it might crush him beneath its weight. "What about the fact that the killings started after Morrison died?" she said. "There were no murders before him, none like this."

"Well, we can't very well have a copycat without something to copy," he snapped, but his voice came out strangled.

If Jackson was bothered, she did not show it. Her fingers beat their steady rhythm on the desktop. "Fine. So he reads about the murder, decides to copy it, and goes on to kill two vics over that next year."

And then the dry spell—a year and a half. Then another spree, three more bodies over eight months. Then another year and three quarters, no killings. Then Webb, three months ago. Whatever he'd been doing, whatever reason he had for stopping…it had to be recurring. "Maybe he was institutionalized." Even if they had two perps working together, it was possible one might not strike without the other.

Jackson's forehead creased. "Do institutions still exist?"

Not really, and a hospital was more likely to send you home with a prescription the second you said you were over whatever homicidal or suicidal impulse had landed you there. Unless… "If you have the money, there are private hospitals. And if a loved one had suspicions that our killer was involved in something like this, had these darker proclivities…" He shrugged. His chest burned.

"Look at you with the big words. Like a walking thesaurus."

"I know stuff, Jackson." He raised his hand to massage his chest—*fuck, that burns*. "There are a million reasons for a dry spell. Maybe he has a job that regularly takes him out of state —or maybe the dry spells aren't dry spells at all. If he changed his MO just a little or committed crimes outside the Ash Park metro, we'd never know."

Jackson nodded, pulling her cell from her jacket pocket. "I'll give Scott a call, see if he's got a few minutes to run a broader search on similar crimes nationwide. You know he loves that shit."

Petrosky nodded—"instant gratification" Scott called those searches. Again, Petrosky looked at his desk phone, hoping Scott was already dialing him up with good news—

He jumped when the phone rang.

Petrosky reached for the receiver, but Jackson was faster. She listened, then met his eyes and mouthed: *Scott*.

Good. Better for her to talk to him anyway. Scott, like his father, probably thought Petrosky was weak. And he was…he was. Hopefully, he could still help Ruby. Maybe she'd already escaped, been found hitching a ride toward—

He blinked at the thunk of the receiver in the cradle; Jackson's face had hardened, her eyes steeped in sorrow. The burning in his chest intensified, but no amount of massage was going to help, not now.

They were too late.

9

THE WARM BREEZE was a gentle pressure against his neck, but the stink lingering in those breathy molecules felt like the persistent fingers of a corpse. Death. Even upwind, you could smell it over the rotten stench of the dumpster, over the acrid, musty fetor of old urine. New death always won out over old—it was the brighter, sharper tang of iron. Of meat.

It was most disconcerting in the dark.

The cobblestones turned their footsteps into an uneven cacophony of rubber on rock that matched the laborious squeezing in his chest. Last time he'd worked a case like this —*Norton, fucking Norton*—he'd had a heart attack. Was he headed that way again? Did it matter? But when Evie's smile flashed in his brain, he pushed that thought aside. It did matter if his heart exploded. Evie and Henry didn't need to suffer another loss, at least not before they had the opportunity to realize what a fuckup he was. After that, they'd know not to miss him too much.

"If only this asshole would stick to one alley," Jackson muttered. "We could stake it out until he came back."

If only. Petrosky squinted, the floodlights at the end of the alley glowing beacons in the dim, but the buildings on either side evoked the shadowed claustrophobia of a minotaur's tunnel, at the end of which was not escape, but a horned monster set to gore them. So far, the gray dumpster blocked his view of the body. *Don't think about it. Don't think.* The flatfoots stood like brawny guard dogs past the garbage, presumably protecting their crime scene. *Cla-thunk, thunk, think-thunk* went Petrosky's shoes, his heart beating tripletime, each pulse sharp as if the muscles in his chest were sitting along the edge of a razor. *It's just a body, just another body.* The corpse fingers scratched more viciously at his neck just above his collar, raising the little hairs at the base of his skull.

He rubbed at the back of his neck. They'd looked for a pattern in dump sites, but had found none; their killer was willing to travel from the west side of Detroit to the east side, and most recently, inside the Ash Park boundaries. Most of the dump sites were in different jurisdictions, but the killer had surely known that dumping a body in Ash Park would raise some red flags if he had been following Norton's career.

Maybe he was tired. Maybe he wanted to get caught.

Petrosky stepped around the dumpster, squinting in the harsh floods, but it did not take long for his eyes to adjust. His heart screamed.

Fuck.

Her red hair, once so vibrant, appeared dull and lackluster next to the lake of crimson spilled over the cobblestones. Her belly was still distended with pregnancy, though softer now, void, and this somehow was a small comfort. Whatever the asshole had done to her, he hadn't sliced her belly open—perhaps she had gone into labor naturally. Had she gotten to kiss the baby before this fucker whisked her child away? The medical examiner would give them more concrete details, but he sure hoped her death had been fast. Maybe she'd died with her baby in her arms. Maybe she'd still had hope.

His heart squeezed, spasmed, vibrating like a fucking taser had been attached to his chest. He rubbed at the sore spot above his breastbone and finally drew his gaze to her head.

Her face—oh, her poor face. One cheek was sunken, crusted, and caved in below her eye socket, making the ridge of her eyebrow all the more pronounced, her nose too swollen to tell what shape it had once been. *Maybe it's not her.* His heart leapt. But the hair, that red hair…

He squatted, his knees aching, and leaned over her face. *Please be someone else.* But what was he hoping? That it was some other innocent girl? He was a monster. And he didn't care. More than anything, in this moment, he wanted this girl to be a stranger. He peered into her mouth—no red lipstick, nothing so obvious, but…that tooth. One chipped incisor.

He closed his eyes. The wet scent of blood gathered in the back of his throat. *I'm sorry, honey. I'm so, so sorry.*

"How close is he, Petrosky?"

"How close to…" But he knew. How close was this scene to that of Lisa Walsh, the postpartum girl Norton had murdered? He forced himself to stand, his thighs aching, his knees on fire. His gaze locked on the brick wall. He couldn't look anymore, not at Ruby. *Poor, poor Ruby.*

But he had to look. It was his job.

"There are differences." His words were a choked plea for help, the final gasping breath at the end of a hangman's noose. He inhaled the thick stink of iron, of Ruby's blood, and peered down once more. *Just another body, just a stranger.* "Lisa Walsh…she had a hole through her shoulder." Impaled. Because Norton had been into medieval torture. But not this killer. "Our suspect appears to take the quickest means to an end." He gestured to her throat—slit open, like the others. "And he sticks to an MO, even if he changed victim profiles." Which decreased the likelihood of a second killer. If the partner had a different victim type, he'd likely have his own preferred way to kill them. Woolverton would check for the type of blade in case the difference was that subtle—just a different weapon—but Petrosky wasn't betting on it. This was the work of one man, he felt the truth of that deep in his guts. His eyes grazed over Ruby's belly. His chest burned.

"He probably couldn't help himself," Jackson said. "Even if he'd planned to kill her a different way, maybe stick closer to Norton's pattern, he needed the rush he gets from using that knife."

Petrosky nodded grimly. "Yeah, so he skipped the pike. But the other details are remarkably similar. He beat the holy shit out of her, and the way he posed her, prone like this, behind a dumpster..." He shrugged. "That was all public information. The details that weren't released—they aren't here." He swallowed hard, trying to keep his heart beating, desperate to take a full breath, and drew his attention to his partner. Her gaze was sorrowful and understanding but also determined. Angry. He latched on to that shared anger, let himself burn there for just a moment, let the heat blister his insides, and when he came up for air, he could breathe easier. He cleared his throat and went on: "Walsh's feet had been mutilated, toes cut off, likely to make it harder for her to run. And she had a scar, a #1 carved into her skin." All of Norton's kidnap victims had. It was possible Ruby, too, had that symbol in an area not readily apparent, but he doubted it— none of the male victims bore that mark. This guy might know the basics of Norton's crimes, but he didn't know the little details that had set Norton apart.

Petrosky blinked at the body once more, then raised his eyes to the sky, a racing stripe of black above the walls of brick. "And he made sure we found her body after we found the kid. Like we did with Lisa Walsh."

But why? Why dive into Norton's backlist now after years of perfecting his own MO? That was a vital piece to the puzzle, one they were missing, and he didn't believe it was simple boredom—they'd have seen other, more subtle, escalations in past murders if their suspect was chasing a waning high. One thing was certain: this man was recreating Norton's crimes. But was he recreating all of them? How far back was he reaching? What was the endgame?

Petrosky's lungs hurt. If this man had recreated Walsh's murder, maybe he'd go back further, seek victims that Norton had attacked in the past, those who'd walked away from him intact, but not unscathed. Shannon's face flashed in his brain—the little puckers around her lips from the crude stitches Norton had put there. And Evie's grin...she'd been tiny when he'd taken her, but that didn't make her less of a victim.

He coughed as if he could clear the metallic foulness from cloying in the back of his throat, but it stuck as did the vise that had grown around his rib cage.

Maybe Shannon and her daughter were next.

10

"ARE YOU SURE SHE SAID YES?"

"Are you actually deaf now?" Jackson rolled her eyes and hit the blinker, the *tink, tink, tink* like a metronome counting down the minutes until he finally lost his shit. He felt oddly okay—but he shouldn't. He'd just spent an hour staring at Ruby's corpse, her throat a gaping wound, her face bloody and raw, this poor girl who had helped him at the diner every morning. He'd cared about her, hadn't he? Was he going numb? Or had he finally checked out? But he said none of that. He stared at Jackson, focused on the lines of her face, the flash of green light across her cheekbones as they zoomed through a dark intersection.

When he remained quiet, she glanced his way. "Seriously? How many times do I have to tell you?"

"One more should do it."

She checked the rearview mirror and sighed. "Shannon and the kids are with Decantor, on their way to your place, even though she thinks you're being overprotective."

He frowned. Was he being overprotective? Sure, it'd only been a few months since he'd had patrols watching to make sure Shannon was okay, but that was important, and even then, she'd almost died. Of course, Shannon said the patrols hadn't helped a fucking thing. And this time, Jackson had already called the chief, who said they didn't have the manpower for a full security detail, especially when there was no evidence that Shannon was in trouble. But the brass always said that until it was too late. He waited for the familiar prickling of panic at the base of his spine, the squeezing behind his ribs. *Huh.* His mouth still tasted like iron, and he probably had blood on his shoes, but his chest…nothing.

And… Had Jackson said *his* place? He'd thought Shannon was going to Billie's—Duke was there with Billie, and there were cameras. He didn't even have an alarm at his house.

And now a more concerning thought attached itself to his brain like a leech. Had he tucked the whiskey away, or was it still on the nightstand? No, he'd tossed the bottle this morning along with the rest of the trash. *Thank god for garbage day.* Not that he'd be able to hide it for long. Shannon wasn't blind. Or stupid.

Maybe you should just quit drinking, old man. Go cold turkey. But he had a feeling he'd need the bottle more than ever in the coming weeks. It wouldn't do for him to be in with-drawal, unable to concentrate while the killer snatched up victims left and right. True, that might have been an excuse to avoid drying out, but he didn't give a shit.

Jackson eased into a parking spot and cut the engine, not in front of the precinct this time, though the squat building next door was equally shitty. Three stories of brown bricks that could use a paint job, or at least a power wash, but you couldn't tell now—the entire lot was painted in wide brush-strokes of onyx, highlighted by the yellow-white glow that oozed from the streetlamp and splattered his sneakers. The breeze hissed against his cheek.

"What about Nace?" he said suddenly. Margot Nace was a girl Norton had kept locked up for over a year and the only one besides Shannon who had survived him. She and her child—Norton's child—now lived out in Pontiac. If their perp was revisiting Norton's older crimes...

"Sloan's headed that way to make sure, and he already spoke to her mother—Margot is at work tonight. He'll watch her and get her home safe, and we'll go out there to chat with her in the morning."

Her mother. *That's right.* Margot was only a teenager when she was taken—thirteen if he recalled, fourteen when they'd found her. How old would she be now? Nineteen? Twenty, maybe? So much childhood to catch up on. At least her mother had been more than happy to take charge of the baby; raise them both. Give them both a chance.

But what would happen to Ruby's newborn son? Both of his parents were dead, and his grandpa, Ruby's father, the only blood relative the kid had left, couldn't even take care of himself.

"Hey, focus, would you?" Jackson said, stepping onto the walk in front of the building. He snapped his head in her direction—had she been talking to him? "It's late, and we've only got ten minutes with the doc." Jackson slung the office door open, the hushed quiet from inside rushing into the evening like a flock of birds in silent flight, the only noise the air beneath their wings. But the air stopped hissing as he followed Jackson into McCallum's inner office through the open door.

McCallum wasn't alone. A tall black man stood in front of the doctor's desk, looming over the shrink, his back rigid, muscles coiled—confrontational. The doctor's eyes flicked their way as they entered, and the man turned. Thick mustache, heavy beard, glasses—Andre Carroll. The chief's husband.

The man glowered, and with one final glance at McCallum, he pushed his way from the office, knocking Jackson's shoulder. Heat rose in Petrosky's chest—finally, something besides that aching, hollow numbness—but it vanished just as quickly. Still, he said: "Watch where the fuck you're going."

"Like you give a damn about boundaries," Andre snapped over his shoulder. The outer door slammed shut behind him, once more taking the night with it.

"What was that all about?" Jackson said.

"Oh, you know. The usual." McCallum's ping-pong-ball cheeks rose as he forced a smile, but it didn't reach his eyes. Had something happened? Was the chief okay? Petrosky had no way to know; he was no longer a part of her life. Again, he waited for his guts to twist, for his heart to react *somehow*, but his lungs kept working, and his heart stayed cold. He was fucking dead—dead inside.

"You're familiar with the case?" Jackson asked the doc, sliding into the leather chair across from McCallum's desk.

The doctor nodded, light eyes shining in the lamplight, irises oddly green against the lime tweed jacket he wore: Elbow patches and everything. Tenured literary professor meets Dr. Freud.

Petrosky's bones ached, knees creaking as he lowered himself into the chair beside her. "So, what can you tell us about our copycat?"

"Well, his recent shift in pattern is significant and concerning—far divergent from his earlier crimes. But I believe you have a fan, not a copycat."

Not a copycat? Petrosky raised an eyebrow. "That doesn't make sense. He positioned Ruby's body"—*Hyde, not Ruby, a stranger*—"just so in that alley, and left the baby in a base-ment. Hyde was even a redhead, just like Lisa Walsh." He hadn't remembered that until this moment, but now the images of Walsh's body in the alley came roaring back. Her swollen belly streaked with purple stretch marks. The gaping hole in her shoulder. Her face crushed, not a single tooth where it should have been. But it wasn't the same alley—the perp had kept them on their toes there. Petrosky went on:

"He even taped up cardboard boxes to mimic the original basement scene. I can't see him bothering with that if he wasn't trying to replicate the crimes." And he'd been careful. The techs hadn't found a shred of forensic evidence, not on the boxes, not on the tape, not on the window frame or the doorknob. They were still combing the place, but Petrosky would have bet Andre's balls that they'd come up empty. Not his own balls, though—he at least had that much hope.

McCallum leaned back in his seat, steepling his fingers and pressing the points of his indexes to his lips—the shrinkiest of shrink moves. "But the more critical pieces of Norton's crimes aren't the same; aren't even close. The note-worthy part of Norton's most recent pattern was the element of medieval torture. And Lisa Walsh's throat was not cut as Hyde's was; Norton impaled that poor girl on a wooden spike, let her die slowly. Her baby was thrown through a window in the dead of winter, suffering significant injuries in the process, and almost died of hypothermia. And the owner of that basement was cut to pieces on her lawn. Your suspect copied none of those things, at least not closely."

"This homeowner was killed, too, just not on the same day." And not on the front lawn—the killer had slit Webb's throat and left him in a car, same as his other victims. Neater than Norton, and far more efficient. "And Lisa Walsh's baby survived, as Ruby's will." Margot Nace and her child…they'd survived too. But only because he'd found them in time.

McCallum was shaking his head, making his steepled fingers wiggle, back and forth, back and forth. "True, but still not the same. His staging of the scene was superficial." McCallum dropped his hands to the desk and leaned over them, and when he met Petrosky's gaze, there was more than professional camaraderie—Petrosky felt like a bug beneath a cruel child's magnifying glass. Was the doc watching to see if he'd crack having to open up Morrison's case file again? But he wouldn't crack; it'd be a slow, quiet slide into oblivion, watching the light disappear inch by shrinking inch until there was nothing. Nothing at all. He could almost hear those words echoing back to him as if he were already in a void.

"I don't think this is about Norton," McCallum said, bringing him back to the room, to the leather chair, to the shiny desk and the rotund doctor wrapped in tweed. "Sure, perhaps he thinks Norton is an evil genius, maybe he obsessed over the news clippings—"

"Clippings?" Petrosky said. "What is this, 1952?"

Jackson snorted. "You asked me yesterday what YOLO means."

The doctor's face remained grave. "It is not a coincidence that he's here in Ash Park. No one knew his crimes were connected until Decantor caught Webb's case—he could easily have kept on with his pattern in other precincts, other states, but he didn't. And no other crimes in Norton's file come close to these serial homicides, except for Detective Morrison's death." With this last line, Petrosky was no longer an object beneath a magnifying glass; McCallum's eyes were focused beams of sunlight, his gaze burning Petrosky's face. "Morrison's killing showed your suspect what he wanted his own MO to look like. And he's been repeating it ever since. Until now."

Jackson rubbed at her temples, but dropped her hands as she asked: "So he watched Norton's coverage and said to himself, 'Hey, that looks like a good idea'?"

"I think he's always had these proclivities, but wasn't sure how to carry them out until that case, and with the sensationalism…" He trailed off, but they all knew the end of that sentence: some psychos loved the spotlight, and if those assholes could copy a high-profile crime and get their own face splashed on the news, they would. "But he isn't interested in just recreating Norton," McCallum went on. "If he was copying Norton from front to back, we'd have seen other crimes similar to those in Norton's file. And we haven't, not until this week. And if his goal was finishing what Norton started, he'd have gone after the survivors too."

"What about Shannon and the kids?" Petrosky blurted. His voice had come out pressured, but without the corresponding tightness in his chest—he hadn't known he intended to ask until the words were in the air. But he was glad he'd done it. Maybe McCallum could convince the chief that Shannon needed better protection than a few patrols and his own dumb ass. Well, and Duke. That big lug would make sure no one got near her.

The doctor shook his head. "It's right to exercise caution on the off chance that he changes tacks, though I suspect he'd have gone after Shannon already if that was his intention. Even if he knows where Shannon is, you've got a hell of a security system at the neighbors', Duke at your place... Shannon and Henry and Evie will be fine. Besides, I hear she's quite good with a gun."

"Yeah, Evie's a regular sharpshooter." Was his voice a little lighter? His throat wasn't as tight, maybe, but it was hard to tell for sure.

The doctor's gaze had darkened. McCallum laced his fingers on the desktop and leaned over his clasped hands. "This jump to kidnapping, to different victim profiles, to the staging of those scenes...it's concerning. We don't know what the killer is reacting to. Or what his next move might be."

Jackson shifted beside Petrosky, knocking his elbow from the armrest hard enough to make him wince, but when she spoke, her voice was soft. "When it comes time to warn the public, what should we tell them to look out for besides the truck?"

Petrosky frowned—publicity could only make things worse with a killer who fed on the tears of the populace.

"Serials of this type tend to be white males in their thirties," McCallum said. "And he's strong to be able to lift those bodies into the vehicles. He's likely working alone—someone this particular about the blade, the scene, is probably a cautious loner who would abhor the idea of involving someone who might out him, or worse, screw up his pattern. But with the shift in MO, we can't be sure about that." The doctor sighed, and in that moment, his eyes looked darker than they had all evening, his usually bright irises circled in navy. "I think all bets are off now—there's an endgame, and this change in MO is not an accident. And if he did follow Norton's crimes—and it's clear he did—he followed you too."

"Me?" Petrosky balked. "You think he's after—"

McCallum put up a hand. "I mean he followed the police—your actions after Norton's crimes. Which means he's learned from every mistake Norton made. And thus far, he's been able to avoid leaving a single piece of forensic evidence. Part of that is planning. Watching. Stalking not only the victims but the scenes and the people who are after him. He won't mess up, not the way Norton did."

"Sounds like he thinks he's smarter than Norton," Jackson said.

McCallum's eyes narrowed, thoughtful, and it was far better than the super-gaze he'd aimed Petrosky's way. "I believe that's true. He's emulating Norton's crimes but changing them—improving them. He's made each killing far more efficient, which means it's safer for him. And if he wants to prove that he's better than Norton once and for all…" McCallum leveled his gaze at Petrosky again. "What would Norton have considered a mistake? What was his biggest error?"

Norton's biggest mistake? The one that had killed him. "Letting me find his ass." And suddenly, Petrosky could feel the stair treads beneath his spine and the tug of fresh stitches in his chest, could see Norton on top of him, grinning, knowing he had won. And then Norton's head exploding.

The stink of gunpowder. The girl, that poor girl, the gun in her hand.

Keeping his victims breathing was Norton's fatal error. If the killer followed on this new path, his victims would not walk out alive.

11

PETROSKY LISTENED to the bright tinkling of the doorbell, the early morning brilliance hurting his eyes. His mouth still tasted a little like the liquor he'd stashed in his Caprice, but i tasted more of mouthwash, and he felt remarkably compose even if his heart was jerking in little fluttery bursts th should probably be checked out. But who had the time fc doctor with a serial killer on the loose?

They'd gotten Margot Nace and Shannon both s squared away last night, Shannon and the kids in his bedrooms. No hint that she'd seen the unopened bo liquor behind the fake panel under the kitchen si damn crafty. *Take that, HGTV.*

But though Shannon and Nace seemed safe moment, there was one other child a Norton admi be interested in: the child Norton's victim had through a basement window years ago. This k seem interested in hurting kids—the docs at the F Hyde's child was perfectly healthy with no sign and Bloomfield was far outside his killing zon house was on the way to Pontiac where Mar her mother lived.

Jackson rang the bell again. This time, footsteps approached, more like a scampering on the other side of the door. Murmuring, a woman. A higher voice answered—a child.

The door swung inward.

Stella, the infant he'd found in the basement, weak and broken and hidden behind walls of cardboard, was no longer a baby—just a year or two younger than Evie. He often wondered whether Morrison would have adopted Stella if he'd lived. He thought so.

The kid seemed happy enough, offering them a gap-toothed grin, eyes shining, hair as red as the woman beside hers was blonde. She waved—friendly. Trusting. This surprised him, though he knew it shouldn't have; she'd been too young to remember the trauma. God, she really did look like her mother. But Lisa Walsh, though she'd given birth to her, wasn't really her mother. The woman standing at Stella's back, her eyes narrowed at Petrosky, questioning but fierce —*that* was a mother. And from the tight set of her jaw, she clearly knew well enough about Stella's challenging first few weeks.

Petrosky and Jackson flashed their badges, and Mrs. Paltrow's brown eyes widened. Was she wearing mascara? Who was she trying to impress?

She led them to the kitchen and sat across from them at the dining table. Stella scuttled off to her bedroom, and good thing—seeing her was making that weird fluttery thing behind his breastbone worse, and he didn't want to have a heart attack before he found this fucker.

"She seems to be doing wonderfully," Petrosky said. "Last time I saw her..." He dropped his gaze to the table, suddenly 'ure he'd see blame in Paltrow's eyes—*You didn't save her 1other, didn't save Ruby, couldn't even save your partner, the 'osest thing you had to a son. What good are you?*

But Paltrow's voice was calm and remarkably non-

combative. This surprised him too. "She doesn't remember anything, just so you know. I've talked to doctors and psychiatrists and psychologists, and they all say the same thing: That she won't ever remember those first few weeks; that no baby would. That she's fine."

Petrosky nodded at the oak table as if approving its craftsmanship. Better that way—to not remember. So many things he'd rather forget.

He raised his head to see Paltrow staring at him. "So, are you going to tell me what this is about?"

Jackson rested her forearms on the table, her gaze earnest and steady. "We don't want to alarm you, but we have a series of crimes that seem linked to the ones committed by Adam Norton."

They wouldn't need to explain who he was—the woman brought her fingertips to her lips, her eyes wide with horror. "You think...are we in danger? Is Stella..."

Maybe. But Jackson shook her head. "We have no reason to believe that anyone wants to hurt your daughter. But the man we're after may be obsessed with Norton, which means he might have wanted to take a peek at Stella. We just want to make sure he hasn't been out this way."

Paltrow shook her head. "I haven't seen anyone." But here she paused, face pale. Her eyes tightened. *Uh-oh.* "We have gotten a few crank calls, but I didn't think anything of it. Do you...do you think those calls might have been him, trying to see if she was here?"

"What did the caller say?" Jackson asked.

"Oh, nothing—they didn't speak at all. Just hang ups."

That might prove to be less helpful, but at least they could trace the calls. He stared dumbly while Jackson jotted down the dates and times, his ears pricked for the slightest shift in atmosphere, the click of a doorknob, the padded footsteps of a killer. What if their suspect was already in the house? Was he with Stella now? He could almost hear her giggling as she skipped to the killer's truck, following him like unsuspecting children trailed after the Pied Piper.

"Any feeling that you're being watched?" Jackson said, pulling him from his bizarre fantasy. What was wrong with him? "Strange vehicles, anything like that?"

Paltrow's jaw dropped. "Excuse me?"

"Just trying to be thorough," Jackson said. And they couldn't lead her. If they told Paltrow they were looking for a truck, she might imagine a truck into existence and send them on a wild goose chase. And they didn't have time to spare. No wonder Decantor hadn't said anything to the more recent witnesses. To Ruby—*Hyde*. His chest constricted and released, angry butterflies erupting from a spot beneath the apex of his ribs.

"No, I haven't seen anyone watching us. Haven't felt unsafe...until now." She sighed and shook her head. "I just can't believe this. When we adopted Stella, knowing that both her parents were dead, that the monster who had been her..." She swallowed. *Her father.* They had all heard the end of that sentence, but none of them would call Norton that; he didn't deserve the title. Lisa Walsh had died to get away from him; she'd paid with her life for Stella to be here with the Paltrows. And Petrosky'd be damned if he saw that destroyed.

Paltrow jumped at a sound in the drive, and Petrosky was on his feet when the front door crashed open. Clomping footsteps. "Mom!" A teenage girl—sixteen maybe—ducked into the dining room, curly blonde hair flying behind her. She froze when she saw them. "Oh, sorry."

His muscles relaxed, but Jackson's hand—she was gripping the flesh of his forearm, her gaze worried. He followed her eyes to...his gun. He lowered his arm. He didn't even remember raising it to his hip, didn't remember snaking his finger behind the trigger.

Luckily, Paltrow wasn't watching him; she was on her

feet, her back to the table, facing the girl in the doorway. The teenager had the same slender build as Mrs. Paltrow. Same hair. Either a biological daughter or Paltrow just happened to get a kid who was a spitting image of herself.

Paltrow pointed to the stairs. "Heather, you can go to—"

"Actually, we might need her," Petrosky said, but that name—*Heather*—drove a dull spike into his belly; before Linda, there was Heather. He pushed the name from his mind. "Just for a moment. It'd be helpful to know if she's seen anything."

Heather blinked at him, her blue eyes wide like her mother's, her lips just as downturned. Frowning. But she slid into an empty seat at the table. And waited for Petrosky to get on with it.

12

THE DAY HAD WARMED QUICKLY, the sun already singeing his arm hair through Jackson's tinted windows. He probably should have asked her to stop for more coffee, a sausage sandwich, something, but he didn't think he could eat if he wanted to; his stomach felt heavy and sour and sick, a far cry from the disconnected fluttering that had started his day. He should have had breakfast. Billie usually shoved a granola bar at him on his way to work, but he hadn't needed to drop Duke off at the neighbors' like he did most mornings, not with Shannon and the kids home.

He rubbed his smarting arm and sighed. Heather hadn't known anything more than her mother—no strange vehicles, no one following her, no one outside the house when she left early for swimming practice or came home late from cheerleading. And the Paltrows had a working doorbell cam: nothing suspicious. That was good; better than good. If their suspect hadn't been watching Stella or her family, he wasn't after them despite Stella's biological connection to Norton. McCallum was probably right—this guy was cherry-picking Norton's crimes and improving them, becoming a more efficient killer than Norton had ever been. It certainly wasn't about the torture; the medical examiner had called, and while there were some ligature marks around Hyde's wrists, the beating had happened postmortem—just trying to copy the scene. No secretions or signs of latex, so he hadn't raped her. No drugs in her system, either, so she had likely gone into labor on her own, given birth, and been killed shortly after. Then the killer had dumped Hyde and her child.

Fast. Efficient. Their suspect's thrill was in the killing itself. But based on the way he was posturing for fame with these more sensational crimes, he wanted Norton's notoriety, too, and damn if Petrosky was going to give it to him.

What else do you want, asshole? Where would a Norton-obsessed fuckwit hide out? Scott had already searched for online chat groups related to Norton but had come up empty; infamous as Norton was during his crime spree, history had mostly forgotten him. But Petrosky hadn't. Nor had the women they were on their way to see now.

Jackson pulled up to a red brick colonial, a tall wrought iron gate leading to the backyard—two huge dogs were currently losing their shit from the other side of the bars. Rottweilers. The animals made the place feel safer, and that calmed his heart a bit. But not enough. Twice, Petrosky stopped as they strode up the front walk, dizziness tugging at him, his lungs tight and ill-equipped to keep him going. Twice, he forced his feet to move on. But when Margot Nace answered the door herself, his lungs stopped working altogether. The air hardened like ice in his throat.

Her hair was a brilliant orange, the same as Norton's other victims—he'd always had a thing for redheads. But unlike the frizzy mess her locks had been when Petrosky found her in that basement, her dead friend tethered to the wall beside her—*Ava, Ava Fenderson*—her hair was glossy, wavy, secured at the nape of her neck with a yellow ribbon. Childlike, maybe, but she'd missed a good portion of her childhood; Norton had stolen that when he kidnapped her.

When he forced her to carry his baby and locked the boy in a cage.

He steeled himself and leveled his gaze at her, waiting for a flicker of recognition, but Margot just nodded to him and Jackson in turn and led them to the living room. The carpeting swallowed their footfalls, which made the sound of crayon-on-paper all the more apparent; the redheaded child on the floor kept his eyes on the coloring book splayed open on the coffee table, scribbling, scribbling, scribbling. Margot's mother was already seated on the loveseat, her tight curls run through with streaks of white as if the ordeal with Norton had aged her. They eased themselves onto the couch across from her, but despite Jackson's assurances that they were only there to ask a few questions, despite Jackson telling her that they had no reason to believe Margot was in danger, Nace's face remained fraught with a worry just this side of abject terror. She surely remembered the kidnapping of her daughter like it was yesterday—surely still felt the pain of seeing her battered child after a year in captivity, the agony of seeing her daughter's scarred flesh, the anxiety of meeting the infant Margot had been forced to bear for her captor.

The child glanced up as if he could read Petrosky's thoughts, a crayon clutched in his fist like a weapon—Norton's eyes stared back at Petrosky, that dark glitter that said more than words ever could. Was the kid a psycho, too? His blood ran cold, and between that and the chilly tightness in his lungs, it felt like drowning in a December lake. The dogs outside bark, bark, barked.

"Petrosky?"

"Hm?" He looked over. Jackson's eyebrows were raised as if she'd said something to him, but he hadn't heard her speak. "I'm sorry, go ahead."

Jackson turned back to Margot, who had settled on the loveseat beside her mother. Margot's eyes burned into him as

McCallum's had, as if she, too, were just waiting for him to fall apart. But of course she was; if he hadn't needed to get Margot out of that basement, he'd have gladly died there with Norton—and Margot knew it. He frowned. Had her trigger finger twitched?

"As I explained on the phone," Jackson was saying, "we just wanted to make sure that things are still going well for you here. That you haven't had any unusual experiences."

Margot and her mother exchanged a glance. Margot's eyes were dull, almost bored, but her mother's face was pinched—the woman really was terrified. Her voice shook as she said: "Unusual like…"

"Have you seen any vehicles around that you didn't recognize?"

Margot dropped her head, her eyes on her lap. Avoiding the question? She had no reason to hide a suspicious vehicle. But her mother's shoulders relaxed. "No, nothing," she said. "And I'm always on the lookout for things like that after what…happened. Trying to protect Martin." She gestured to the child, who looked over his shoulder at her, smiled, and went back to his coloring book. Should they be doing this in front of him? Maybe he was too young to care.

"What about people on the street?" Jackson asked. "Anyone that made you feel uncomfortable?"

Margot's head snapped up. "Is that a joke?" Her face had paled, her eyes no longer bored—fire blazed in her irises. "I can't go anywhere without people making me feel uncomfortable. I'm always waiting for him to come back. For someone else to snatch me up. I can't even get on an elevator, because the second the doors close, I'm right back there with him. Even here, in this house…" She shuddered, and her mother put an arm around her shoulders. Margot did not respond to her touch. Martin went right on coloring as if these outbursts happened all the time, and maybe they did—these women would be on high alert for the rest of their lives. It sucked, but damn if that didn't make the ice in his lungs melt. They were safe. If anyone would notice a rogue pickup lurking in the shadows, these two would.

"We're sorry to bring all this up," Petrosky said, his voice low. "But we had to ask."

"You didn't even tell us what this is about," Margot said. "You just wanted to ask about unusual experiences? Why? Is someone trying to hurt me? I haven't slept at all, spent the whole fucking night with my nose pressed against the window."

Jackson raised a hand. The kid at the table looked back at Margot, eyes wide, his expression less like Norton's now, and more like a scared child. *God, he's just a kid, what was I thinking?*

"We don't believe our current case has anything to do with you," Jackson said.

"Then why are you here?" She was practically yelling. "Why the fuck are you here?"

The child dropped his crayon and scampered toward the loveseat, but he did not approach Margot—he climbed into his grandma's lap and buried his head in her chest. Outside, the animals began their barking again in earnest, a sharp, agitated symphony of howling, snarling, and snapping.

"Look what he did to me!" Margot yanked her T-shirt down, exposing a shiny pink scar on her chest, the one Norton had branded all his victims with—*#1.* "I don't want to do this anymore." She bolted to her feet and stalked from the room; her mother watched her go without a word. The boy pressed his face harder into his grandmother's shirt.

"Listen, detectives, I'll help however I can, you know that." Her gaze remained on the hallway, where Margot had disappeared. "But you owe us the truth. Are we in danger?" She finally turned back to them, her eyes glassy, her nose red.

Petrosky looked at Jackson, but his partner was focused on the woman across from them. "We don't believe so, ma'am. But between us, we might have a man out there who worships Norton. So far, there is no indication that he'd come here, that he'd go after any of Norton's previous victims, but—"

"But you can't be sure." Her voice held less panic now—resignation, like a nervous man with a crusty mole who gets a cancer diagnosis and sleeps for the first time in months. Real you could deal with. Real was easier than the demons inside your head.

Petrosky cleared his throat. "If you see anyone suspicious, call us. Do you have an alarm?"

She nodded. "Absolutely. Door alarms, glass break sensors, the whole deal. And those dogs sleep with Margot and my grandson here. Watch them extra carefully." Her face had hardened, her eyes steel—no longer glassy. No longer scared. Determined.

"Good." Anyone coming near this property would be dog food before they could claim another victim. *This was a waste of fucking time.* He pushed himself to standing. "Let's head back to the station, Jackson. Leave these nice people alone."

Back to the station. Where his car was. His little bottle of Jack. And god help him, he needed it.

13

———

"GOT THE TRACE BACK," Jackson said, collapsing into the chair at his desk.

Petrosky pushed his keyboard aside, along with the useless DMV printouts. Decantor had looked at the trucks already and checked any and all security cams around their crime scenes—nothing. What had made him think he was going to do any better? Decantor was a good cop. And he was sober.

"The trace?" he said. So far as he knew, their suspect hadn't left even the tiniest bit of forensic evidence at any of the crime scenes. He hadn't even jimmied the door on the house where he'd left the baby—the guy had probably taken an old key from the homeowner when he'd murdered him.

"The phone trace. From the Paltrows.'" Jackson laid a page on his desk: a name and address.

Oh yeah. Right. "And?" He didn't think their killer would be so sloppy as to call, especially not when his only point of interest should be a kindergartner, but maybe they'd gotten lucky.

"The calls came from a cell, the owner of which lives

three miles from the Paltrows: Tanner Beattie. Paltrow says they know the kid; he's an ex-boyfriend of Heather's."

"So just a punk kid prank calling his ex?" Very anti-climactic.

Jackson nodded, but she didn't look upset, and neither was he, not really—better a punk ex-boyfriend than a serial killer looking for Norton's daughter. But a phone number might have helped them catch the bastard. As of now, there were no leads, no evidence that their guy might be stalking past victims, and no evidence that he'd known any of the victims before he killed them. Which left...the truck. That goddamn truck. At least four or five years old, since it had been seen at the earliest crimes, but that didn't narrow it down much.

"You heading out soon?" Jackson's voice came from behind him—her seat at his desk was empty.

He turned to see her shrugging into her jacket. "Yeah, I'll be out of here in a few." He just had one stop to make. And he didn't need Jackson watching him do it.

———

THE AIR HAD COOLED with the setting sun, leaving behind a chill laced with the subtle scent of moonflower and fresh-cut grass. He parked at the curb three houses down from his destination in the shadows of an old oak. A shot of Jack burned in his gullet, liquid courage in normal circumstances, but not tonight.

He didn't need courage for this.

The Beattie home looked just like the picture on Google Earth, a little white picket fence that only reached Petrosky's hip—any animal worth its salt would jump over as it pleased, so they probably had one of those little pissant dogs. Over-grown rats, really. But no tiny creature yapped from beyond the fence as he headed up the wide driveway. No growls rumbled from the oppressive darkness along the side of the house as he slipped behind the back gate. He had it on good authority that little Tanner had hockey practice tonight at a rink ten minutes away. And it had ended five minutes ago.

He didn't have to wait long. Petrosky pressed himself against the bricks as a Sebring convertible squealed into the drive and came to a halt dead center, the ultimate "fuck you" to his parents or any other person who might want to park alongside him. The kid who emerged from the driver's side had blond hair shaved close to his scalp, the floods above the garage making the tips glow white—his head looked like a fucking dandelion.

Tanner headed away from Petrosky toward the front door with the swagger common of upper-middle-class white boys who just knew Daddy's money would get them out of their next date-rape accusation—but he'd never met Petrosky.

Petrosky stepped over the gate and emerged from the shadows. "Hey, fuckface!"

The kid turned, gaze dropping to the gun at Petrosky's hip—he'd left his jacket in the car along with his badge. Oops. Tanner's eyes widened. "Mom!"

"I wouldn't do that if I were you," Petrosky said, raising his hand. "Then we'd have to tell her how you've been harassing your ex-girlfriend." He stepped closer, the *thwap* of his sneakers like an audible punctuation mark. "Do you think Heather's scared of you, Tanner? Are you hoping she might be nervous enough to take you back if you call her a few more times? Breathe all hot and heavy in her ear?"

"I didn't call her." He looked to the house as if expecting someone to come out, but his dad worked in the ER and wouldn't be home until morning. Mom was at yoga, though Tanner clearly didn't know that. Funny how easy it was to find people who weren't actively trying to evade you.

"Oh, but you did call her, Tanner." *Thwap. Thwap.* "And when Heather stopped answering your desperate, pitiful begging on her cell, you started calling the house phone."

Tanner had paled—was the kid even breathing? "I don't want any trouble, man. I just miss her."

"You've got trouble, kid, whether you want it or not." Petrosky grimaced, baring as many teeth as he could. "Did she say anything that would indicate she wanted you to keep trying?"

Tanner pressed his lips together. He shook his head.

"You are not entitled to her. You don't get to call her. You don't get to see her. And it doesn't matter how you feel about it."

"I'm sorry," Tanner whispered. His voice was shaking.

"You fucking should be." Petrosky crossed his arms and stared the boy down. "Now I'm going to need you to say it— say she isn't yours. Tell me you're going to respect her boundaries."

"I'm sorry, she isn't mine, I'll respect her, I'm not going to hurt her."

"Say you'll leave her alone."

"I will, I swear, I—"

"Say it!" His voice echoed off the garage door and startled the night birds in the oaks, who took flight with an irritated cackling.

"I will leave her alone, I won't call her, I'll leave her alone." He was talking so fast it all came out as one word. The kid hissed a breath, eyes darting to the house and back to Petrosky, then said, lower, "Who are you?"

"Let's call me a concerned party." He leaned so close he could smell the salt of the kid's sweat and a horrid pungent aroma that could only be body spray. "And if you ever bother her again, I'll rip off your balls and feed them to you."

He turned on his heel to another burst of squalling from the sky. By the time he slipped behind the wheel of his

Caprice, the shadows felt lighter, the world less oppressive. He lit a cigarette and smiled.

14

HE AWOKE TO GIGGLING, the high tinkling sound not near as abrasive as his alarm. He opened one eye.

Evie and Henry stood beside the bed, the girl with her hands clasped over her mouth, Henry staring at his sister as if waiting for instructions—he was the one laughing. Julie… she used to do that. And Linda would groan into his ear, ask if it was time to get up yet. They'd been good together once; Julie had been their glue. But she was gone now. As was Linda, so far as he was concerned.

Evie apparently could hold back no longer—she burst into laughter and climbed onto the bed, jumping, jumping, jumping. Last night's booze rolled in his belly, but at least he hadn't left anything incriminating on the nightstand.

Evie squealed, Henry giggled from his spot by the bed, pans clanked against the stove, then a thunk that might have been dishes on the dining table. "Kids! Breakfast!"

"Oh yeah!" Evie's eyes widened, and she dropped to her knees on the mattress, onto the pillow where Duke usually rested his head. Where was the big dog now? "Mom said she made oatmeal and that you should come eat before you have to go to the pee sink."

Henry laughed harder. *The precinct.* A pee sink was probably more fun. Petrosky smiled, stretching his arms above his head. "She did, did she?"

"That's why we're here!" Henry said, then laughed again, his words softened with the lisp common of smaller children.

"Yeah, and she said to ask why all the windows were closed when it was so nice."

Petrosky glanced at the window behind him—cracked, but not open all the way. "I just like the breeze. And it makes the mailman a little more comfortable." He gestured to Duke, who had sauntered into the room and was now peering at him over Henry's shoulder. The dog wagged his giant tail. "Can you imagine this beast snarling at you through an open window?"

"He snarls?" Henry's blue eyes widened. Duke licked his face.

"Not at you, son." *Man, he looks like Morrison.* He reached out and ruffled the boy's hair though his heart suddenly felt like it was breaking. "Never at you."

THE RIDE to the prison felt like it took far less time than the four hours allotted by his GPS, though he knew the time had passed—he'd watched the sun drag itself into the sky inch by gilded inch, watched the pink and purple clouds give way to white cotton on a background of searing blue. It was probably the quiet; as much as he loved seeing Shannon and the kids, having people in his space all day was not the most relaxing experience. Maybe it was because he couldn't drink at will, but he'd pretend it was just an old-codger-introvert thing.

He slammed the door to his Caprice, the scent of tobacco clinging to his suit jacket like the familiar embrace of a favorite blanket. Always comfortable. Comfort*ing*. And he needed that. Jackson had elected to stay behind at the precinct, working with Decantor to review the recent serial files as well as Norton's closed cases—Morrison's case file, photos of his boy with his throat slashed open front and center. The thought of having to see that, examine it again, had made his guts turn and his chest brighten with pain, but this…this he could do.

High brick walls painted the color of stale Dijon mustard surrounded the prison complex, all topped with savage-looking barbed wire that glittered like diamonds against the cerulean sky. His footsteps against the asphalt quickened. He couldn't wait to see this bitch in the flesh.

The trip through security was quick, as was his stop at the warden's office, and before he knew it, he was seated across from Janice Lynwood herself. Norton's second partner. The woman who'd helped Norton kidnap Shannon and her infant daughter. Without Janice, would Norton have stayed in Ash Park? Petrosky didn't think so, which made Janice just as much Morrison's killer as Norton himself.

Lynwood's red hair had lost most of its luster, the ends frizzy and split, her scalp showing through at her hairline. Balding—it was the very least of the terrible things she deserved. Her eyes were dull, too, even more so than the bland beige walls; no bars in this room, just painted concrete blocks, a raw concrete floor, and a metal door with a plexi-glass window beyond which a guard stood with his arms crossed. She blinked at him slowly and leaned back in her chair, the metal legs scraping against the concrete floor with a grinding like that of a bone in a wood chipper. "What do you want?"

"No hello?" Petrosky said, laying the manila folder he'd brought on the table in front of him. "This is probably the most exciting thing you've done all week."

She grunted but shrugged, probably trying for nonchalant, but the telltale twitch at the corner of her eye told him she wasn't nearly as bored as she was pretending to be. "So, what is it? Did someone else go missing?"

He raised an eyebrow. Did she know about Hyde? They'd put out an Amber alert when they thought they had a kidnapping, but they'd said nothing about Hyde's connection to the Norton case. Even the 300-word news article reporting that she'd been found dead had not mentioned her baby or her connection to Webb or Adam Norton. And connection was the reason he was here. If their killer was interested in Norton but wanted to make sure he improved on that psycho's technique, as McCallum had speculated, it might make sense to go to the source: A woman who had worked with Norton. A woman who knew what errors they'd made, why they had gotten caught. If nothing else, a copycat would be fascinated by Norton's second partner—the only one still alive to tell about it. About him.

"What would make you say that, Janice? Do you think someone's missing?"

"You're here. You wouldn't be here unless there was a good reason." Her front teeth had grayed, one incisor missing. Only a few years inside, and she was literally falling apart. *Good.*

"Weird that you went immediately to missing—to kidnapping."

She shrugged one thin shoulder, one corner of her mouth turning up—*smiling?* "It's what I know."

Fucking cunt, you almost killed Shannon. Rage burned in his belly.

Perhaps she saw the fire in his gaze or the rigidity in his shoulders because her lips turned down once more. "I know what you want me to say: That I'm sorry. That I know something else, that I can help with whatever you're after now. But I was never as much of a planner as you wanted to believe. I thought we were in it together, but Adam used me like he used everyone else—he had friends I knew nothing about."

Liar. "You helped torture Shannon. Let's not pretend you didn't like it, that you didn't get off on it." But he did believe Norton had kept her and any other partners separate; Norton was too smart to tell her about anyone else he associated with.

"Maybe I did help, and maybe I did like it." The corner of her mouth twitched up again, so briefly he almost missed it. "But I think—"

"I don't give a fuck what you think." His fists were tight balls of bone and sinew against his thighs. "You abused her, abused my granddaughter."

"You aren't related to either one of those people, and you know it—your only kid's dead." Her eyes glittered meanly.

Don't punch her, don't punch her. But there was no danger of that, not really. Though he was angry, though his belly was hot, it was a fire dampened by wet timber—too weak to make him lose control. "It takes more than blood to be related, not that you know anything about relationships. Otherwise, someone would have come to see you." That was the first thing he'd checked, hoping their suspect might have shown up here in person. She hadn't had a single visitor outside of Petrosky, partly because of her tendency to get thrown in the hole—inconvenient. Even if the suspect had come, they wouldn't have let him visit, making it more effective, and safer, to contact her another way.

Lynwood was scowling.

"No visitors at all," he repeated, releasing his hands; his knuckles popped like muted gunfire. "All you get are these." He opened the manila folder and spread the pages over the table, one by one by one: Notes from other psychos or people who worshipped psychos. Assholes who thought Janice and Norton were heroes worthy of admiration. The type of assholes who might copy their crimes. "Do you recognize these letters?"

She did not appear to see the papers; her eyes remained focused on him. "The days all run together for me. Can you imagine being locked up? Eating the same thing day in and day out?" She sniffed and leaned back, crossing her arms across her wasted breasts. "Maybe it'd be worth looking harder if you made things more interesting."

His chest was forged of molten steel, but though he was aware of it, there was a disconnect between his body and his brain as if someone else's chest were burning. "What do you want, Janice? Some thread? Want to sew your own fucking lips closed?" He slammed his palms on the table and leaned over the pages. "I generally frown on giving sharp objects to inmates, but in your case, I'd make an exception. Maybe your roommate could use a shiv. Who hates you most in this place?"

Her nostrils flared. "You want me dead, Detective?"

Fuck yes, I do. "I want my family safe. I want the citizens of Ash Park to be safe. Any of them are worth a hell of a lot more than you." It was a risk, putting it like that, but she'd helped mold Norton into what he became. After Lynwood got arrested, Norton had started kidnapping girls who looked like her—McCallum had speculated this was because Lynwood had emasculated him. Sure, maybe he just had a thing for redheads, but taking them so young, when they couldn't fight him off...he'd been making up for something.

Petrosky glared at the sheets, wishing he could drag every letter-writing asshat into the station by his balls. Maybe he would unless Lynwood gave him some insight. He raised his head, ready to stare her down, but Janice had dropped her gaze to the table.

"Tell me what you know about this man." Petrosky slid one of the pages across the table, his top choice for copycat fuckbag. The letter had come from a man in Ohio—gun lover, survivalist, conspiracy theorist, anti-cop in every sense, and what McCallum called an "internet troll" which made him statistically more likely to be a psychopath or a narcissist. But more critical here, the man was a hunting knife enthusiast, someone who might be particular about the kind of blade he used—who'd know how best to slit through the musculature of a human throat. "Maybe I can read you the top line? Where he praises you for being close to a great man, for helping to plan the death of a cop." The letter had come in mere months before the first killing on Decantor's list—just after Morrison's death. He waited for his heart to squeeze, but the steel in his chest had solidified, leaving his lungs tight but cold.

"I don't know this man, and I didn't kill a cop, didn't plan it either—I was already locked up. And you'd know if Adam contacted me, just like you know about the letters." She waved a hand over the table like a tired magician. "You had to ask the warden for a favor to get these, didn't you? They don't save anyone else's mail, they just read it." Her tone had gone haughty, her eyes brighter—smug. "Seems like you're more obsessed than any of these guys."

He inhaled a thin breath and leaned back, as far from her as he could get. Yeah, he'd asked the warden to keep careful tabs on her incoming correspondence, which was how he knew Norton hadn't involved her in Morrison's death. But the idiots who sent her letters didn't seem to understand that. And with Norton dead, Janice was the next best thing.

"What about this guy?" Petrosky said, tapping another page. "He asked what drew you to Norton, said he watched your trial, wanted to be your boyfriend. Promised he could make you happy." He slid the page across to her; she rolled her eyes. "Did you tell him what he could do to make you happy, Janice? Maybe told him to keep on with Norton's legacy? Because if you did, that's another crime added to your already very long list."

She chuckled. "That's why you're here? You want to see if you can keep them from paroling me? I've got another twenty-five *if* I'm lucky. By then..." She shook her head. "It won't be worth living. It's not worth living now. If only I had a needle and thread, maybe people would stop asking me stupid questions." She narrowed her eyes at him, and he planted his elbows on the table and leaned in close, bile bitter in his throat—just looking at her made his skin crawl.

"I'm not here about your sentence. I'm here to protect innocent people the way you didn't do for Shannon. I'm here because of that little boy Norton killed—I know that one wasn't on you." The tiniest flicker of guilt crossed her features, then vanished. "Janice, I'm not here about the past, and if you have information that helps with this case, I'll put in a good word for you." *Like hell.* "I need to know what you wrote to these men." The warden hadn't had any outgoing mail in the file, so either she hadn't replied, her letters hadn't been saved, or someone else had mailed them out for her. "Did you tell any of these men to find a victim? Did you help them figure out how sadistic they were the way you did with Norton? You always were good at that." He paused, waiting for another arrogant smile, or a narcissistic glimmer in her eye, but her face remained still, bland. The table pressed into his belly. "Did you tell them about me, Janice? About Shannon?"

"I have better things to do than talk about you." Now, a half smile. "And I wouldn't tell you if I had."

He hated her. Suddenly, every molecule of his being wanted to reach across the table and snatch her up by the throat, and if he hadn't thrown back two shots of Jack in the car, he surely would have. He forced his voice to stay even. "Last time, Janice: Did you write to anyone who seemed intent on hurting another person? Maybe someone who likes knives as much as you do?"

The silence stretched. From somewhere beyond the door

came the clank of cuffs on bars, steel on iron. "I think lots of them have a thing for knives," she said softly. "But I can't help you." She leaned closer to him, their noses almost touching—her breath was foul. "I hope they kill everyone you love," she whispered. "That they ruin you the way you ruined me."

———

HIS FURY HAD EASED by the time he stepped onto the asphalt once more as if the beige concrete had absorbed his hatred. Perhaps it would leach back into Lynwood's cell, take care of her for him. If she killed herself, the world would be a better place.

He sighed, letting the blaring sun sear the flesh of his forehead, burning off the cobwebs that had spooled themselves through his brain as he watched Lynwood led back to her cell. He'd had the warden hold her mail altogether for the time being, and the man had agreed to send Petrosky copies of any correspondence. But he didn't think that would pan out. If their killer was trying to prove himself better than Norton, he wouldn't keep going back once he had his MO firmly in place. Lynwood would have been a source of information, a stepping stone. The killer was past that now. And if any of the men from her earlier correspondence were involved, they'd know soon enough. He glanced at the folder in his hand, the copies of the letters—return addresses to go with each. And it had only cost him a case of premium bourbon.

He slid into the driver's seat and tucked the file beside the passenger. His phone blinked from the cupholder: missed call. Another query from Jackson about one of Norton's crime scenes? Maybe a question about Morrison's body.

How deep was the gash in his throat? Did your fingers touch his spine? Did you really put your gun to your head?

He shoved the key into the ignition and eased into drive,

watching the prison recede in his rearview as he slugged back a shot—just one more. Then he drove. He let the summer breeze caress his cheeks. Let the setting sun heat his forearm. Let the smoke blow out into oblivion.

He watched the sun sink.

He was half an hour from home when the cell buzzed again. This time, he lifted the phone and peeked at the caller ID. Billie.

"Part of your harem?" he could practically hear Jackson asking.

"My family," he said to the empty car. She was probably calling about dinner. Or she wanted to take Duke out somewhere—Billie loved that old dog as much as he did. He smiled and drew the phone to his ear. "Hey."

"You have to come home." Not Billie. Candace? Her voice was shaking—it took him a moment to figure out what she'd said. And why did she have Billie's cell? He tried to force his mouth to work, tried to force air into his throat, but he couldn't catch his breath.

"Billie...she..."

His chest felt like it might collapse. *Don't say it. God, don't say it.*

Candace said it anyway. "She's gone."

15

THE ROAD SIGNS blurred past his car window, the setting sun burning a hole in the back of his head, his fingers too tight on the wheel to even smoke. He'd managed a few cigarettes with shaking hands on the highway, but the booze was the only thing keeping him even—keeping him sane.

Jackson's Escalade was already parked in the neighbors' drive when he squealed up, his tires spraying gravel onto the lawn and pattering against the undercarriage of his old car like a hail of bullets. Shannon opened the neighbors' door and stepped onto the porch, Henry in her arms, his knuckles white on Shannon's shoulder—scared. The puckered scars around Shannon's lips appeared all the more pronounced, pink and angry as if Norton had sutured them closed just today. He squeezed her arm and ruffled Henry's hair as he headed past her into the house.

Candace was sitting on the couch beside Jackson, her silk blouse shiny in the lamplight, a towel in her hands, wringing it like she was trying to throttle the person who'd stolen her friend. Her dark eyes were cast down at her lap, her shoulders slumped. He knew that posture—shame. At the dining table, Jane, too, appeared both grief-stricken and guilty, her muscles coiled, her lip trembling, but her hands were steady as she handed Evie a crayon for her coloring book.

He knelt beside Candace, and she turned his way. Tears had run streaks down her face, little rivers of salt and mascara—dried now. But her eyes welled again when he put his hand on hers. "It's okay. We'll find her. It's not your fault."

She collapsed against him as if she were a marionette whose strings had suddenly been cut. He wrapped an arm around her, letting her wet his shirt with her tears. "It's okay. I'm going to do everything I can."

She shoved herself back to seated. "But what if you can't do anything? What if—"

He put his hands on both of her shaking shoulders. "You trusted me once when you had no reason to—got into my car out on that street. I might not be good at living up to anyone's expectations, but I need you to trust me now."

She blinked and nodded, a breath shuddering from her lungs in a rhythm that matched the fluttering in his chest. His belly felt oily—sick.

He glanced at Jackson and sat back on his heels. His partner's face was grave, but not panicked—logical. Panic wouldn't help Billie. "What happened?" he asked Candace. Though Jackson had surely asked already, probably had pages of notes tucked away inside her brain, he needed to hear it from her.

Candace swallowed hard, but her breathing had steadied. "I heard tires. I thought it was you, actually." Her words were pressured, but she squared her shoulders and continued, "And then Duke... I could hear him all the way from here, even though he was at your house." Petrosky nodded, though it made the muscles in his neck cramp. The dog must have been at the window, per usual, but he was too big to make it through the crack. Shannon had been right—he should have left the windows all the way open. Then Duke would have leapt through the screen, would have gone after the man who'd taken Billie. Duke would have protected her.

Fuck. Why did I think they were fine? He should have demanded an around-the-clock detail on both houses, but the neighbors hadn't even been on his radar. Why Billie? She had nothing to do with Norton. They'd had no reason to think she was in danger.

"Please go on," Jackson said, her cell clutched in her hand.

"I looked out to see what Duke was barking at, and I saw Billie struggling with him down by the road—up past our house." Up past the house where the camera couldn't see him. But they'd still catch him driving up the street. "He hit her really hard in the head, like punched her, and she kinda…" She swallowed again. "Do you think she's alive?"

Yes. The killer had plans for her, didn't he? Another alley? Another of Norton's crime scenes? But which one? The sick feeling in his guts intensified—he smelled blood, tasted it in his throat. "He probably just knocked her unconscious."

Candace nodded, though she didn't look convinced. "He picked her up and put her inside, and I was running for the door, but I… I couldn't get to her."

"Can you describe the vehicle?" They'd be able to tell make and model from the camera, but not the color—the camera was black and white.

"I mean…a truck. A blue pickup truck."

Blue. That was better than the earlier witness statements, even if there would still be thousands of options. Jackson's thumbs were flying across her phone's screen, probably texting Decantor—they'd surely put out the APB already. A description of the vehicle would have been the first thing she asked for.

Petrosky cleared his throat. "What about the man? What did he look like?" Jackson had probably asked this, too, but it was always good to ask twice in case there were discrepancies.

"I couldn't see his face; he was wearing a stocking cap."

"Like the kind a bank robber might wear?" That wasn't how people usually robbed banks these days—that was becoming a crime for the hackers—but Candace understood the reference. She nodded. "Yes. A ski mask."

"Tall?" Petrosky asked. "Short? Thin?"

"He was average height. But he was a white guy—I could see his neck." She closed her eyes as if she could see him clearly behind her lids. "A little overweight, around the middle, especially. But he was strong; he had to be strong to pick her up like that. It was like she didn't weigh a thing. And when he had Billie over his shoulder…he waved." She opened her eyes. "Then he jumped in the truck, and he was gone."

"Waved?" Jackson frowned. This seemed to be new information.

"Yeah, like peeked back at me and kinda…" She raised one hand and made a tight flicking motion with her wrist.

Petrosky narrowed his eyes. That looked less like a wave and more like he'd been shooing away a bee. And even the fact that Candace had been here… "Wasn't I supposed to pick you up on my way home?"

She blinked at him, the fine web of red around her irises like strands of bloody hair. *Like Ruby's hair.* "I got off early— Dr. Gifford had a couple of cancellations. Dropped me off."

He glanced back at the dining table, and Jane looked over her shoulder at him. Evie kept her eyes on the coloring book, red crayon held deftly between her fingers. "What about you, Jane? Did you see anything?"

Jane shook her head. "I wasn't here. I came home from school early because Candace called me."

And if she hadn't called… *Shit.* Billie was supposed to be here alone. And their suspect knew it. He hadn't bothered with Norton's offspring, the women who'd gotten away; no, this guy was after a whole new batch of victims, and they all appeared to be…

McCallum's voice rang in his head: *And if he did follow Norton's crimes...he followed you too.* The doc had gone on to explain the statement away, said he meant that the killer had watched the police for ways to exploit their shortcomings, but what if his first interpretation was correct? What if this wasn't just about being a better Norton; what if the ultimate thrill would be to succeed where Norton had failed? The killer was already waving his successes in Petrosky's face by taking people Petrosky knew, and Norton's ultimate failure was the one that had led to his death—he'd let Petrosky find him.

This asshole wasn't trying to prove he was better than Norton—he already knew that. He wanted to be better than Petrosky.

He pushed himself to standing and met Jackson's eyes. "I'll pull the camera—"

But Jackson was shaking her head. "Already sent the feed off. No truck. He must have backed up the street; he knew exactly where your lens was pointed."

Fucking hell. "Okay, let's get Scott over here, have him pull what he can on the tire tracks."

Hopefully, that would narrow their search. He turned back to Candace. "I'll get some photos together for you, okay? See if we can narrow down the make and model of the truck you saw."He turned away from the couch, but Candace grabbed his hand. "Wait," she said. "The truck. There was a mark in the back window."

He raised an eyebrow.

"Like a bumper sticker?" Jackson asked.

"No…something written in the back window, in the dust. Like a symbol, but it might have just been letters."

At his back, the dining chair squealed against the wood floor, and then Jane was there, handing Candace one of Evie's crayons and a piece of paper. His heart vibrated, sting-ing. He closed his eyes, inhaling deeply, trying to ease the horrible tightness that was trying to squish his heart—trying to stop it from beating.

"Petrosky…" Jackson said. Her voice was strained.

He forced his eyelids open and peered at the page on the coffee table. The squeezing sensation in his chest turned to a bright, fiery stabbing.

On the page, Candace had drawn a capital *G*. And an *H*.

The last thing Morrison had ever written. As he lay dying, his son had scrawled those two letters in his own blood.

16

THE BASEMENT STANK OF MILDEW, though she'd smelt far worse, and the breeze from the open window was pulling the most pungent edge out into the night. But the concrete was cold and hard beneath her, the zip tie biting against the flesh of her wrists, her skull aching where he'd sucker punched her like an absolute asshole. And more than that—the fear. It tugged at her chest from behind, as if electricity had snuck up her spinal column and made its way forward past her lungs, leaving them quivering with current as it wrapped her heart in a sparking fist.

"Do your wrists hurt?" His voice was kind and oddly genuine—caring. He'd been remarkably pleasant so far, had even smiled as he pulled his fist back to hit her, and that alone made gooseflesh rise between her shoulders. The men who smiled too much, those the neighbors called "quiet and shy"—they were the ones the news later referred to as "madmen" in the aftermath of some atrocity. But Billie knew better. Those men were never mad, nor were they crazy. And that was the scariest part of all.

"No," she said as calmly as she could manage. "My wrists don't hurt."

"Good." He sounded like he was smiling, but she couldn't see his face. The room was too dark to see much of anything except the vague outline of the window off to her right and her own thighs, tinted gray by the moon. She wasn't even sure the place had electricity now that she thought about it. She strained her ears, listening for the telltale click of the air conditioning turning on upstairs, the monotonous hum of a refrigerator or a dryer, even the distant buzz of a freeway, the whistle of a train, something to indicate where they were. Nothing but the breeze from outside and the subtle hiss of her captor's breath, low and threatening despite his good-natured words. Like a snake.

"Why are you doing this?" When Eddie found her, when he got her out of here, she could give him some tidbit of information that would help him catch this guy before he killed another man. Not just men though—he had killed that waitress, hadn't he? She wasn't supposed to know, not really, but Shannon had mentioned it because she was worried about Eddie, she always worried about Eddie, but this…

No. Billie'd been through so much, and finally, *finally*, she was alive—free. Happy.

She forced herself to smile, hoping this would somehow change the tension in the air, that he'd let his guard down even if he couldn't see her, but her wrists were burning too much to do more than wince. Her fingers were wet. Was she bleeding? The man remained silent—of course he wasn't going to answer her. She leaned back, trying to ease the pressure on her hip joints, but then he laughed, and she startled, scraping her back against the wall as his voice vibrated out of the dark in the far corner.

"Why, huh?" It was disconcerting that she couldn't see him, like talking to a ghost. "It's weird, I know," he said. He laughed again, and if not for the bindings on her wrists, they could have been chatting about why he preferred soccer over baseball. Weird? That wasn't the word. Shocking, maybe. Sadistic.

Fucked up for sure.

"I could have kept on leading this perfect American life, this life everyone dreams of—I had it. You follow the rules, good things happen, right?" He shifted in the gloom, leaning out of the shadowed corner with his elbows on his knees, but still, his face remained hidden—all she could see was the glint of moonlight off his teeth. "Did you follow the rules, Billie?"

Rules? She'd done things she wasn't proud of, sure, but she'd finally grown to accept all those pieces of herself that had once made her stomach hurt. "No," she said. "But I follow the rules now. Everyone makes mistakes, right?" Tears stung her eyes, but she blinked them back before they could fall, before he could see them sparkling in the moonlight. The most important lesson she'd learned from her family— maybe the only one—was never let anyone see you cry.

But then he stood, and the desire to cry dried up along with her mouth. If she focused, she might have been able to see him; maybe she could have discerned the outer edge of his eyes, the shape of his lips, see the straight line of his nose, but all of it was remarkably average and not near as horrifying as the collar in his hand. Even in the dim, she could see the sharp bits, an appendage like a double-sided barbecue fork; the vertical metal made a sinister cross with an open collar. *What the fuck is that?*

"Mistakes are mistakes. I'm talking about actions— patterns." His voice had gone quiet. "Some people do everything they can to follow the rules, but your friend...he's a screw-up. And he still comes out on top. Everyone he loves protects him." He spat the last line—*protects.*

Is he talking about Eddie? "Please." Her voice hissed through the air and vibrated the little hairs in her ears. *Rein it in, I'll be there, just hang on.* But it wasn't her own voice in her head this time: Eddie's voice. And she believed him—she'd always believed him. She'd believed him when she'd gotten into his car the night he pulled her off the street. She'd believed him when he told her he'd take care of her so she could go to school. Believed he didn't want anything from her except to spend a little time with Duke while he was at work, and even that had been her idea. She didn't believe him when he said he was sober, but that lie was self-protective, guilty—not malicious. Unlike the man approaching her now beneath the shadow of night.

Why isn't Eddie here yet?

When the man spoke again, his voice had regained its friendliness. Calm—too calm. "You'd think I'd have people to protect me as well. Hell, the last time I had a drink was at my high school graduation. But even my own blood..." He shifted with a scratchy sound, fabric on fabric—a shrug. "I guess it doesn't matter now. And I still can't convince myself to throw caution to the wind." He chuckled. "Maybe your friend will help me with that too."

He'll be here; even this guy thinks Eddie will be here. She just had to make it a little longer. She hissed too-hot air into her lungs and held it there, trying to force her heart to slow as he bent over her. He smelled musky, but not like sweat —cologne.

"Hey, it's okay," he said. He brushed the hair from her neck, and she flinched away, grimacing. "Sorry, did I hurt you? I worry about that a lot, you know."

And this more than anything made her heart act up again; friendly men were dangerous. They always wanted something. "Why are you being so nice to me?"

"You don't have to be scared," he went on as if he hadn't heard her. "I promise. Just a bit of theatrics to send a message."

"Theatrics," she said, but the word was a whisper that didn't reach her ears—had she spoken at all? But she knew she had by the way his fingers tensed at the edge of her collarbone—hard and warm, the skin smoother than she'd have imagined.

He laughed again and went back to fussing with her hair, securing loose strands behind her ears, first one side, then the other, each gentle press of his hand making her skin crawl like he'd deposited a nest of writhing maggots in her flesh.

"I hate dramatics too," he said, righting himself. "It's silly if you ask me."

"Then why do it? Why not just write a letter?" Her voice was shaking—her whole body vibrated, head to toe to fingertips. But her hands…were the bindings looser than they'd been before? She gently wiggled her wrists, the blood making the plastic slippery and…yes, they felt looser with the lubrication. If she worked at it, maybe she could get her hands free, and when he wasn't looking—

He knelt abruptly and brought the collar to her throat. She flinched away from him once more, but he wrapped his fingers around the back of her neck and gripped her tightly as he affixed the collar, the material cold and somehow moist like damp human skin. And the metal appendage attached to it…oh god. One sharp point pricked at the soft spot beneath her chin, so close to her jugular, the bottom half stabbing into the flesh of her chest just above her heart. It would kill her if she moved the wrong way, and this man wouldn't have to do a thing. He'd just stand there smiling.

She sat as still as possible, and even with the brighter, colder metal against her chest and throat, she could feel the dull ache from the zip tie, the band tight across the bones of her wrist. If she could just—

He secured the clasp against the base of her neck and stood. "It's okay, kiddo. Just don't look down or you'll be put down." He chuckled again, the thick cackle of a laughing hyena.

"Fuck you." It slipped out before she could catch it, and the moment the words were in the air, she regretted them. The skin on the front of her neck stung; metal bit into her chest. She sat straighter, holding her neck higher, trying to keep the pressure off.

"Now that's not very nice," he said, but his voice still managed to sound jovial. "If you were my daughter, I'd put you over my knee."

"If I were your daughter, I'd kill myself." That, too, was the wrong thing to say—definitely the wrong thing—but he simply turned his back on her and headed for the corner. She closed her eyes, rotating her wrists, careful not to move her shoulders too much, clenching her jaw when the sticky plastic slid over the fleshy pad below one thumb. In minutes, she'd be free. Maybe Eddie would even be here by then.

17

G. H.

G. H.

The killer knew about Gertrude Hanover, of course he fucking did. Morrison had used his dying breath to paint a *G* and an *H* in his own blood on the only paper he'd had, then stuffed it in a travel mug. For Petrosky. And at the Hanover house, Petrosky had found Margot Nace and her child, Ava Fenderson's body, chained to the wall nearby, a *#1* carved into her belly. If he closed his eyes, he could see the blood trailing down over her rib cage, the deep punctures in her chest and throat from that bizarre contraption around her neck—he could smell the blood and Ava's shit, could hear the horrible wet noise the sharp metal had made when he'd tried to raise Ava's head, hoping against hope that he'd made it in time to save her. And while Petrosky couldn't recall telling the world how he'd finally figured out where Norton was keeping the girls, he was sure it was public knowledge.

Morrison's blood had saved Margot and her child. But would it help save Billie?

Jackson seemed to think so. The Escalade's engine whined as she pushed harder on the gas pedal.

The home where Norton had hidden his victims was just a block or so from the house where they'd found baby Stella on the basement floor, and right up the road from where Norton had killed Morrison. As Jackson pulled onto Beech, his muscles knotted, the spot above his breastbone throbbing, aching; he hissed a breath through clenched teeth. Dr. McCallum would call it muscle memory, maybe a panic response or a traumatic reaction, but fucking hell, why did it always take his breath away? The past shouldn't hurt so damn much. But he couldn't think about current events either; if he let himself imagine what the killer was doing to Billie, he'd go insanc. He rubbed harder at his chest.

Unlike the snow-covered walkways from years past, Hanover's green yard glistened in the light from the streetlamp across the road. Pots of magnolias perfumed the air as they made their way up the steps to the porch, but he couldn't tell the color—the porch lights weren't on, the space beneath the eaves a mysterious watercolor done in shades of gray. But Hanover still lived here; the same wide-open lace curtains peeked from behind the window glass.

Jackson rang the bell, and Petrosky's muscles twitched, his hand on his gun. He stared into the darkness, straining his eyes to locate anyone hiding outside the halo from the streetlamp, but he saw only the verdant grass. The house across the road had been demolished, leaving behind an empty shell of a lot. A builder's sign stuck from the dirt on spindly metal legs, the lettering a garish pink—it looked like a flattened flamingo.

Shuffling from inside. Dim yellow light spilled onto the porch from the foyer as the door swung wide to reveal a young man with dark eyes and darker hair tousled with sleep. *Is it you, fucker? Do you have my girl?* What better way for the killer to get into Norton's head than to live in the same place Norton himself had stayed? But he could see no reason for the killer to tell them exactly where he was hiding. No, this was something else—another sign, another message, though he'd be damned if he knew what it meant.

"Can I help you?" The man's voice was wary, tired—unless he was acting. Who was this asshole? The man froze when he saw Jackson's badge, squinted, then stepped back inside the house, his hand shooting out to the side behind the doorframe where they couldn't see. Was he going for a weapon? Petrosky's fingers tightened on his gun.

"Don't move, sir," Jackson barked.

"I'm just turning on the porch light." He raised his hands in the air, though Jackson wasn't aiming a weapon his way, not yet. The porch light stayed dark.

"Your name, sir?"

"Sorry, yeah, I'm Lev, Lev Hanlon. What's going on?"

A deep scraping sound came from somewhere beyond the foyer, and Petrosky's gaze darted past the man as another voice echoed up the hall. "Richard? Who is it?"

Richard; he'd almost forgotten her nephew's name. Richard had never actually lived here, but dementia was tricky, and poor Gertrude saw him in every young dark-haired man she met—the real Richard's hair had long since gone gray.

"It's the police, Gerty."

"The police?" she practically squealed. "Why I'll be! Turn on that light and let me get a good look at them—the light shouldn't be off this time of night anyhow."

"You turned it off again, Gerty," Lev replied as if he'd said it a million times before. "Just stay there, okay?"

"Don't be ridiculous." And there she was. Gertrude Hanover looked the same as she had the first night they'd met, right down to the cane and housedress, though it had been orange before...hadn't it? And neon yellow slippers. Her hair was a shock of white spouting wildly from the top of her head. "You're lucky I had my ears in, that's all I gotta say, coming out here to save your ass, Richard." Her eyes roamed to Petrosky; she leaned more heavily on her cane. Did she remember him? Could she even see him out here in the dim of the porch? "I'm Gertrude Hanover," she announced. Then she leaned forward, reaching past the man in the doorway—

The glare blinded Petrosky for a moment, but he recovered when she said: "Just Gertrude to you...sir." She winked at him.

Petrosky dropped his hand to his side, suddenly overcome by déjà vu so strong it pulled the air from his lungs like someone had stuck a vacuum hose down his throat.

Gertrude did not appear to notice; she kept her gaze locked on Petrosky, blinking her wide eyes like an attention-seeking puppy. "Now, what can I do for a big strong man like you?"

"First, you can introduce us to your friend here," Petrosky said. Lev still had his hands in the air, but he looked too wussy to be a threat to anyone. "Maybe tell him to put his arms down."

"That's just my nephew," Gertrude said, waving a hand as if waving off a fly—a man utterly unimportant. But her nephew...that was how Norton had conned his way into her house. He'd pretended to be her nephew, Richard, and the old bird's dementia had been too advanced for her to realize he wasn't. And that hadn't changed.

Petrosky's back tensed again. Was he wrong? Was this another dangerous man living beneath Hanover's roof? But Lev was already shaking his head, his hands now clasped at his waist. "No, Gerty, I'm not your nephew." He looked first to Petrosky, then to Jackson. "I'm her caregiver, a home health nurse. I work through Grand River Medical. My credentials are in my room if you'd like to see them." He swallowed hard, and the ping-pong ball in his throat bobbed.

Jackson's muscles relaxed; she nodded. "We'll take a look at those before we leave, sir. May we come in?"

The man hesitated, but Gertrude elbowed him and snapped, "Now, Richard, you just get on out of the way, you're being rude to our guests." Gertrude winked at Petrosky again, and Jackson chuckled, nodding toward the door—*after you*.

They stepped into a sparse linoleum foyer, not even a chair—lighter than he remembered, but the last time he'd been here, he'd snuck inside in the dead of night. And he highly doubted they'd find any victims this time. So what were they looking for? Why had the killer traced a *G* and an *H* on his truck for them to see?

"Have you had anyone else in here recently?" Jackson asked Lev, closing the door behind them. "Maybe delivery people, or someone out to fix the roof? Even a package you don't remember ordering?"

The nurse shook his head, but Gertrude was nodding. "There was that one man, the nice boy who brought my mail while you were in the shower."

"Oh…yeah." Lev's brow furrowed. "He came and brought a few letters that got dropped in his mailbox by mistake. Gerty made him tea."

"And he fixed the washer." Her eyes were gleaming chips of stone in a sea of wrinkles. "But don't you worry, Detective, I like my men with a little salt and pepper."

Lev balked. "The washer…. Wait, he went into the basement? How did he open the door?" Petrosky frowned. Was the door difficult to open? Or did Lev keep it locked the way Norton had? Petrosky swallowed hard as Lev shook his head, his mouth open as if prepared to say something else, but the nurse stopped himself short, his gaze questioning—skeptical. *Interesting.* He wasn't trying to figure out whether to admonish Gertrude for letting the man into the basement; he didn't seem to believe her at all.

"Did you see this man?" Petrosky asked.

"No, he showed up while I was in the shower. I didn't have reason to doubt her, though; I saw the letters and the extra teacup, even if it was still....full." His gaze drifted to Gertrude once more as if trying to decipher the truth from the lines of her face.

"When was this?" Jackson said.

Lev squinted. "I guess it would have been...Sunday?"

Sunday. The day Ruby was killed. Had he left a nasty surprise for them? Was this washer repairman their suspect? But those weren't the questions he really needed answers to. *Will this help us find Billie? Is she already dead?* Heat flared in his chest and settled.

"We'll need to take a look at the basement," Jackson said, following Lev's finger to the kitchen. Petrosky made it to the threshold and froze—his feet were glued to the floor, his legs numb. Last time he'd been here, the basement door had been completely hidden behind a bookcase—Gertrude hadn't even known it existed. Now, that bookcase was gone, as were the metal bars he'd unscrewed to get downstairs; the room glowed with neon orange paint, the white basement door a spotlight at the back of the room. But...not everything was different.

He forced his feet to move, a disconnected trudge toward the door, and fingered the padlock, then the combination keypad just above the door handle. "What's all this, Lenny?"

"Lev. And it's for Gertrude's safety. She likes to poke around, go downstairs, but her legs—"

"Don't you tell me my business, asshat," Gertrude huffed.

Same old Gertrude. "Anyone else have the combination?"

"Not a soul, and even if she watched me do it a time or two, she never remembers. Zero-four-two-six. You're welcome to go down, just don't let her go with you unless you want to carry her."

"That man can carry me anywhere, Richard." She grinned.

"If you wouldn't mind, Gertrude, I'd like you to stay right here," Petrosky said, shocked that his voice sounded steady. "That way, I know you'll be safe. I couldn't forgive myself if something happened to you." This, at least, was true.

She giggled like a schoolgirl, bright and happy, not a care in the world. "Oh, *Detective*, you always did know the way to a lady's heart."

"And here I thought you didn't remember me." He forced a smile—the banter was helping release some of the tension in his shoulders, but it wasn't going to help for long because he had to go down in that basement and *Billie's out there, Billie's out there somewhere waiting for me.* He swallowed the thought back, wishing it were whiskey.

"Of course I remember," she chided. "You're Richard's friend, right?"

No wonder Lev didn't believe her about the washing machine repairman. He met her eyes, nodded, then tapped in the first number on the keypad. His chest constricted. *Four-two.* His heart ached. *Six.* The hinges creaked... No. Not a creak. Someone was screaming.

His breath caught, but no one else responded to the noise, and when he paused, his heart in his throat, he realized he could hear nothing else from the room below—only a thick, empty silence. *Just because someone was screaming last time, doesn't mean anyone is screaming now.* He found the switch with a trembling hand.

In the light, the basement stairwell was as unrecognizable as the kitchen: Carpet on the treads, fresh paint on the walls, brilliant sconces as yellow as Gertrude's slippers. And the staircase was wider, far wider now, plenty of room for his shoulders and then some. But despite the new decor, every time he blinked, he could see the claustrophobic sound-proofed padding Norton had wrapped over the walls.

Though he could feel his shoes thudding on the steps, he did not hear his footfalls, only the steady *thunk, thunk, thunk* of Margot Nace as she banged her own head against that pole, half-insane with the horrors she'd been through. He'd gotten her out, but not soon enough. Never soon enough. *Where are you, Billie? I'm sorry, I'm so sorry.*

He hit the bottom landing and turned the corner. The window had been replaced with glass block, the bricks removed from the outside where Norton had closed the room in. Yellow—all of it yellow. Before, one small lamp had made the room look yellow, hadn't it? He followed Jackson with his eyes as she strode through the space, peering at walls, looking inside a few boxes, squinting at the carpet. No cages to keep children. No chains on the walls. And as he advanced into the room, every step heavier than the last, he saw no hanging weaponry, no scythe with a wicked-looking metal ax on one side, a sharpened, jagged hook on the other. Now, the nook that had contained those horrors held a washer and dryer and a set of cupboards, a stack of folded towels atop the dryer's closed lid.

He reached the back wall and turned, eyes on the pole, a support beam; no amount of remodeling would be able to change that. He could almost see Margot's blood on it, and when he looked beyond it, from this angle…

Ava. Her red hair gleamed, her blood garish against the golden glow, her wrists nailed to the wood behind her —*crucified.* Ava's head lay against her chest, the prongs of that fork sunk deep into the soft place under her chin. Iron, iron on his tongue. The stitches in his chest tugged tight.

He blinked. The dead girl wasn't there. The air wasn't thick with the stink of shit and blood. He had no stitches in his chest, not now. Yellow walls. Just yellow walls.

He hissed an inhale, but the sound was far more ominous than the silence—the warning hiss of a rabid cat. Jackson peered at him over her shoulder. "Are you okay?"

Absolutely fucking not. I'm seeing things. "Fine." He forced himself to examine the walls, the little spots that used to hold Norton's security cameras—just drywall now. The open space beneath the stairs where he'd crouched with Margot had vanished, too; someone had built a little rectangular room like the one in the Harry Potter books Evie loved. Unless it was a false door—a decoration.

He crept closer and knelt. No handle, but there was a little indentation with a pull latch, half a step fancier than a knotted rope.

The door did not squeal. The dark beneath was absolute. He pulled out his phone and tapped the button for the flashlight, then peered into the opening.

"Whatcha got?" Jackson's voice came at a distance as if she were speaking underwater, but he couldn't answer—he couldn't breathe.

Footsteps behind him. "Fuck," Jackson muttered.

He stared at the blade, stained dark near the wooden handle, the knife's edges smooth and wickedly sharp—he could almost feel the prick of the metal against his flesh. The small square of thick plastic beneath it shimmered in the light from his phone—Visqueen. The same plastic used to wrap the bodies.

The bastard had planned all of this, every detail. Candace's presence when he'd taken Billie hadn't been an error—he'd waved at her for fuck's sake. He had known Candace was home, that she'd see that message—*G.H.*—that Petrosky would link it to Hanover.

Their killer had lured him here.

But he hadn't led them to Billie.

Petrosky's eyes locked on the knife, on the stained handle —*blood, there's definitely blood on it*—the smell of Ava's shit cloying in the back of his throat.

Please don't kill her. His heart—fucking hell, his heart. The room wavered, the blade going dark, and he finally closed his eyes, trying to calm the pain in his chest where a deep chasm was trying to rip open wider—a bigger hole for one more person he loved. One more person he lost. But one more he could not bear.

Please just let Billie live.

18

"It's late," Jackson said.

"I don't fucking care." He grabbed the bear claw from his desktop, Decantor's gift to him; the paper sack had been sitting beside his computer when they returned from Hanover's. But the chocolate was tasteless, slimy on his tongue, the donut beneath dry and crispy with dried sugar.

Jackson slipped into the seat beside him, though she'd just told him he should go home and get some sleep. Maybe she'd figured out that telling him to rest was fucking pointless. What was he going to do, sit at home beside his insufficiently cracked window and stare at the house where Billie had been abducted? Imagine their suspect taking her over and over again? Imagine what that sadistic fuck was doing to her? And god forbid he actually closed his eyes. Even now, every blink contained a flash of Ava Fenderson's body, her skin slippery with blood, except her hair wasn't red, it was gray, and her eyes were blue, and Billie wasn't smiling or scratching Duke's ears anymore, she was dead, dead, dead.

"We can't wander around at midnight, banging on doors, and expect that anyone will help us," she said. He frowned at her—what had they been talking about?—as she continued:

"We'll go back to the neighborhood and canvass first thing. But it might help to know who we're dealing with first; maybe one of these names will sound familiar to you." And it would be even better if one of them resembled the guy Hanover let into the house—the "washing machine repairman" who just happened to know the code to the padlock. But how? Lev hadn't given it to him, and Gertrude didn't know it. *Fuck.*

He choked down another cardboard bite and chased it with coffee, squinting at the pages they'd spread on the desk. Hanover's neighbors from Norton's old case file, all the people who'd lived nearby while Norton was torturing women in that basement, each page adorned with lettering too neat to be called scrawl—Morrison's. He rubbed at his chest, absentmindedly. There were only a few new arrivals to the neighborhood, but they didn't look promising. Jackson glowered at the sketch in front of them, the same thing he'd been doing for the last hour.

They had gotten a sketch artist out to the house to draw the "nice washing machine fixer," but the picture Gertrude had given them was absolutely not the "thicker around the middle" strong man that Candace had seen—this guy was handsome, strong-jawed the way her nephew Richard was from the photo in the hallway, though this man was far younger. And Gertrude had once told Petrosky she liked Justin Bieber, right? The sketch looked like someone had taken Justin Bieber and her dark-haired nephew and merged him into a nineteen-year-old social media hottie. And maybe that's what Gertrude had done; the man didn't match any neighbor they'd found. One thing he did trust her on: she'd said the man had a backpack, tossed that little detail at them on their way out the door. But it made sense; Gertrude wouldn't have let a stranger walk in with a large blade—forgetful or not, she wasn't stupid. Well, unless he'd distracted her by raising his shirt—maybe a six-pack was enough to give a hunting knife a pass.

But why would he give them the knife at all? Did it signify a more drastic change in MO was on the horizon? Was this bastard getting ready to go full Norton, torturing and confining his victims? And if so, did that mean Billie had more time? *Is she still alive? Please let her be alive.*

He met the eyes of the hunk in the sketch—Gertrude's ideal man. He tapped the corner, then pushed it away, grabbing his coffee instead. Tomorrow, the image would go live in the press, along with Candace's description of the suspect and the truck. They were beyond the point where silence might be useful. With the conflicting sketches, the public might believe they had a pair of murderers, but they couldn't rule out a serial-killing team anyway.

Jackson pushed herself to standing. "Scott won't have anything on the knife until the morning, so we might as well—"

"What'd he say about it, though? Just first glance?" The kid's first impressions were often more useful than a full examination by someone else.

She lowered herself back into the seat. "He said that it's a hunting knife, which is the type of weapon used by Decantor's serial." Which they knew. He swallowed more coffee and forced out: "But the blood on the handle... If it is the weapon used in Decantor's cases, the fact that he's giving it to us means what? That he doesn't need the knife anymore because he's planning to change things up?"

Or the blood is Billie's. He wants you to know she's dead even as he hides her body—maybe he'll make sure you never find it. His chest spasmed, a bright, angry, shooting pain, but it was his shoulder that made him wince; the muscles there hurt like a bitch.

"I don't think so," Jackson was saying. "We can't be sure of his next move, but he hasn't changed his killing method at all despite the changes in scene. He used a knife on all his male vics, used a blade on Hyde—he didn't let her suffer." The thought that she'd said this last part for him, that she was trying to soften the blow for when they found Billie dead, surfaced in his mind, and he shoved it away and planted his elbows on the desk, squinting at the files. She was probably right; this bastard was set in his pattern, at least with the way he killed. He surely had another knife. But he wouldn't give this one away unless the act itself meant something.

Petrosky straightened. "Did we get the medical examiner's report on Hyde back yet?"

She nodded. "Yeah, it's in this mess somewhere." She shuffled a few pages and handed him the printed sheets, and he flipped to the description of the wounds.

"Here, this part—Hyde's wounds show that a section of the knife is serrated. And didn't Decantor say there was a striation pattern on all of his victims? From the blade?"

She nodded, realization dawning. "And the one we found at Hanover's is smooth."

It was a different weapon. "He just wanted to send us a message, not give up his pattern or his knife."

"You're right." She pushed herself to standing once more. "But there's nothing else we can do tonight—if you can't sleep, go hang out with Shannon, go see Candace and Jane." When he frowned, she raised a hand and her voice. "We've got the sketch out, the descriptions. Scott has the blade. At first light, we'll comb that neighborhood top to bottom, look for anyone who might have seen Gertrude's washing machine guy or someone snooping around the Hanover house. For now, we need to get some rest."

But they didn't have time; they didn't have fucking time. Billie was gone.

Jackson met his eyes. "You can't find her if you're out of your mind, Petrosky," she said quietly.

But he could.

19

THE SUN EMERGED from its blanket of cloud just as they pulled in front of Gertrude Hanover's home. This time, instead of parking in the drive, Jackson eased to a stop at the curb. Then they were off, off into the slowly lightening morning to find a killer before Billie ended up like Ruby Hyde.

Petrosky hustled to keep up, his lungs aching a little but not terribly. Better than he'd have expected from a guy who'd smoked three packs in his car the night before and topped off today's to-go coffee with more alcohol than he'd had any morning this month. But whiskey was probably the only thing that kept him following Jackson down the road and up the steps to Hanover's neighbor's place, skirting the pot of dead tulips and the deader ornamental grass. The only reason the thunk of the door knocker didn't make his head want to split. The only reason he felt like he could breathe.

If Jackson, or Shannon, found out about the liquor, they could judge all they fucking wanted.

The young woman who answered the door had lanky dishwater hair tangled with sleep and an oversized T-shirt to her knees, but the dark-skinned man behind her was every bit as pressed as Jackson's pinstriped blouse. He sipped from his mug and put his arm around the woman's shoulders. "Can we help you?"

Petrosky's arm felt too heavy to lift the corner of his own jacket, but he didn't need to. Jackson flashed her badge and explained why they were there.

The woman shook her head in response to whether she'd seen someone matching Candace's description, but the man, who identified himself as Bernard Faral, shrugged. "White guy with a paunch? There are probably thirty in this general vicinity, but I can't say I've seen a truck around. I'm in residency at Henry Ford, though—I work long hours, so the only way I'd notice is if someone left their car out in the street."

Neither of them had seen anyone snooping around the Hanover place either. "I'd remember that," Faral said. "I always have to watch that place."

Jackson cocked her head. "Watch for..."

His cheeks reddened—blushing. The woman, his wife, based on their matching gold bands, raised an eyebrow Faral's way. "Well," he said, "every time I go out to get the mail, that lady catcalls me from the house. Talks about my... my butt." He glanced over when his wife chuckled.

Jackson nodded. "Of course she does." The man's face grew darker still—even the tips of his ears looked hot.

Petrosky could absolutely see Gertrude on her front porch, whistling at this poor gentleman, trying to get him to come in for tea and maybe for far more than that. He wanted to smile. But his lips simply wouldn't cooperate.

No one was home at the next house, and the owners in the house after had similar responses to the Farals—no one had seen anything. But Petrosky paused on the corner of Beech and Whitmore, the world under his shoes as familiar as if the stones had once pricked those very same pads of flesh. The red brick house stared back at him. Those barred windows. The twitching curtain...*the twitching curtain.* Someone was watching them.

"You alright?" Jackson asked.

"Yeah." He forced himself to start forward. "Let's go see Mr. Lockhart."

The stairs felt steeper than they looked, far steeper than he remembered, the doorbell's ring shrill and angry. The man who answered was scrawny, just as he'd been last time. His jeans hung from his skin-and-bones frame. But his hazel eyes narrowed when he registered Petrosky's badge. "You again?" The jailhouse hula girl tattoo quivered on his forearm.

"It's been a long time, Lockhart," Petrosky said, shocked at the cool evenness of his tone. "You miss me?"

"With every bullet so far," Lockhart quipped, then appeared to realize that was the wrong thing to say to the cops.

"Getting ballsy in your old age, aren't you?" Petrosky leaned an elbow against the doorframe. Lockhart worried his bottom lip with yellowed buck teeth. "Molest any little girls lately?" Was that why Lockhart had been arrested? He couldn't recall.

Jackson glared at him, annoyed, but he ignored her. Lockhart's already pale flesh had gone gray. "This is harassment. You can't keep coming here when you know I haven't done anything wrong."

"We don't know that." Had Lockhart admired Norton from afar and figured he'd jump on board the murder train once Norton was dead? But this guy didn't match Candace's or Hanover's descriptions, and...he hadn't even molested anyone, had he? No, this guy had whipped out his dick in front of some lady at a bus stop. And it was a big jump from flashing to homicide.

Lockhart took a step back from the door as if considering whether to slam it on them. "Maybe I should call my lawyer."

He crossed his arms, and the hula girl's terrible misshapen face shuddered—it looked like she was screaming.

"That seems like an overreaction," Jackson cut in. "We just want to know if you've seen a blue truck rolling around."

He shook his head, lips tight.

"What about this man?" She held up Hanover's pretty-boy sketch.

Lockhart sniffed—agitated, but no glimmer of recognition in those beady eyes. "No." And before Petrosky could push himself off the doorframe, Lockhart slammed the door closed in a burst of stale air.

"Well, that was useful," Petrosky muttered. But his anger was dull, a mere whisper of heat near the apex of his ribs. *Maybe there really is something wrong with me.*

Jackson's jaw was tight—for once, she was more agitated than he was. "I'm going to dig into that fucker's history when we get back to the station," she said. "If there's so much as an unpaid parking ticket, we'll arrest him."

"Hey, that's my line." He glanced over in time to see her shrug. "We both know he's a cagey shithead, but he doesn't fit." Even Gertrude would know if she'd let her neighbor inside, though Lockhart wasn't much to look at. Petrosky frowned as they made their way back up the block on the other side, across from Hanover's. They'd checked on new residents last night, thinking that if this guy wanted to get close to Norton, maybe he'd try to live near Norton's torture dungeon—dead end. None of the new residents matched Candace's description or Hanover's sketch. None had a blue pickup either.

He squared his shoulders and went on in an unthinking haze. Knocking on doors. Moving up and down the block as quickly as possible, but it felt like they were moving through molasses—or in circles. He was the one who had history here, every step on this road like a record player on repeat, a song you hated that just kept going and going and going. But what else was he supposed to do? The press had put out the sketches, the descriptions, and the whole force was looking for the truck. Billie's smiling face had been front and center on the news today. He needed to be here; it had to be him— that message was *for him*—but his nerve endings tingled with the desire to fight an enemy he could not see and protect a woman who was not here.

Please let Billie come home.

He squinted at the For Sale sign as they passed the Salomon house. The place where they'd found Lisa Walsh's infant in the basement, the homeowner slain on the lawn, was currently owned by the bank. It was hard to sell a murder house, it seemed, and with good reason—he could almost see poor Ms. Salomon on the front lawn now, her bathrobe soaked through with blood. They hadn't even bothered to put a real estate padlock on the door. Why had their current suspect hidden Hyde's child in Webb's home when it would have been just as easy to leave the infant here, Norton's original ground zero? Just to prove he was different? But if this was a game to their killer, if this bastard was trying to prove he was smarter than Petrosky, he'd want to make sure he had a worthy opponent able to connect the dots when they weren't so obvious.

They hit the corner of Pike and hooked a left. "This is turning into a goddamn treasure hunt," he muttered. But it didn't matter so long as the prize at the end was a living, breathing, Billie. He wiped sweat from the back of his neck, and though he knew his fingers were wet, he could not feel the dampness. Just cold.

"What the hell does he want us to see?" Jackson said, more to herself than to him. "Was it really just about the knife? He had to know we'd check the block." Their footsteps echoed in his chest instead of in his ears. She stopped halfway up the street and turned, craning her neck, scanning the houses as if some new information might appear out of nowhere. Everything was familiar, everything, but none of it the same—here, new paint glared from the shutters, there, flower beds bloomed unencumbered by ice, and running through it all were dry concrete walkways unmarred by the snow and salt that had been present the last time he was here.

His eyes lingered on Zurbach's old house, and he could almost hear the man's voice: "Wendell Zurbach, with an *H*. It's German." Zurbach had sold the place years ago, according to the records. Too bad. That old geezer had been the neighborhood watchdog, and he'd had a complaint about everything, from a stray dog across the road to Lockhart's noisy parties and the too-young girls he'd seen there, to...

Petrosky guts twisted into a rat's nest of fire. But he drew his eyes to the house across the street from Zurbach's: Unattached garage. Cracked driveway. A lawn like a jungle.

That's where he did it—that's where Norton killed your partner. Cut him to pieces like he was nothing.

"Is that place still abandoned?" he asked, but the words sounded foreign, faraway. Jackson had pulled files on all houses directly related to Norton, but he couldn't bring to mind the property he was staring at now. Maybe his brain was trying to block him from thinking about it. But he could smell the basement from here—metallic. Sour.

Jackson nodded; if she'd noticed the strangeness he heard in his voice, she did not show it. "As of today, yes. It was bought recently at auction, but no one's been in to do any work on it, hence the disarray."

He squinted at the haphazard lawn once more, then the door, then the path, then the window on the side of the garage, the glass spiderwebbed with cracks—the tiniest bit of pressure, and it would all fall apart. Like him. But... "Whose is that?"

Jackson followed his gaze. She frowned. "The bike?"

Not just any bike. A blue ten-speed. A blue... His lungs

stopped working. They'd never found the bike back when he was working Norton's case, but he would always remember their little witness who'd seen it speeding away from a crime scene. Had that been Norton's first kill?

And then Petrosky was running, his sneakers flying over the concrete, toward the garage, toward the bike, his breath wheezing in his ears, but he could feel nothing, see nothing but the blue of the metal, the faded rubber tires.

He knelt, the splintered driveway sharp against his knee. He fingered the bike chain—slippery yet gritty—and a chemical scent wafted into his nose. Oil. *Not a coincidence, no way.* They'd found oil normally used for bike chains embedded in a scratch on the side of Morrison's car...where Norton had dumped his body. He didn't know if this was the same bike Norton had used, and they never would—forensic evidence would be degraded if the killer had left anything at all. But the bike felt like another message. The killer knew about the blue ten-speed, and his truck...his *blue* truck. An homage to Norton's blue bike, but still an improvement over his predecessor.

Faster. And far more efficient.

20

THEY WENT in through the back door, Petrosky jimmying the lock with shaking fingers.

The kitchen was much as he remembered it, but the Crock-Pot that had once sat abandoned on the kitchen tile was gone, and that more than the empty linoleum counter-tops or the dingy carpeting in the living room felt somehow profound. It was as if without that little appliance, the room had suddenly lost all humanity. No dog, of course—that's what he'd come in to find the first time he'd been here. A little dog the previous occupants had left. Gigi. That little bitch had been a biter, and her, he did not miss.

Jackson opened the cupboard nearest the door and eased it closed with a hollow *thunk*. "Maybe we should call for backup." She dragged her gaze along the edge where the ceiling met the wall, then down toward the hallway. "If he led you here on purpose, if he knew you'd understand what the bike meant, if he knew you'd be in this house...maybe he wired it."

Petrosky shook his head. "That's not his game—too easy." There was no reason to show himself to Candace or to leave the bike or even to plant that knife; those things were messy.

Risky. When it came to Petrosky, their suspect wasn't looking for a means to an end. Every piece he'd left was a clue—and who would he taunt if Petrosky was gone?

"I don't mean a bomb," Jackson said. "I was thinking a camera, so he could watch you. And we really don't know what his game is; he's changed it up enough times already."

Petrosky barely heard her. He pressed on to the living room, his eyes narrowed at the flattened carpet, the rat—or even rabbit—droppings in the corner, the front window shaded by dust and yellowed fabric and dirty screens. Nothing more to see, but he could feel the fucker in the place, feel him like the oil dripping down between his shoulder blades, a presence that merged with the insistent nagging thought that he'd been here before, done this before. The killer was in his blood.

And Morrison had died in the basement—if the perp had left a clue, that was where it would be. He headed up the hall, past the bedroom where Jackson stood peering at the closet, his nose prickling with the metallic tinge of iron; his mouth tasted of dust. He could practically hear Morrison's voice, whispering from the bowels of the house, calling up from the cellar: *Come on, boss!* But...

No, this wasn't right.

He squinted back over his shoulder at the entry to the kitchen. The rooms hadn't changed much, a door on either side. One bathroom, one bedroom, though there was no mattress in it now, no used condoms scattered about. Cleaner than before. But at the far end of the hallway...

He frowned at the blank wall.

There had been a door there; he was positive there had been a door.

What are you doing, Petrosky? Morrison's voice whispered, but it sounded as if he were drowning, trying to speak through a rising surf. *Help me!* And then Petrosky could see him, lips red with blood, his arms and hands gouged by defensive wounds, the white bone of his forearm glaring from beneath severed flesh. Fighting to survive on that damn basement floor. And when Norton had gone to get the blade to finish him off...Morrison had written that note in his own blood and secured it in a coffee cup. *For me.* Because that had been his only choice. Petrosky hadn't been there that night, hadn't been there to help his boy. *I was a fucking drunk.* Just like now.

He did not recall walking to the dead end of the hallway, but now he placed a hand against the wall, the paint cool despite the heat outside, despite the clammy air that was sticking his shirt to his skin. His heart throbbed, uneven and sharp; sweat prickled on his brow.

"Hey...there's a basement, right?" Jackson said from somewhere at his back. Ah, yes, she'd read the files too. "Where the hell is it?"

"Here." He knocked, ran his hand down the wall, and knocked again. Hollow.

"It looks like a wall." Closer now. "You think he covered—"

"Yes." He felt the certainty of that in his marrow. He looked around, seeking a hammer, a wrench, a shovel, even another Crock-Pot, anything that might help him, but the floor was empty. Jackson laid a hand on his arm. "Petrosky?"

He took a step backward, drew his foot up, and kicked with all his might.

His shoe went through the drywall easily—nothing beyond, no insulation, no support beams. *I knew it—I'm not crazy.* At least not about this. The skin of his calf ached where the drywall had splintered against it. He yanked his foot free and went again, again, again, his skin smarting, his muscles screaming, and Jackson—she was yelling too.

"Enough!"

He paused, panting, and peered down the stairs, the slow descent into blackness.

THE STEPS WERE STEEP—CLAUSTROPHOBIC. He felt along the wall, easing himself down one stair, then the next, the rotting wood crying beneath his shoes. Unstable. Like him, like him.

He could see light from the darkness below, a gloomy kind of haze that barely penetrated the shadows of the landing. His lungs weren't acting right; every step created a weak ballooning sensation inside his chest that deflated when he tried to inhale—like trying to suck air from a plastic sandwich bag. And though he knew his heart was actually working, knew his pacemaker would ensure it kept going, knew he didn't have fresh stitches in his chest now, he could feel them, god, he could feel them—sharp little points tugging at his flesh as if someone was yanking out his chest hairs.

He stepped off the stairway and into the basement—slow, everything was moving *so slowly*. He didn't recall pulling his gun from its holster, but there it was, glinting dully in his hand. Jackson shouted something into the dark that sounded like "Police!" but he couldn't immediately see who she was yelling at in the fuzzy dim. A breeze brushed its cool fingers against his scrubby cheek—a breeze from the row of glass block that ran along the top of the concrete wall, one wide section missing. But it didn't take away the thick musk of mildew. Didn't take away the metal on his tongue. Blood, Morrison's blood, clotting in his throat, plugging his nose with iron. His boy was here; he'd died here. Maybe he was still here. Was that who Jackson was yelling at? No, that didn't make sense.

He squinted, his phantom stitches tugging harder, dragging a grunt from his lips, but he could not be sure what he was looking at; he knew only that it was silver, brighter than his gun. An orb about thigh level, barely visible in the shadows near the floor—the light from the window did not reach there, as if the sun were purposefully staying away. It wasn't until he blinked again that he could make out the tendrils of hair trailing down toward the floor, the wisps of gray making the orb appear more like a slow-moving comet aimed at the ceiling, the gas tail edged in a fiery crimson even in the dim.

A wicked hand grabbed his imaginary stitches and yanked, the threaded edges ripping through his chest.

It wasn't dust or a gas tail. The ball wasn't a comet.

"Oh shit," Jackson said. "Oh shit."

He didn't feel the gun fall, but he heard it hit the floor, a bright clatter that pulled him from his stupor. Billie was sitting just as Ava Fenderson had been, but her arms, her hands, were tied behind her—he didn't crucify her, thank god he didn't crucify her. Her clothes were intact, too, her T-shirt laying limply over her frame, the fringe of her shorts visible beneath. All of it soaked through with blood. His knees screamed as he threw himself to the floor at her side, but it didn't matter, nothing mattered if she was dead.

He reached for her bound hands and gingerly sought the curve of her wrist, pressing lightly, trying to locate the throb of a pulse beneath her cool, sticky flesh. Her radial artery remained still—was it just him? His heart was vibrating so hard that perhaps he just couldn't feel the life still pulsing through her. And she would be tired, dehydrated, of course she would be—a weak pulse didn't mean dead. He put a hand on either side of her face. "Billie." The word was a croak, timid and awful.

She said nothing. Her jaw was cold against his thumb. His cheeks were wet—tears or blood?

"Billie," he said again, louder, and this time he tugged, raising her face, pulling her chin away from her chest. For a moment, it stuck, oh god, that sound like wet tearing, and then he could see the fork, the prongs were driven into her chest, the sharp metal emerging from deep inside her chin. But that wasn't what had killed her. Just above the wicked collar, Billie's throat was a chasm that would gape like a bloody second mouth if he leaned her head back. He held her steady, traced her cheekbones with the pads of his thumbs, and stared into her face, into her beautiful blue eyes—wide, cold, the life drained from them.

He'd killed Billie as soon as he'd taken her. They'd never had a chance.

21

TIME PASSED IN AN INSTANT, a blur of memory and blood.

Morrison's body in the back seat of his car, his throat slit, the Visqueen shining beneath him.

The crime scene techs scurried around Billie. He sat on the concrete beside her, but could not look at them as they picked, poked, scraped.

Ruby, that chipped tooth in her shattered face, the yawning gash in her throat, the streaks of crimson over her distended abdomen.

He pressed his leg against Billie's, imagining he could feel the last of the heat slip from her body and release itself into the air. Into oblivion.

Billie's bright-blue eyes, the blood on her shirt, the silvery gleam of her hair.

He vaguely heard himself threaten the man who wanted to put her in a bag. The sky went orange, then purple.

He held her hand in the ambulance—no sirens. They didn't need any.

Someone in the ambulance was talking to him. Someone touched his arm. He watched Billie's eyes, the little slivers of white beneath her eyelids. They left him alone.

The vehicle stopped, and for a moment, he believed it was his heart that had ceased to work, one final pulse, then nothing. And then he was running to keep up with the gurney, the wheels so fast, so fast. Woolverton looked over when they wheeled Billie in. He blinked.

The gurney wheeler talked.

Woolverton pushed his glasses up his nose.

Petrosky held Billie's hand. He held on to her so she wouldn't be alone. Woolverton didn't count. He was poking, prodding, scraping at her too.

Woolverton thought she was dead.

HIS MOUTH WAS DRY. His eyes burned. His legs ached from holding himself upright beside the stainless table.

Clink-scrape went Woolverton's instruments. *Clink-scrape. Clink-scrape.*

Jackson was in the doorway, holding up her phone. Was it for him? Was it Billie?

She met his eyes and lowered the cell. "Do you want to do it? We have to tell Candace and Jane; we can't just leave them hanging."

"Tell Candace what?"

She bit her lip. "Petrosky…"

The *clink-scrape* stopped, then began again. *Clink-scrape. Clink-scrape. Clink-scrape.*

He was supposed to say something. He didn't have anything to say. "You call them."

"They need you; they'll want to talk to—"

"You call them."

She met his eyes. Then she was gone.

He squeezed Billie's hand. She was cold—when had she gotten so damn cold?

Clink-scrape. Clink-scrape. He watched Woolverton work.

The blade. The Y-shaped incision. Her heart, her good, good heart. But he couldn't move. He couldn't do anything.

He was much too cold.

Like she was.

HE SAW ONLY BLACKNESS—WAS he dead? He opened his eyes. And groaned.

His hips hurt from sitting in the hard plastic chair, and his head...shit. At some point, he'd leaned his head back against the painted bricks, and now the bone was aching as if someone had taken a bat to his skull. He heaved himself to standing and peered at Woolverton's stainless table—empty now. And no Woolverton. He glanced back; where had the chair come from anyway? They didn't have a waiting area in the morgue, and... *Billie.* Where was Billie? He did not remember sitting down, did not remember them taking her away, but he remembered the basement, remembered trying to lift her head...

He resisted the urge to collapse into the seat once more. He felt hollowed out, his nerves scraped raw—he was not a man; he was the aching chasm in the middle of his chest. He blinked, but his eyes refused to focus; maybe they had realized there was no point in looking when everything he saw eventually turned awful.

Billie's dead eyes, the blood, the blood.

A sound drew his attention from off to his left, just outside the door. Jackson? Ah, and there was the medical examiner, talking to his partner. But though he strained his ears, he could not make out their words. "Hey, Jackson?"

Her gaze remained locked on Woolverton. The doctor, too, appeared not to have heard him. Maybe he really was dead. Just as well.

"Jackson," he said again, louder, but still, she did not

turn. A wave of heat rose from his belly to his chest, and though he could identify the sensation, though he knew logically that it was rage, he felt incapable of reacting to it. His brain had come undone, the wires severed from his body.

"What the fuck is happeni…? What…?" He couldn't complete the sentence—his brain, his lips, something was broken. And his muscles…they were twitching, weren't they? His arm was almost convulsing. Was he having a seizure? He had the vague idea that it should hurt, but nothing did, not really.

Jackson turned toward the door, toward him, Woolverton at her heel, and as they both stepped into the morgue, the horror on her face tripped a live wire in his head. His brain suddenly cleared, the neurons snapping together and chasing the cobwebs away.

Jackson met Petrosky's gaze. "Sorry about that. How are you feeling?"

Woolverton offered no such apology. He stepped around Jackson for his table, casting barely a backward glance at the chair against the wall—*he put it there. For me.*

Petrosky forced his mouth to work. "Did Candace take it badly?" In that moment, he could think of nothing else to say.

"She took it as well as can be expected." Her nostrils flared—she was twitchy, too, almost…nervous. Had something else happened?

"What is it?"

She cleared her throat. "There's something you need to know."

Oh shit. Shannon? The kids? "Spit it the fuck out!" Woolverton wheeled around and stepped away from his table once more, heading back their way, his eyes wide, his spindly muscles taut. *Did I scream that at her?* Woolverton edged sideways as if to position himself between Petrosky and Jackson, but Petrosky raised his hands and stepped back.

"Just tell me." He could barely form the words. "Goddammit, just—"

"Scott got the results back from the knife we found at Hanover's." *Oh, thank god, Shannon's okay, everyone's okay.* The silence stretched, Jackson's mouth moving as if she were trying to find the right words but kept failing. Finally, she finished, "The blood doesn't belong to any of his recent victims."

"We…" Okay, wait, was that news? His brain felt fried, but he could have sworn… "We knew that, didn't we? The knife we found doesn't have a serrated edge, it—"

"The knife at Hanover's was covered in Morrison's blood."

Woolverton was no longer there, the morgue a mere memory.

Morrison…no.

How was that even possible? Sure, they'd never found the weapon used to kill Morrison—they'd tested all the blades in Norton's little basement hideout for DNA but had come up short. And now Norton was dead. How had this man gotten his knife? Norton wouldn't have given it away. Had Norton had another hideout, one this guy knew about? Had this asshole just found the weapon? But even if he'd come upon it accidentally, he wouldn't have made the connection to Morrison's death unless…

He knew exactly what the knife had been used for. The blood in Petrosky's veins congealed in an instant, the world pulsing around him. Norton hadn't done it alone. Norton might have tortured those girls alone, maybe even killed them alone, but when it had come time to take out a cop… he'd had help.

The man who'd killed Morrison was still out there. He'd kept himself hidden all these years because he'd known better than to use the same blade. Now he was ready to come out of hiding—ready to announce to the world who he was and what he'd done.

Petrosky blinked at Jackson. Morrison's dead blue eyes stared back from her face. Billie's hair gleamed from her skull.

The bike. The blade.

They'd never had a copycat. Their killer was someone who'd been involved with Norton. Someone who knew him.

A hidden partner. Smarter. More careful.

But just as savage.

22

PETROSKY DIDN'T REMEMBER the drive home. Didn't remember getting into bed. He remembered the girls next door—Jane and Candace had been waiting for him on his porch, wanting to hug him, telling him it was okay. It wasn't fucking okay. He didn't remember sending them away, but he must have—he did remember their tears.

The Jack burned a hole in his guts until the bottle was empty, and even then, he refused to let it go, holding the glass neck in a stranglehold against his pillow. Duke's giant tongue massaged his hand, the dog's heavy panting hissing in his ear. But the dog made no other sound, unlike every other damn day as if the old boy realized it would not be welcome tonight.

"I'm sorry." He said it to the ceiling, to all the people he'd failed, wheezed it until his voice was raw, and his eyes dry. Duke licked his hand. Petrosky rolled onto his side, buried his head in the dog's silky fur, and found more tears. A killer who idolized Norton, who had Norton's fucking knife, was still out there. And Petrosky's heart was too heavy for him even to breathe, let alone chase the bastard. What was the point?

Nothing. He was nothing. He hadn't protected Morrison from Norton, and he hadn't protected Billie—he couldn't protect anyone from this new asshole. *I hope he finds me. I hope he fucking finds me and takes me out.*

He dozed on and off, and by the time the sky lightened, he had a new kind of ache in his head, a deep pain throbbing in his temples like being shot over and over by a weak bullet —eventually, it would break through the fragile bones of your skull and kill you, but not before you suffered first.

———

Tap-tap-tap.

He squeezed his eyes shut. Shannon had already knocked twice but had stopped short of sending the kids in, which would have been emotional blackmail—thank god she was better than that.

The tapping came again.

"Go away. I'm sleeping."

"The hell you are." Not Shannon. Jackson.

He heaved himself to seated, and the room spun, his eyes bleary with sleep and booze. "Go away, I'm masturbating."

"Oh, for fuck's sake," Jackson snapped. "Open this door, or I'll break it down, and I'm not paying to replace it."

He sighed. Duke stretched his big paws, grazing Petrosky's back as if to push him forward off the bed. "I'm going, boy. I'm going." Damn fur ball always thought he knew best.

His feet felt heavy, and his muscles unsure—weak but still tight like a rubber band someone had stretched beyond usefulness as he pulled the door inward. The hinges were remarkably silent. "Well, fancy meeting you here, in *my own fucking house.*"

Jackson narrowed her eyes at him, her arms crossed— appraising him, maybe trying to decide what to say to make things better. *Good luck with that; you gonna try to hug me too?* She did not; Petrosky was suddenly jostled backward, and before he knew what was happening, she had pushed past him and was yanking out his dresser drawer.

He whirled around, one hand out to steady himself. "What the fuck are you—"

"I'm getting you dressed. And then I'm taking you to work."

"I'm not going to work." Billie was dead already. And they had flatfoots watching the houses now, keeping an eye on the neighbors, on Shannon, on Margot and Stella. Jackson had told him that...hadn't she?

He staggered back again as a black T-shirt hit him in the face.

"If I thought you were grieving and sober, fine." She slammed the drawer and nodded to the empty bottle in the bed, the cap off, the base hidden beneath the pillow. Duke's ears pricked up. He wagged his tail at her, weakly, but laid his head down once more when she turned back to his master. "Put that shirt on. We have a case to solve."

"Did Carroll send you?" He frowned; his teeth were fuzzy and foul.

She raised an eyebrow. "You'd like that wouldn't you, having Stephanie Carroll all worried? Maybe you're hoping she'll come over and take a nap with you." She stalked closer, shoulders square, jaw hard. "How is the chief these days? Seen her lately? Maybe in this very room?"

She's fucking with me. "I don't need a babysitter, Jackson."

"You might not need a babysitter, but you have information even if you don't know it, and I'm not about to let anyone else die while you sit here and feel sorry for yourself. This was your case. Your loved ones. You need to fucking finish this with me. Then you can fall into your hole and drown." Her eyes glittered. Angry.

I do need a babysitter. I'm a goddamn useless piece of shit.

He looked down at his boxers, his gut peeking from beneath the hem of his undershirt. *Fuck it.* Not like he could make things worse. He stripped off his shirt and dropped it to the floor. Jackson vanished into his closet—the hangers on the rod screeched.

By the time he had tugged on the new shirt and a pair of jeans he'd found on the floor, she had a jacket held out for him. "Do you want to piss first, or are you going to hold it?"

"Jesus Christ, Jackson."

She crossed her arms.

"I'll meet you in the kitchen," he said, but his legs felt rubbery again—would he make it? Yeah, he would; the powers that be didn't like him enough just to let him fucking die.

"Brush your teeth too," Jackson said to his back. "You smell like a goddamn brewery." A steady pressure on his shoulder made him pause—her hand was firm, determined, her breath warm against his ear. "And this will be the last time I give you a pass, grieving or not. Do you understand?"

The last time. She didn't have to tell him for what. He nodded his agreement—*I'll stay sober*—but he didn't believe it, not even now when he was still a little drunk.

PETROSKY DID his business and headed for the front door, expecting that Jackson would be ready with her SUV, intending to whisk him off to the precinct. Instead, she ambushed him in the kitchen. Shannon and Evie were already sitting at his bistro table, Shannon with a mug of... urine? Probably tea. Jackson shoved something into his hand and dragged him to the living room, his legs still unsteady— off-kilter. The coffee table was littered with files.

"I thought you were taking me to work," he said.

"I am." She grabbed a roll of yellow crime scene tape from

the couch and taped one side to the entryway arch. "We'll just make our own little zone. Don't want to freak the kids out." She nodded to the dining table. Evie smiled and waved, her hand full of smashed ham and cheese sandwich. A piece of cheese fell to the table. Shannon snatched it up and put it in her mouth, but her face...all narrowed eyes and flaring nostrils. She was pissed at him too.

Just what I fucking need. But he didn't feel irritated; his insides were a cold void. And damned if he didn't like that better.

"We both need a little time to work away from the office," Jackson was saying. "It'll be fine." She secured the other side of the crime tape and tossed the roll onto the Lay-Z-Boy.

Fine? Maybe, but this was an all-hands-on-deck situation, and the precinct was where Decantor was working... He squinted at Jackson. "Carroll doesn't know I'm on this case, does she?"

"Papa Ed!" *So much for the crime tape.* Petrosky stumbled as Henry plowed into the backs of his knees, but the boy saved Petrosky from falling by wrapping his arms tighter. "What's mas-er-bating?"

"He was hiding in the next room when I knocked at your door," Jackson said. "Good luck with that one." Henry was still staring at him, arms locked around his legs—waiting for an answer.

Fuck. "It's a kind of cookie."

Henry released him and stepped back. "Why d'they call it that?"

"Because of all the extra baiting."

"What's bait—"

"Whoa, is that a T-Rex?" Petrosky pointed to the kitchen.

Henry scampered off, giggling, craning his neck as if he expected to see an enormous reptile holding vigil near the fridge. When he realized the room contained only his mother and sister, he joined Shannon at the table—attention on his lunch. No more questions.

Jackson rolled her eyes. "Nice save, Gramps. Now let's get to work."

He settled himself on the couch, Jackson beside him, but his hand was on fire. He glanced at it, vaguely surprised to see a waxed cup in his grip—Rita's. When had he gotten coffee? Had they gone to Rita's today?

"This is obviously connected to the Norton case, but in a way we didn't see," Jackson said, her voice probably normal, but to his ear, the words were muted. "Likely a partner, but maybe just a friend. Either way, I don't think our guy had anything to do with the girls Norton kidnapped."

Petrosky nodded, blinking as his head began to clear. Too many inconsistencies with Hyde and Billie. Neither was tortured or raped as Norton's victims had been, which wasn't any consolation—if their killer had taken the time to torture Billie, maybe they'd have had time to save her. He waited for the telltale tug at his heart, the shooting pain, but felt only a heavy numbness. Like his chest had quietly collapsed into a yawning cave.

Creak—he jumped. Shannon had moved from her spot at the table and was peering into the living room from behind the tape; the kids had vanished. "Maybe we should work somewhere else," he said quietly, too low for Shannon to hear.

It wasn't quiet enough, though. "Like hell," she hissed, ducking beneath the tape. "Norton and his asshole buddy… they took my husband from me, from my children. I'm not walking away from this." Her voice cracked, but she drew her shoulders up, rigid. Her hands were fists.

Jackson leaned back against the couch, gaze even—unsurprised. *That's why we're here: Shannon knows as much about Morrison's death as I do.* Again Petrosky waited to feel something, hell, he *should* be feeling something about the way

Shannon's voice had cracked, about the thinly veiled pain in her face. Nothing. The room itself looked different, too, he realized, a shaded gray landscape like he was watching an old movie of his life. Maybe his shirt wasn't black at all. Maybe it was some blue or green hue—did it matter? Did anything? He dropped his gaze to the table. *You owe her this much, old man. You let her husband die.*

He sighed. The only way out of this, the only way to put this to rest for Shannon, was to solve it, and worthless piece of shit or not, he had to try. Then, as Jackson had said, he could drown. Alone. It was better that way.

He flipped open the case file.

Interviews, names, dates; he could almost see himself talking to the mothers of the victims, giving them the bad news and watching the hope drain from their eyes. Then came the sketches: line drawings of blades—medieval weapons Norton had in his possession, the shapes and sizes gleaned from his victims' wounds. Page, after page, after page of missing girls and weapons and blood and torture. But he didn't need the notes, not for this. The horrors in these pages he could recite by heart.

The back cover of the file approached, and with it, Morrison's small, even print—his partner's notes, marred by dark splotches of ink from the copier. The originals had been stained with blood.

11/12 6:45pm: Block casing complete. Three teenagers, African American, approx. 17-19 y/o, approached, all noted no suspicious activity in area.

The day before Morrison died. *What am I missing?*

11/13 2:20pm: Block casing: Hanover, getting mail—assisted back into home. Notes no suspicious activity, notes nephew will be home tonight. To follow up.

But her nephew Richard had never come home; she'd probably said that every day for years until Richard had hired that nurse. And 2:20 p.m.... Mere hours before Morrison's death. He'd been casing the blocks around the Salomon house, looking for clues as to where Lisa Walsh had come from—canvassing alone. *Because I was a drunk piece of shit.* But even that thought didn't hit Petrosky the way it should have. Maybe because it was true.

11/13 4:20pm: Decantor indicates Alicia Hart may know Walsh. Address in file. To follow up.

11/13 5:50pm: Jewelry stores: dead end. Untraceable. (Specifics in file.)

11/13 6:30pm: Alicia Hart not at residence. To follow up tomorrow.

11/13 7:45pm: Block casing: Caucasian male, approx. 65, walking Labrador, identified as Wendell Zurbach. Indicates suspicious activity at home on corner, party one year prior. Poss. trafficking/prostitution of underage females.

And Morrison had headed to Lockhart's right after. Spent his last hours with that creepy dick-flashing asshole. *It should have been me—I should have died instead.* It wasn't the first time he'd had that thought, and years later, it was just as true.

11/13 8:22pm: Sex offender database identified owner of home at 584 Pike Street as Ernest Lockhart.

11/13 8:50pm: E. Lockhart interviewed, allowed search of premises, nothing suspicious. To look into underage party: Lockhart denies wrongdoing, to follow up with others present in the a.m.

11/13 10:30pm:

And then the bloody letters. An uppercase *G*. And an *H*. For Gertrude Hanover. That was how Petrosky had figured out where to go, where to find those girls. But something was missing. He glanced Jackson's way. "Did you remove the photos?"

Shannon turned to his partner as well—he hadn't noticed her taking a seat in the recliner, but there she was, the roll of crime tape discarded on the floor, her elbows on her knees. Beyond the arch to the kitchen, the bistro table was still empty. Were the kids watching TV in the bedroom?

Jackson sniffed, bringing him back. She was nodding. "Decantor's examined every inch of those shots, compared them to the current serial case when he thought it was a copycat. But..." She averted her eyes.

He frowned, the fog finally lifting as his heart rate spiked. "Did Decantor find something?"

"Not in the pictures."

"Somewhere else?" Shannon this time—her voice shook.

"It's just... Decantor had a thought." Jackson ruffled the pages and snatched up the one Petrosky had been looking at. "About the lettering itself—the...scrawl."

The blood, his boy's blood forming those letters. No wonder she didn't want to bring it up. "The *G* and the *H*? What about them?"

"What if it wasn't him at all?"

"Wasn't who?" He narrowed his eyes at the page in her hands—*what the hell was she...* "Wait, Decantor thinks Morrison didn't write this? Then who the fuck did?"

"Decantor doesn't think Norton was involved in Morrison's death." Shannon's voice rang hollow, her eyes locked on Jackson. "Does he?"

Petrosky waited for her to deny it, but Jackson shrugged. "It's a consideration."

His jaw dropped along with his stomach, and for a moment, he didn't have the words to respond. Then he sputtered: "Morrison died because he figured out where Norton was. Are you telling me that Decantor thinks Morrison was randomly attacked by a second serial killer? That the timing is coincidence?"

"No, not coincidence; he thinks Morrison's killer was involved with Norton, that the perp knew exactly who Norton was and what he was doing. But that doesn't mean they were working together in the end, that they planned Morrison's murder." Jackson lowered the page and studied Petrosky and Shannon in turn as if trying to gauge their reaction. "He might have gotten tired of Norton's bullshit, wanted to strike out on his own. Or maybe he knew we were getting close and didn't want to get caught. And by planting this note in a coffee mug no one else would have noticed…"

The words hung in the air, and suddenly he could feel the stainless coffee mug in his hand—Morrison's cup that had been tossed in that basement. The cold of it against his palm. He looked down; he still held the Rita's coffee, the wax dented from his fingertips. He brought it to his lips and took a long, tasteless swallow.

Shannon watched until he lowered the cup, then said, "Maybe he wanted you to get rid of Norton for him."

But he hadn't—Margot had killed Norton when Petrosky was too weak to fight him off. "Why orchestrate all that? Why not just kill Norton himself?" They knew this guy was good with a blade.

"Maybe Norton got suspicious," Jackson said. "Wouldn't let him get close enough."

Petrosky shook his head. "He had to assume Norton wouldn't live to talk. Norton had no qualms about saving his own skin; he would have given this guy up in a heartbeat." That's why Janice was locked up tight—Norton had left her behind to take the fall.

"Of course he thought Norton wouldn't make it out," Shannon said quietly. "He'd know killing Morrison would push you to the breaking point." She dropped her gaze to her knees.

He set the coffee on the table; his belly had gone sour. It was true. Anyone might figure Petrosky would lose his shit—would catch Norton with those girls and rip his spleen out through his nose. Perhaps this killer *had* outsmarted them all.

He'd used Petrosky to kill Norton, then kept himself hidden. For five more years.

And now Ruby was dead—Billie was dead. And it was his fault.

Jackson was sorting through the pages on the coffee table but paused when her cell buzzed with a text. Her eyes brightened as she read. "Oh shit." She set the cell on the table, her brow furrowed.

"Are you going to tell us?" he demanded, too loudly—a harsh bark. He lowered his voice: "The suspense is killing me."

She ignored the question and rifled through the file, then pulled a mug shot to the top—Ernest Lockhart, the skinny dick-flasher. *Him? No fucking way.* Jackson kept her gaze on the table. "This guy... Okay, based on Morrison's notes, Lockhart was the last person to see him alive." Which they knew. "But Lockhart isn't just a flasher anymore. Decantor pulled his history. In the last four years, he's been arrested for watching a little boy get undressed at a department store, and most recently, he was arrested for molesting a twelve-year-old, which almost matches the profile of Norton's first accomplice."

Petrosky frowned. Norton's first accomplice had been a pedophile who'd raped little kids and watched Norton kill them, but he'd been a sadist too. Their current serial was going after adults, not even close to the same victim type. "I don't get it. We already knew he was an asshole; now he's just an asshole with a longer record and more reasons to punch him in the taint."

But Jackson's eyes were sparkling. "It's not the crimes themselves. It's the arrests. Decantor says that those dates match the killer's dry spells. Every time this guy goes away, the murders stop."

What the fuck? "Why didn't we see that before?"

"We were cross-referencing, looking for an ex-con who

also had a dark-colored truck. Lockhart's never had a vehicle like that registered to him. And he's been on the back burner, especially because he was cleared during Norton's case. You searched his house yourself."

True—he had. The place had been clean. Lockhart was smarter than they'd given him credit for. But...Lockhart? *Really?* "If he doesn't have a truck, what kind of car does he drive?"

Jackson shook her head. "Couldn't find one at all."

That seemed strange—most people had a car. And years ago...the guy'd had a classic car in his garage, even had the place padlocked to keep people from stealing it. He should at least have that beast, though if he didn't drive it around town, he wouldn't necessarily have it registered.

But Petrosky frowned when his gaze dropped to the mug shots. Lockhart was thin; he was so damn thin... "He doesn't match the description Gertrude gave us. Candace either."

"That's what Decantor said too, but..." Jackson grimaced. "So, it's a stretch, but Candace said he was wearing a hoodie and a ski mask."

"She did?" He remembered the mask, but—

"Yes, before you got there. I'm thinking she misinterpreted the sweatshirt pouch as a belly. Or he was carrying something in it, a tool to hit her with. Woolverton did say there was blunt force trauma present, more than you'd expect from a punch to the skull, so he probably hit her with something else before Candace got out there."

He blinked. He was supposed to say something, but he couldn't find his voice. Shannon reached across the table and touched his arm. He flinched back. Coffee speckled his hand —he was holding the cup again.

Jackson grabbed her phone once more and checked the time. "Decantor's picking him up, but he said he'd give you the honor of interviewing him." Her eyes said: *For Morrison.*

He pushed himself to standing on rubbery legs; color was

leaking into the room at the edges, though much of the world remained muted—dull. Shannon met his eyes, and this time, he held her gaze.

I'll get him. For Morrison. For Billie. For Ruby.

I'll fucking get him.

23

THE INTERROGATION ROOM was colder than usual, making the gooseflesh prickle on Petrosky's arms, but Lockhart's upper lip was slick with sweat. Petrosky's determination had waned during the ride to the station. It wasn't that he didn't want to catch the killer, but Lockhart? That meant they'd missed it— no, *he'd* missed it, looked right into this creepy fuck's eyes so many years ago, and let him go on to murder five more men and Ruby. And Billie.

Did you kill my boy?

Lockhart's lips twitched, as squirrelly as ever, his same malformed tattoo twisting with his arm muscles; hell, even his jeans appeared to be the ones he'd answered the door in a few days back. But the lawyer was new. The fiftysomething man who sat beside Lockhart had a moon face, a forehead speckled with healed acne scars, and arms and hands covered in thick black hair like the goddamn rat he was. Glen Haverford made his living defending the assholes Petrosky worked to put away. He hated the guy just as much as he hated the pedophiles the lawyer defended. Maybe more.

"So, do you really like saving pedophiles, or is letting child abusers walk just a bonus?"

Lockhart's jaw dropped, and he bolted upright in his seat, but Haverford pressed one fuzzy hand against Lockhart's chest until the man sat back. The lawyer met Petrosky's eyes. "Are you charging my client with something?"

"I haven't decided yet."

Lockhart's eye twitched, then his fingers. The terrible hula girl tattoo on his forearm twitched too.

Petrosky glanced at the mirrored wall behind which Jackson was probably watching, hawk-like, waiting for him to lose his shit on the guy. But he wouldn't, not today when he felt so empty, when the world was so dull—his muted senses were probably a good thing. If he snatched the guy up and forced a confession, it'd get thrown out, but more than that...maybe he didn't want them to be right. If their killer was someone else, it was less his fault—Billie was less his fault. *Who the fuck are you kidding, old man?* Petrosky cleared his throat. "How well did you know Adam Norton?"

"The killer? Like from...years ago?" Lockhart frowned. "Not really at all."

"But you knew him a little, right?"

Lockhart shook his head, fast and twitchy—nervous. "You guys asked me all this before. I don't know the guys from your pictures the other day, and I didn't have anything to do with Norton."

"Maybe not." Petrosky folded his hands and leaned over them, the table a tight band across his belly. "Or maybe you decided to pick up where he left off."

Haverford's hairy fingers stilled on the tabletop.

Enough fucking around. Petrosky sat back suddenly and slapped his file open. "Lance Frank." He tossed a photo of the man on the stainless steel, the victim's throat a gaping hole, the plastic shiny around his shoulders. Blood on his teeth.

Lockhart's jaw dropped. "Wait—"

"Curtis Brazinda." He slammed another crime scene

photo beside the first, his eyes on Lockhart's twitchy face, on his wide, staring eyes. "George Fernsby."

"Hang on, just wait a damn—"

"Henry fucking Shanker." His palm hit the table with enough force to make the other pictures flutter, his palm tingling with the vibration—but he felt no pain. Maybe he was beyond that. "Where were you on the evening of August fifth?" *Did you take Billie, fuckface?*

Lockhart shook his head again, like a dog after a bath. "I...no idea. Probably at home?"

"Alone?"

His eyes were locked on the photos. "Yeah."

"What about August second?" When Hyde was kidnapped.

"That was a while ago, I really can't rememb—"

"Morning of August third?" When the baby was dumped. "Close enough? They're all less than a week ago, shithead. Just this past Tuesday is the day someone kidnapped a woman from my front yard." He snatched another image from the folder—Billie, her silver hair, her shirt soaked in red. He was glad he couldn't see her eyes; he had the sudden understanding that if her dead blue gaze had been aimed at the camera, something inside him would have broken for good, and he probably wouldn't even have felt it.

Both the lawyer and Lockhart stared at the photos. "This isn't something my client would have done," Haverford said finally, raising his gaze. But his eyes didn't look so sure. Still, he put a furry hand on Lockhart's shoulder. "If you're going to arrest my client, have at it, but it sounds like you don't have a case. Like you're digging." He released Lockhart and gestured to the table—the photos. "What possible reason would my client have to kill these people?"

"Serial killers don't need a reason you and I would understand." But even as he said it, something tugged at him, a strange déjà vu sensation deep in his guts like the memory of food poisoning—the nauseating *oh shit* moment when you realized that gas station hot dog had been a mistake. Petrosky held Haverford's gaze for a beat longer, then let his eyes drop to the table.

Lance Frank. Curtis Brazinda. Henry Shanker. George Fernsby. Evan Webb. Five victims, no connections. But…

Lance Frank. Curtis Brazinda. Henry Shanker. George Fernsby. Evan Webb.

Lance, Curtis, Henry, George. *Huh.* The names, at least the first names of the victims, matched those of people Petrosky knew. Lance was Jackson's son. Curtis Morrison. Henry…little Henry. George, a man who had been his friend up until Petrosky'd fallen off the wagon again. Even Evan Webb, the last man killed, the father of Ruby's baby… Evan was their forensics guy's first name and George's son. Paranoia? Maybe. Coincidence? *You don't believe in coincidence, old man.*

He raised his head once more and stared Lockhart down, ignoring the daggers coming from the priggish attorney. "What do you drive, Mr. Lockhart?"

"I…" Lockhart swallowed hard.

"My client doesn't have to answer that," Haverford said.

Petrosky glowered at the lawyer. "True. So let me ask you this: is driving an unregistered vehicle a violation of his parole? Say, if I had him on a traffic light cam driving around without a care in the world?"

That was a risk; he had no camera footage, no evidence that the man had a vehicle, and there had been no car in Lockhart's garage—they'd checked that on the way over. But Petrosky needed something, some way to get this bastard talking. And Lockhart used to have a car. Kept his baby padlocked and everything.

Petrosky narrowed his eyes. If the man had no access to a vehicle, he'd expect Lockhart to look confused. But Lockhart did not look confused. He looked worried. He bent his face close to his attorney, lips moving rapid-fire.

Finally, they pulled their heads apart and turned their attention to Petrosky. "I want assurances that my client will not be charged," Haverford said.

"That all depends on what you're about to tell me." He crossed his arms. "I don't give a shit about a parking ticket, Haverford. I'm looking for a goddamn serial killer. If your client isn't involved, his assistance could help us—goodwill never hurts for a guy so prone to getting locked up. And you and I both know he'll be back here again on some child sex charges, so how about we stop fucking around?"

Haverford's nostrils flared, but he nodded.

Lockhart cringed, then met Petrosky's gaze. "I've been driving a truck—got it off Craigslist maybe...six years back? It was cheap; I paid cash, and I never changed the registration."

A truck. He had a goddamn truck? "What color?"

"Blue. A pickup."

Fuck and double fuck. Jackson was right—this was their guy. And Lockhart still seemed to think he was getting away with it. He clenched his fists and leaned away from Lockhart, afraid if he got too close, if he could smell the bastard's sweat, he might snap—in his current half-diluted state, he probably wouldn't even feel it coming. "Remember us asking you about a truck a few days ago? Did it just slip your mind?"

"I didn't want any trouble."

You've got trouble now, asshole. Petrosky tried to keep his voice even; he could feel Jackson's eyes on him, burning a hole in his shoulder. "Why didn't you register it?" *So you could use it to kill people and hide it from the police?*

Lockhart sighed. His shoulders slumped. "Because I was going to move, put the new address on the truck. Everyone who lives nearby knows about the offender registry. I get hate mail. They spray painted my garage door twice, and the third time, they broke in and trashed my car." He swallowed hard. *Sad story, fuck-o.* "I even started keeping the truck in the garage up the street so no one would vandalize it—that abandoned place with the burned-out kitchen." That would be easy enough to verify; they'd put forensics on it, see what kind of DNA was smeared across the back seat. Petrosky nodded for him to go on; the attorney crossed his arms as if that would protect him from whatever his client might say next. "I thought maybe if I moved…but then I couldn't find a place. And the months went by, and I just… The house is paid off. The truck is mine, even if it does break down every other month. When I was locked up, I had enough to pay my taxes. I just… I don't know."

"Is the truck in that garage now, Lockhart? We need to take a look at it."

Lockhart straightened and leaned back, his hands pressed against his thighs. "Nah. In the shop again. Busted radiator."

"How long's it been there?"

"A day or so."

"So, you still had it in your possession through Wednesday?"

"You don't have to answer that," the lawyer interjected, his flat face tight—anxious—but Lockhart frowned.

"Is that what this is about? Did someone take my truck and…" His eyes widened at the photos once more. "Did they use it to do this?" His breath was coming in frantic little huffs. "I brought it to the shop on Thursday, but if someone took it, if they used it for—"

"Do you know this man?" He turned over the last sheet in his folder: Gertrude's sketch of the young hunk who'd come to her home, who'd planted that knife in her basement; the same man Lockhart had denied knowing…was it just two days ago? "This man delivered a murder weapon to your neighbor's house, a hunting knife from a cold case." A cold case—is that what Morrison was? *Yes*, a little voice whispered, and he tried not to think about the fact that it sounded entirely too much like his boy.

Lockhart's chest heaved. Haverford's lips still held that smarmy twitch, but they turned down at the corners when he looked at his client. "Ernest?"

Lockhart was shaking his head from side to side, mouth gaping like a fish out of water. "It's not…possible."

He definitely knows him. Fucking liar. "Who is he, Lockhart?"

Haverford put that bear paw back on Lockhart's shoulder. "Ernest, perhaps we should speak privately."

Petrosky rapped his knuckles against the sketch. "This man might be a serial killer, and you want your client to keep it to himself?" He'd left that door open on purpose, hoping Lockhart would blame this other man for the murders, confess whatever he knew in exchange for a lesser charge. Lockhart stayed silent, head swinging side to side to side. Petrosky pushed himself to standing and leaned over the table, his face inches from the attorney—the man reeked of butterscotch. "If this man ends up being our killer and your guy keeps protecting him, I swear to god, I will charge your client with accessory on every one of these homicides."

Haverford half smiled—haughty as fuck. "It'll never stick."

"Juries like pedophiles, do they? They tend to think child molesters are trustworthy?"

Again, Haverford's nostrils flared. He turned to his client, then back to Petrosky. "I want it in writing that—"

"I'm not giving you shit. He's already lied to us—we're two days behind this killer because your client decided to protect him. This is a limited time offer." He addressed Lockhart. "Tell us what you know about this man, or we'll take you down with him."

Haverford patted Lockhart's shoulder once more but nodded—*go ahead.*

"He's...a friend." Lockhart's voice shook. "I didn't do anything, I swear to god, I—"

"Name?"

"I never knew it, he never—"

"When was the last time you saw him?"

"I'm...not sure. A week ago?"

"I need you to call him, Lockhart. Let's get all this cleared up." *Lure the bastard down here so we can arrest him.*

"I...can't. We just talk on the internet." The hula girl on his forearm shuddered, but his face had stilled. "You have to send a message, and then he calls back. But he never calls back from the same number."

Probably burner phones. "Sounds like a very careful guy." Smart. Efficient.

Lockhart nodded. "He has to be."

Does he now? "And why is that?"

Haverford raised a hand again. "He'll give you the man's information. Are we done here?"

"Not until I have what I need." He kept his gaze trained on the skinny bastard across the table, and when Lockhart finally looked his way, he said, "Ask your attorney how long I'm allowed to keep you in custody before I have to charge you. I think you already have a good idea."

Lockhart's lip trembled, the twitch returning to his eye.

Petrosky scowled, trying to muster the right amount of irritation, but his rage wasn't as hot as usual. Stunted. "I want to search your truck, too."

The lawyer put up a hand—*stop*. "Absolutely not. Get a warrant."

Fine. Petrosky headed for the door, rubbing at the little spot above his breastbone, though it didn't really hurt—not now. "See you in a couple of days, assholes."

24

Jackson wanted to take him to eat. He refused. She asked if he wanted a cigarette—in her car no less, a concession she was apparently willing to make to keep him off the bottle. Oddly, he didn't want to smoke either.

He didn't want anything except to throw Lockhart to the wolves, let the community have their way with him. Jackson had called Reyansh Acharya, her ex-boyfriend and their contact with the press, to get Lockhart's face out there, hoping someone could connect him to one of the earlier crime scenes. Decantor was running around, too, taking Lockhart's photo and Gertrude's sketch to the families of the previous victims, and checking in with the witness who had seen the truck. If a witness could connect Lockhart with it, they could arrest him—but what they really needed was to find their mystery hunk from Hanover's. Lockhart had messaged him from the precinct, but the guy had yet to call back. His IP was untraceable. They didn't even have a fucking name. And despite all it had taken to get here, it felt too...*easy*. Remarkably easy for a killer who'd planned this for years, and it had taken years; he'd started spree killing right after Morrison's death. Started picking people off—

people who shared names with Petrosky's loved ones. He still hadn't mentioned that to Jackson, couldn't tell if it was a coincidence. Or paranoia.

Jackson pulled her SUV into a restaurant over his objection, a Mexican joint they'd gone to once before...a lifetime ago, it seemed. He followed her inside, dumbly, slow, sniffing the air, hoping frying tortillas would whet his appetite, but all he could smell was dust. He let her order for them with a wave of his hand—*I'll have what she's having.*

She adjusted the napkin on her lap, watching him. "The interrogation took a lot out of you, eh?"

He nodded though he didn't think that was it. "Yeah. Sorry, I'm just..."

"You don't have to be sorry. You're allowed to grieve. But you're not allowed to starve, or your cranky ass will bitch me out in a few months once you're all skinny."

He couldn't even fathom what that meant. And when he blinked, it was Lockhart sitting across from him with his twitchy little eyes, smiling with those yellowed buck teeth, that goddamn pixelated hula girl gyrating as he flexed his spindly forearm. Petrosky blinked again, and his partner returned. "Does...does Lockhart seem like a killer to you?"

Jackson set her pop aside. He hadn't even registered the waiter bringing the drinks. "You think he's innocent?"

"I don't know what to think. All I'm sure of is that he knows the man who snuck that blade into Gertrude's house."

"On a first-name basis with her, are you?" She winked at him, but he couldn't force his lips to smile.

"It's just so strange. Lockhart has no history of violent crimes."

Jackson raised an eyebrow. "He's a child molester, so I think I'm going to have to disagree."

"It's still a big jump from molestation to murder, especially this kind of serial crime. No sexual assault on our vics, and the victim profile, adult men and women..." Then again, the killings had stopped when he went inside, and they both knew that jail was basically crime school. Going inside might have turned Lockhart more violent, or aimed his rage at grown men, especially with the way they treated pedophiles on the inside. Convicts had children too.

"Maybe Lockhart knew Norton back then, decided to pick up where Norton left off, like you said." She raised her drink again, eyeing his still-full glass—ginger ale. He grimaced at it as Jackson went on: "It's also as possible that Gertrude's repairman is the killer."

Is he the guilty party? Is Lockhart? Shit. Neither felt quite right. "I just want to know who the fuck is murdering the people I love." The words burst out before he registered his intent to speak, but he didn't regret them. His nerves were suddenly on fire, electric and sparking, and yet the twitchiness didn't reach his flesh; his limbs were heavy. He did feel a little like puking, but the nausea seemed to be the only real thing in the world, and he leaned into it even as bile rose in his gullet.

"Finding the guy from Gertrude's sketch should help us answer that," Jackson said from somewhere far off. "Either he's the killer himself, or the killer gave him the blade, but there's no way to know until we talk to him."

Dull. Dull. Dull. Outside the restaurant windows, the sun was setting, the sky surely awash in color, but the horizon remained gray. He squinted. Something was wrong—something was really, *really* wrong with him. Even Jackson didn't seem real, a silhouette of her normal self—a shadow.

Salt wafted into his nose, and he turned in time to see the waiter set their plates down. Enchiladas. He loved enchiladas, didn't he? But he left his fork where it was. "Lockhart took a long time to get caught on the pedophile thing." His cheese was gray, but it brightened to yellow as his chest heated—was it rage? Nerves? He couldn't tell. "Why the fuck did he get so goddamn stupid all of a sudden? He hides his abusive tendencies for years, and now he's driving an unregistered murder mobile? Involved with some guy who's planting evidence?" It was all so obvious, blatant like he was trying to get caught. But the slit throats, the plastic, the staging—that was meticulous. *Planned.*

That's what was bothering him: none of Lockhart's crimes had been planned. Jacking it at a bus stop? Peeping into a dressing room? That asshole wasn't careful, not at all. He was downright reckless. But maybe someone meticulous had decided to take advantage of that and set him up. Someone smart enough to hide his IP address and his phone number. "That handsome fuck from Gertrude's better call back," he muttered. Until then, they had to look at Lockhart. And the victims. Maybe there'd be some connection between Lockhart and the dead men that they hadn't known to look for.

He shoved a cardboard bite of enchilada between his lips and chewed slowly. "That name thing is weird, right?"

She cocked her head. "What?"

"All of the names of the victims. Each one matches the first name of someone we know. Someone I know."

"I mean, we know a lot of people…"

"People who are close to me, though. That's a very small circle." Petrosky raised one finger for each name: "Lance, Curtis, Henry, George…"

But Jackson was shaking her head. "Larry was the first victim, wasn't he? And Kent, not Curtis, I'm almost positive." She looked at the ceiling, fork raised halfway to her lips. "Yeah, Larry, Kent, John, and…Avery?"

He frowned. No, that wasn't right, he'd read the names, he was sure…

Jackson set her fork aside and leveled her gaze at him. "Are you okay?"

No. I'm not. The room was too small; his jacket was too small. He needed to leave.

As if on cue, his cell buzzed in his pocket, but he heard it instead of felt it: Shannon.

"Hey," he forced out, but it sounded more like a cough than a greeting, and somehow foreign to himself, though he'd felt the words leave his mouth. "You want some Mexican? I can get some to go."

The silence stretched. "Shannon?" *It's him, oh god, it's the killer, he's got Shannon, he's got the kids.*

But then Shannon sniffed. "Can you come home?"

His heart was made of rock, heavy and cold. "What's wrong?" He didn't want to know; he would have done anything not to know. He closed his eyes, hoping the cell would die, that his signal would vanish, but he could still hear her breathing.

"It's Duke. He... Petrosky, I'm so sorry."

He opened his mouth, but he couldn't speak. Or breathe. He closed it again. Morrison's face flashed in his head, then Billie's, then Julie's, then his sweet old dog—he could feel Duke's giant sloppy kisses. He could smell him, too, that weird mix of the floral dog shampoo Billie always used and the musty edge of dirt.

"Are you there?"

His heart splintered, the jagged edges slashing at his insides. He hit *End* and re-pocketed the phone without another word. Jackson was staring at Petrosky, but he couldn't bring himself to talk to her either. *Cold.* His face, his chest, god he was cold.

He forced himself to inhale, though he really didn't want to. First Ruby, then Billie, now Duke... Closer, closer, closer.

This fucker was pushing him. Seeing if he'd break.

And he would. Oh, he fucking would.

Maybe he had already.

25

JACKSON DROPPED him in the driveway, but he could still hear her engine idling as he opened the front door. Shannon stood in the kitchen, her arms around her daughter, Evie's head against her belly—the girl was crying. The crime scene tape had been torn. The case files were gone.

He drew his gaze to Shannon. "What happened?" *Duke was an old dog—maybe it was natural causes.* But that was stupid, and he knew it. Hope was always stupid.

"After you left, I played with the kids for a bit, did some coloring. Then I realized we hadn't seen Duke for a while."

He frowned. He'd thought the same, hadn't he? When he was in the living room. He'd wondered where the old boy was. *I should have looked. I should have checked.*

"Evie ran in there ahead of me. I thought he'd gotten locked in the room or had gone back to sleep on your pillow." She swallowed hard. "Evie jumped on the bed, and… he'd thrown up. On the sheets."

Fuck. He'd woken up sick. That's why he hadn't bothered standing when Jackson had come in. He should have known —Duke always got up to play with Jackson. Petrosky could suddenly smell the dog's fur in his nostrils again, could feel

Duke's flank beneath his palms, sticky with salt from Petrosky's tears. Had Duke been sick when Petrosky had wrapped his arms around him last night? Had he been so preoccupied with his own grief that he just hadn't noticed how ill the dog was?

Evie pulled her face from Shannon's damp shirt and looked at him with glassy eyes. "I have to use the bathroom." She trudged off, her head held low. Evie…she'd found him—oh, poor kid, she'd found him like that.

Shannon wiped at her shirt as if to dry the tears the way you'd swipe away crumbs. "I tried to get him up. He was panting really heavily, and his back legs…it was like they were paralyzed. And he was shaking. It didn't look like a seizure, but…" Her eyes drifted to the back hallway where Evie had disappeared.

"How'd you get him to the car? Duke is thin, but…" *Was.* Was thin. But tall and heavy. Like most Great Danes.

"The neighbors came over and helped me. Jane stayed with the kids while Candace and I took him to the vet."

And then she'd come back here to meet him. He frowned. "When did all this happen?"

"Maybe twenty minutes after you left."

"Wait…hours ago? You knew this hours ago, and you didn't bother to call until now?" Was he yelling? He couldn't tell.

"I knew you were in interrogation, and there wasn't anything you could do." She chuckled, but there was no humor in it. "The craziest thing is that I was really hoping the vet could help. That I'd take Duke in, and by the time I had to call you, it'd be with a report that he was going to be fine. That they could save him."

False hope. He was well familiar. *Stupid, stupid, stupid.*

"By the time I got there, it was already too late. I told the vet I'd have you call when you got in. That we would need to know what happened to him, in case…"

In case. In case their serial killer murdered Duke too. "You asked the vet to do an autopsy." He should have thought of that. He crossed his arms, wishing he had a sweatshirt, maybe a blanket. Had Duke been cold like this too? Had Billie?

Shannon's mouth twitched up, and the little spots where Norton had sewn her lips together puckered like they always did when she smiled, as if even when she was happy, those scars were there to remind her of her fallibility—to drag her back down. Like the ruined tattoo on his shoulder: Julie's face torn apart by a bullet, the world trying to kill her again. Norton had done that. Norton had tried to erase his daughter. His guts rolled, bile burning his throat, a sudden burst of pain exploding through his chest and into his lungs—hot. Sharp.

The hallway door banged open, and Evie returned to the kitchen. Eyes still glassy. Face less red. He rubbed at his chest. Evie, sweet Evie; how long until she died, too, until Shannon died, and Henry and Candace and Jackson—

"I might have told him the autopsy was an official police matter," Shannon said, bringing him back. "He'll probably still charge for it, though."

Petrosky patted her shoulder. She reached up and grabbed his fingers, but he couldn't feel her hand. At least his chest had stopped hurting. "Good girl," he said. He released her and headed for the door.

Shannon followed. "Wait, where are you going?"

"To see the vet. I want to talk to him in person." But that wasn't really true. He needed to get out of there. The timbre of her voice—sorrow and guilt and fear, *definitely fear*—was eating away at the tenuous grasp he had on sanity. Besides, if he hurried, he could find a bottle with his name on it.

THE VET WAS PRETTY, or as pretty as a man can be: thin fingers, effeminate features, blade-like cheeks, a jaw like glass. "I found some cerebral edema," he said, his voice a booming bass that didn't match his appearance. "That coupled with the symptoms your partner described suggests that he ingested bromethalin—it's the main ingredient in some rat poisons." He met Petrosky's gaze. "I've seen it before. Sometimes people forget and allow their pet into the basement or wherever they have the box stored..."

His rib cage was a prison, but a larger prison than it had been an hour before—the airline liquor bottle from beneath the floor mat had helped. Yet it was not enough to keep his tongue in check. Petrosky glared. "You think I fucking did this?"

The vet's eyes widened. "No, of course not. I know there might be suspicious circumstances here, I'm just letting you know the most common cause."

"Fine. Let's pretend I'm not a complete fucking tool and know how to keep rat poison away from a dog," he growled. "How long does something like this take to kill?"

The man's eyes wandered to the adjustable steel table in the little exam room, the place he'd led Petrosky, perhaps to keep him away from any unsuspecting visitors in the lobby. Was this where he'd done it? Was this where he'd taken Duke apart? "That's hard to say. Could be a few hours, but more than likely two or three days. There are usually a few symptoms—lethargy, shaking, decreased appetite, even paralysis of the hind legs—but there are often no signs until the body starts to fail. And at that point, there's not much anyone can do, myself included."

He's placating me. Petrosky's face heated. "Are you bullshitting me, doc?"

The vet raised his hands. "For goodness' sake, Detective, of course not. There's a reason the best treatment for poisoning is prevention—pet owners often have no idea until there's nothing I can do. Some poisons I can counteract with vitamin K, but…"

"Not this one."

He shook his head. "Once your partner noticed the symptoms, it was already too late."

His partner? Ah, yes, Shannon had told the guy it was a police matter. He must have assumed. "So two or three days incubation?"

"Incubation isn't really the word, but yes." He nodded. "It depends on the amount ingested, obviously, but a dog that size would have to eat a good bit."

A good bit—purposeful. *He poisoned Duke.* And it wouldn't have taken much planning either; it wasn't hard to toss a ball of tainted hamburger meat into the yard. Duke was a very good boy, but he'd eaten a moldy pepperoni out of the trash a few weeks back. There was no accounting for taste.

But two or three days ago… Had the killer dropped the poison the night he'd taken Billie? They hadn't found anything suspicious after Billie's abduction, but Shannon had opened the door when she heard Candace screaming—Duke had taken off down the street after the truck. They wouldn't have noticed if Duke had found something at the curb.

"Is she here for you?"

Petrosky blinked. "What?" The vet was squinting at him. How long had he been standing there? Then he heard it—footsteps. Behind him.

Shannon? Maybe Candace? Had someone else he loved gotten snatched? The ruined tattoo on his shoulder throbbed, his chest brightened with pain, then it all vanished with an almost audible *bizzt* as if in a puff of electrical smoke. He turned.

Jackson stood in the doorway to the exam room. She held up her phone. "Sorry. I tried calling."

"What are you doing here?" Had she followed him? Had she seen him scavenging for the tiny bottle of Jack? But her face was drawn, her eyes tight; she didn't look pissed —*worried*.

"We have to get back to the station. Acharya got something on Lockhart from his press release. It won't wait."

Petrosky looked at the vet.

"Would you like him cremated?" the man asked, his voice low, compassionate surely, but Petrosky just heard pity. "I can have it done this week. Get you his remains in any number of vessels so you can take him home with you."

Take him home? Petrosky shook his head. "No thanks, doc. You keep him." Duke, poor old boy, was as gone as Julie, as Morrison, as Billie. But he paused in the doorway. "I'll take his collar, though." He'd keep it on the pillow so he'd remember until the day he finally went to join him.

26

BACK TO THE PRECINCT. Back to interrogation.

It felt different in the dark.

And this wasn't the regular dark of night—it was a blackness so complete that when he inhaled, he felt the oblivion on his tongue, in his lungs, mingling with the acid in his hollow guts. But it didn't hurt. At least it didn't hurt.

The woman in the interrogation room was a surprise: curly blonde hair that bordered on frizzy, thick red glasses, pale, thin lips. Watery eyes. Not who he'd expected to be the nail in Lockhart's coffin, perhaps because she seemed like the type of person who'd have reported something suspicious up front, a woman who might ring the police if someone's cat edged too far onto her lawn; not the sort to ignore a man or a truck skulking around. And her presence was not nearly as much of a shock as was the boy sitting next to her. Same light hair as his mother, but with shorn sides, the top pulled into a miniature man bun. The boy was covered forehead to nose with freckles, but there were none on his lower cheeks or chin as if he'd been painted with a spray gun that had suddenly run out of juice. His eyes shone, glassy—sad. And anxious.

"Have you seen this man, Mrs. Wyndham?" Jackson showed them the composite sketch of the man Gertrude had described—the young hottie she shockingly hadn't tried to bed. Petrosky frowned. But…Jackson said they had something on Lockhart, hadn't she?

The woman turned to her son, slow and careful as if trying to avoid sudden movements. "Jared?"

The kid nodded.

They all turned their attention to the boy. "Where did you see him, Jared?" Jackson asked.

"He was at Mr. Lockhart's house when I went to collect the money for cutting the lawn."

Wyndham sniffed. Her eyes were spiderwebbed with red, her cheeks streaked with tears, her lips tight—angry. *Fuck*. She wouldn't be sobbing because her child had seen one of these men. She was crying because…these men had done something to her son.

He turned back to the boy and waited for Jackson to go on. If something had happened to this child, if he'd been hurt by Lockhart or his hunky buddy, it was better for Jackson to ask the questions; Petrosky's fists ached with the desire to punch the photo, though that heat did not reach his chest. Maybe he shouldn't be here at all. But he couldn't bring himself to leave.

"Is this exactly what he looked like?" Jackson said. "Anything you'd change?" She pushed a pencil across the stainless table, but the boy didn't even look at it—his eyes were locked on the sketch.

"He looked just like that, but he was wearing a baseball cap," Jared said, his voice small. "And a jersey like one from the team I used to play on."

The suspect had gotten hold of a jersey from this boy's baseball team? Had the man been watching Jared, chosen him to be a victim?

"The same team?" Jackson rested her clasped hands on

the table and leaned over them. "Had you ever seen him before? Maybe he was a coach."

Jared shook his head. "The shirt wasn't exactly my *team*, just…like…the *style* from my team. It had buttons on the front and little stripes." His brow wrinkled. "I can't remember the team from his jersey, though. He was leaving when I was coming in. I only saw him for a minute." His eyes filled, little beads of glistening shame. "I'm sorry."

"It's okay, son," Petrosky said, though the words made his guts twist as if he had a gnarled mass of briars hooked around his intestines. *Because you're lying, old man—it's not okay.* He nodded to Jackson, who tapped the sketch. "Did this man say anything to you?"

"Just goodbye, but I think he was talking to Mr. Lockhart. It was kinda like…I wasn't there."

At least he wasn't attacked by both of them. Mrs. Wyndham wiped at her eyes, knocking her red-framed spectacles askew, and sniffed again. Petrosky leaned back in the chair, as far from the family as he could get—he had the sudden, undeniable urge to run. *You just don't want to hear any more. You don't want to know what Lockhart did to him.* But if he couldn't listen, he was finished—the inability to handle trauma was a death knell for a cop.

Jackson clearly had no such qualms. She went on: "Did you see what kind of car he was driving?"

Jared shook his head again. "I didn't see. I wasn't really looking, but I don't think there was a car in the driveway."

A gasp from Mrs. Wyndham made them all turn. She covered her mouth with her hand.

Petrosky sat straighter—did she know something more? "Ma'am?"

"I want him in jail!" Her voice was high, tight. "He *touched* him. Your sketch, that guy was out doing god knows what, and that…that *monster* Lockhart was *hurting my son.*"

"When did this happen?" Petrosky asked, keeping his eyes on the boy, on his trembling shoulders.

"Sunday," Jared said. "That's the day I collect for the lawn."

Sunday. Not a week ago, as Lockhart had said. Just two days before they found the knife in Hanover's basement.

The boy looked down. A tear dripped onto the table.

Mrs. Wyndham put her arm around his shoulders. "This never should have happened," she hissed. "He never should have been out on the street."

Petrosky said nothing. She was right. But maybe this time they'd be able to put him away for good.

THE DOOR to interrogation sucked closed behind them with a tiny *thhhhp*, locking in Mrs. Wyndham's sniffling and her son's quiet sobs. Petrosky headed for the break room while Jackson went straight to the bullpen to call the district attorney. *Fucking Lockhart.* He wasn't the man who'd put that knife in Gertrude's house, but he might be an accessory to murder, and he was definitely a fucking pedophile. With Jared's statement, they didn't need anything else to hold him—and now they had all the leverage they needed to get him to cough up his friend. Though cutting deals usually chapped his ass, today, Petrosky didn't care if they had to drop the assault-of-a-minor charge. Lockhart would get out far too soon as it was. But if they nailed him for accessory to homicide six or seven times over...

He filled two cups with the acrid charred sludge that passed for precinct coffee and made for his desk. Arguing hit his ears before he made it there, the indistinct rumbling of two female voices that solidified into actual words as he stepped closer.

"And that makes it okay?" The chief stood with her back to him, her braided black hair hanging down her spine, looming over his desk and Jackson, who was sitting in his chair. And Carroll looked thinner than she had in weeks past. Was she sick?

"I didn't say it was ideal," Jackson said, her voice pressured as if she were trying desperately to keep her temper in check. "But this is the best chance we have of solving this case. And I know him as well as you do. He can't just be at home..." Jackson caught sight of him over Carroll's shoulder. She dropped her gaze. And pushed herself to standing.

"Now, now, ladies, don't fight over me." Petrosky waited for them to say they'd been talking about someone else, or offer some snappy comeback, but Jackson turned on her heel and stalked off to her own desk. Carroll whirled on him, her brown eyes familiar and yet foreign, like an estranged family member who comes to see you after years apart, eyes full of new ideas...and new demons.

He frowned at her navy jacket, bagging loosely from her frame. "Are you okay?" He extended one Styrofoam cup.

"What are you doing here?" She glared at the coffee and crossed her arms.

Fine, two coffees for me then. "I'm just asking a few questions. Locking up pedophiles. Trying to find a killer." He sniffed. "And you?"

"Stop fucking around, Petrosky. You just found your friend dead in a basement. It's a conflict to have you on this."

"It's necessary, and you know it. If we can find this asshole even a day sooner with me working—"

"The moment you fall off the wagon, we don't need you anymore, you understand? You pick up the bottle, don't bother coming back." Carroll met his eyes, but her gaze was heavy—this wasn't just anger or concern for him. A million unsaid words flew between them, the electricity in the air palpable. Agitated. The uneasy tension of addicts—you could feel it on any street corner at the right time of night if you paid attention. And…her husband had been with McCallum; Petrosky had thought him furious, but maybe it was panic.

"Maybe that goes for you too," he said, his voice low. "Wagons can be slippery."

Her eyes turned to steel. "This isn't about me."

"But I'm right."

Her jaw was so hard, he was surprised he couldn't hear her teeth squealing. "Keep your shit together," she said finally. "And don't fuck up."

27

THE NIGHT WAS a black void outside the bullpen window. Jackson had returned to sit at his desk as soon as Carroll left, perhaps to work on the case, or maybe because she'd seen he had coffee. Probably both.

"The bike is a no-go," she said, blowing steam off the Styrofoam cup Carroll had refused. "Not new, and it's common enough that there's no way to track who bought it. Decantor's been working on the construction angle."

Ah, yes, the construction. The suspect had removed a section of glass block in order to get the victim—*not Billie, the victim*—into that basement after drywalling over the door. A treasure hunt custom made for someone who'd been in the house in the past, someone who knew the basement door should be there. *For you*, Morrison whispered.

"What'd he find?" Petrosky asked.

"Not much. The materials needed to build that wall aren't exactly hard to come by. Decantor and I canvassed while you were"—*plastered*—"gone, asking if the neighbors saw someone driving by with sheets of drywall, but only one resident noted anything like that. Guess what the suspect was driving?"

"A blue truck."

"Nope. Gray. We ran gray trucks, but I honestly think she just made a mistake."

He nodded. Witness statements were notoriously unreliable, even if Gertrude's sketch thus far appeared accurate. "She see the guy behind the wheel?"

Jackson shook her head. *Of course she fucking hadn't.* "She said the guy used the garage. Opened it like he owned the place, so she assumed it was someone moving in. She was glad the house would be taken care of."

Dammit. Their killer had learned from every single thing that happened to Norton. He knew exactly how to cover his tracks, how to get people to look the other way. Petrosky brought the coffee to his lips, but though steam was still billowing from the top, he didn't feel the heat on his tongue. A little dry going down, a little abrasive…but no warmth.

Jackson sipped at her own coffee, winced, and put it back down. "But get this: the witness said it was three years ago. She didn't connect it to this case because of the timetable."

Years ago? How did that make sense? "Maybe someone else was working on it." Coincidental, but it was logical. And any contractor would have a pickup.

Jackson shook her head. "I pulled every owner, and talked to the bank; no one should have been working there at any point in the last four years."

Which meant the killer had been planning this for far longer than Petrosky would have guessed. Hell, he'd been there working on the crime scene before Billie had even moved into Petrosky's house. *Shit.* Three years? And going on five since Morrison's death. He'd waited an awfully long time to return after covering that door. "What the hell was he going to do if someone sold it out from under him?" And… they had sold it, right? Wait, was that why he'd chosen to use it now before someone else moved in? Webb's house where he'd hidden the baby…that had been on the auction block, too. Maybe the killer waited for someone to buy the homes to make sure the bodies were found sooner rather than later. His game ended if no one picked up on his clues, and he didn't strike Petrosky as the type of guy to call in a random tip. Petrosky sat straighter. "I know Decantor pulled the auction records..." But Decantor hadn't found anything useful, or he'd have said. Unless he *had* told them—had he? Petrosky's brain felt like a thousand pieces of loose thread, fraying more by the minute. "Who bought the place, again?"

Again. In case Decantor had already told them. In case Petrosky was losing his shit.

Jackson's eyes narrowed—concern?—but she nodded. "The thirty-year-old couple who purchased the house was planning to move here from New York City. They were looking to invest."

"Invest? There?"

"They have no children, so they don't have to worry about schools. He lost his job recently, and she does graphic design work, but with all the house flipping they keep seeing on TV..." She shrugged.

"There's going to be shiplap everywhere."

She raised an eyebrow. "What do you know about shiplap?"

"I know everything, Jackson." Except who was killing off his friends and family one by one. His heart squeezed, dully, like it had simply given up caring. He was so damn tired. But his partner did not respond; her eyes were locked on the room behind his chair.

"Evening, Officer." The voice at his back was familiar, but he couldn't immediately place it. *What the fuck now?*

"Detective." Petrosky stood, bristling, turning to face whatever idiot had decided this was a good time to bother him. Haverford? *Word travels fast.* He crossed his arms. "Are you here to be the mouthpiece for your piece-of-shit client again?"

He grunted, but a self-satisfied grin touched his lips. "I just wanted to tell you in person that Lockhart's family will be filing suit."

"Lockhart doesn't have any family," Petrosky said.

"He has a kid in Texas. And I'm filing on behalf of that boy."

"For what?" Jackson scoffed from her seat at the desk. She hadn't even bothered to stand up. "Is he pissed that we protected him from his pedophile father?"

Haverford narrowed his eyes. "Oh…you really don't know, do you?"

"Know what, asshole?" Petrosky snapped.

Haverford shoved a manila envelope his way, and when Petrosky didn't grab it, he tucked it in the space behind Petrosky's crossed arms. "My client died this afternoon while in your custody. Someone smashed his head into a metal toilet because of your press release."

Well, fuck. That meant they couldn't wring any more information out of him, but maybe he'd already told them all he knew. Petrosky opened his mouth to ask if they'd caught Lockhart's killer, but he closed it again; he didn't give a shit. Death was the only way to make sure guys like Lockhart never hurt anyone else, and Mrs. Wyndham would probably send Lockhart's killer a cake with a file in it. Was he smiling? *I am going crazy.* He forced his lips into a straight line once more, but Haverford's shoulders had tightened, his eyes hard —glaring.

"If I didn't know better, I'd think you did this on purpose. And I think a jury will too." He smirked.

"You don't care if you get anything for that kid," Petrosky snarled. "You just want to milk Lockhart's estate for every dime you can fit in your slimy hand. If you're going to be a dick, at least own it."

Haverford's nostrils twitched—definitely agitated, which

was a small consolation. He turned on his heel and stalked off.

Petrosky dropped his arms and let the envelope fall to the floor.

28

IT TURNED out they didn't need to wring Lockhart for information—not that it was possible now. Gertrude's hunky knife-hider himself called in the next morning in response to Acharya's article. The press release had informed the public that the man in Gertrude's sketch was wanted for questioning, that he might be a witness—did he know why they wanted to see him? Was he concerned that he, like Lockhart, might end up a casualty of vigilante justice? Whatever the reason he'd decided to make that call, Yannis Getzel had refused to come into the precinct, and Acharya, the journalist who had taken the call at his fancy newspaper office, hadn't wanted to scare him off. Neither did Petrosky. If Getzel was calling them, it was far more likely that he knew something than that he was their killer. Their suspect didn't feel like the turn-himself-in type.

Jackson drove. Petrosky rubbed at his aching cheekbone. He'd slept at the precinct, his face planted on his desk until Acharya's arrival had dragged him from a dark and dreamless unconsciousness. He hadn't been able to fathom lying in bed, staring at Duke's pillow or looking at the house next door, knowing he'd never see Billie again. Listening to the silence. There was an urge to see Shannon and the kids, a pull deep in his bones as if their presence could stitch his heart back together. But what kind of selfish bullshit would that be? He'd used the people in his life enough; used Carroll to get clean, put his demons on her, and now it appeared he'd dragged her down with him. That wasn't fair, and he wasn't going to do it to his almost-daughter, to his grandkids. Besides, Decantor had been posted on Petrosky's place last night—he trusted Decantor to keep them safe more than he trusted himself. He was a liability. And he hadn't even been able to save Duke.

Jackson pulled to the curb, eyes narrowed. She hit the lock button twice. Getzel's apartment was a little place in downtown Detroit near Caffrey Corridor, and the open stairwell smelled less like piss than the closed stairwells in the neighborhood. Not *no* piss, but less—a moderate amount of urine.

Getzel bore an uncanny resemblance to the sketch Gertrude had created for them: dark hair, wide-set eyes, a strong jaw speckled in barely there stubble like a young John Stamos. Gertrude had her moments of confusion, but damn if she didn't get this one spot-on. He met them at the door wearing jean shorts and a Pink Floyd T-shirt, though he looked far too young to know anything about the dark side of the moon.

"So tell us about yourself, Mr. Getzel," Petrosky said when they were all seated on his tiny balcony. The inside of the apartment smelled like urine too.

Getzel leaned a shoulder against the chipped railing and pulled a cigarette from his pack. "Are you going to offer me a deal or something?"

Petrosky and Jackson exchanged a glance. "A deal?"

"Yeah, for like...coming forward?"

Jackson leaned toward him on her plastic seat. The legs tottered dangerously. "Do you need a deal, Mr. Getzel?"

"You tell me." The lighter flicked, and soon smoke was curling around his head.

Petrosky's mouth watered, and when Getzel met his gaze, he gestured to the pack. Jackson glowered at him, but Getzel passed it over. *Just bonding, Jackson. Just bonding.* Besides, letting him smoke was the least she could do; he hadn't had a drink since the day before, and his spine felt like it was vibrating—like it might shake his flesh clean off, leaving behind a skittering snake of bone.

"So, were you Lockhart's dealer, or what?" Petrosky asked. The whole burner cell thing was pretty common when you were slinging dope around, but Petrosky wasn't sold on the idea. This was the guy seen at Hanover's place, and drug dealers didn't randomly play hide-and-seek with hunting knives. He just needed to soften him up. Best to start small.

Getzel chuckled, expelling smoke from his nose like an angry bull. "A dealer? I guess in a manner of speaking."

"Let me be straight with you, Mr. Getzel. We don't give a fuck what you do for a living—I don't care about arresting you unless someone paid you to diddle a little kid, in which case we have a problem." But Petrosky didn't think he'd done that either; Jared said the guy didn't even glance at him. Did Getzel know about Lockhart's perversions?

It did not appear so; Getzel's eyes widened, his jaw gaping, the cigarette forgotten in his hand. "Whoa. No, no way, I would *never* touch a kid."

"Then what were you doing hanging out at Lockhart's? And wearing a baseball uniform, no less? You got a thing for popcorn and crackerjacks or what?"

Getzel crushed his smoke in the ashtray; the metal table beneath wiggled on spindly legs. "No, you're misunderstanding. He asked me to wear that."

Jackson frowned, her faux-confused expression. "And you just wear whatever people ask you to?"

"Well…yeah, that's kinda my thing." He cocked his head, the hair along his jaw glinting in the sunshine. "You're really not going to arrest me?"

Petrosky dragged on his cig and let the smoke burn his eyes as he said, "Not unless you hurt someone, Mr. Getzel, but I don't think you did. I think Lockhart was paying you for sex."

Getzel met his eyes, inhaled sharply, then nodded once. "Yeah. He was."

"And the jersey?" But he already knew the answer. Lockhart was into kids—he'd wanted this guy to *look* like one.

"I don't know; I don't ask questions. People are into all kinds of weird shit."

"Did he ask you to do anything else?" Jackson said. *Like hide a knife?* That was why they were there. Was Lockhart really their killer? Was this over?

"He always asked that I shave real close—*everything*." He inclined his head, eyebrows raised to emphasize the point. "And I always wore that baseball shirt he gave me. Sometimes I just…stood there while he watched." An expression that might have been disgust flickered across his face and vanished. "I mean, he was a weird guy, and he couldn't always get it up, but that happens sometimes." He shrugged. "I don't take it personally."

It wasn't personal—the only thing this guy had done wrong was be of legal age. Lockhart had been trying to take the edge off his child abuse fantasies with someone who looked young enough to trick his brain. But it hadn't been enough.

"Is that why you're looking for me?" Getzel raised an eyebrow. "I mean, my buddy called, gave me the number of the newspaper because I was a person of interest or something, but I kinda thought there was a reward. Like, maybe I knew a fugitive." He grinned, confident—almost cocky. Did he really not know he'd done something wrong?

"Oh, you know a fugitive, all right." Petrosky tapped ash into the tray, setting off another round of table-wiggling. "But there's no reward except staying out of jail."

Getzel's eyes widened. "But you just said—"

"We're not worried about your whoring around," Jackson said. "We're worried about a knife you delivered to a house right up the street from Lockhart's."

The guy's jaw dropped, but he recovered quickly, though his confidence had vanished—he looked like a scared kid. "You know about that, huh? Man. He said if I didn't do it right, I had to give the money back, but I already spent it."

"Who?" Jackson asked. "Lockhart?"

He shook his head. "No, not him." He sighed and leaned back against the railing once more, and Petrosky suddenly saw him plummeting over the side to his death, taking whatever clues he was hiding with him—his head shattering against the asphalt into a useless abstract of blood and bone and brain. Like Ruby's head. Lisa Walsh. He dragged harder on the cigarette, the butt burning his fingertips. *Stop thinking, you crazy fuck.* He blinked as Getzel righted himself.

"Okay, so this guy came up to me when I was leaving Lockhart's place. He gave me a thousand dollars cash and said to knock at exactly two thirty. I was supposed to tell his wife I was a washing machine repairman and hide the knife in the basement, somewhere she wouldn't find it; he said if she found it too quickly, he'd want his money back." He shrugged as if he'd just told them he was given a dollar to deliver a ham sandwich. What the fuck was wrong with this guy?

"What did he look like?" Jackson said.

"Um…white, I think? Average build, not as big as… well…" He gestured to Petrosky's bulk, then frowned as if realizing it was a bad idea to piss off the cops after admitting to prostitution and knife smuggling. "No offense."

"None taken." He waited for the man to go on; Getzel's mouth was already moving like he had a million words fighting to escape his lips.

"He wore a mask," Getzel continued. "One of those cheap plastic ones that look like Michael Myers, which is kinda why I thought it was part of their kink. And he seemed spry —maybe too young to be married to the lady in that house— but I guess I can't really assume that. And if some older lady wanted to take care of me, I'd probably say yes no matter what kinky shit she was into."

But that wasn't the part nagging at Petrosky's brain— Norton had liked masks, too, his favorite modeled after those worn by doctors during the Black Death.

"What happened next?" Jackson prodded.

Getzel smiled, but it was without humor. "I remember thinking he was going to ask me about some kinky bondage shit, but he just passed me a note with the door code and that bag." The code—ah, yes. No wonder this guy thought their perp was the homeowner. But how the hell had the suspect gotten the combination? Had he watched through the window?

"You didn't mention a bag," Jackson said.

"Oh yeah. Like a backpack."

Gertrude had told them about that too. Maybe they could pull DNA off it. The only prints on the Visqueen had been smudged, unusable, and there'd been nothing on the knife. Except blood.

Morrison's blood. The air thinned. He coughed.

Jackson shifted in the plastic seat, wincing—uncomfortable. He couldn't even feel his ass, which was probably a good thing. "Where is the bag now?" Jackson said.

"I left it outside the house afterward like he told me to."

And he still thought nothing was wrong with this? Was this guy a fucking idiot?

Jackson seemed to be thinking the same. She was staring at Getzel like he'd just said he preferred cauliflower to cake. "Why would you do that?" Jackson asked. "Leaving a knife, dumping a bag... That didn't seem even a little suspicious to you?" But even if it had, Getzel was already doing enough illegal shit, and a grand would pay his rent for a couple of months. What did he have to lose?

Getzel shrugged. "Not really. It was his bag, his house; why wouldn't I leave it there? Plus, he gave me the money up-front, and the job was just a delivery—easy. He also said he knew Lockhart, so I guess I trusted him a little more."

"That still doesn't make sense to me, Getzel." Jackson shook her head. "I don't think it'd make sense to most rational people."

"I imagine it wouldn't." He let his eyes drift past them, toward the door to his piss-smelling apartment, less like he was concocting a lie and more as if considering his life. "Listen, I play all kinds of roles. Plumbers, firemen, pizza delivery guys... Acting like a repairman and delivering a package wasn't even the weirdest thing I'd done that day."

"And the knife?" Jackson said. "With blood on it, no less? You thought that sweet old woman needed a package like that?"

"Nah, there wasn't blood on it; it was just rusty." *Huh.* Petrosky had pegged it as blood right away, but would the average citizen jump straight to that conclusion? Maybe not, and this guy had fewer working brain cells than average. Getzel shrugged, tapped another cigarette from his pack, and lit up. "I thought it was *a game*, okay? You'd be surprised what kind of packages people need. I once got a request from this guy in his midseventies to show up with lubricant, a lead pipe, and—"

Petrosky put up a hand. *Dear god, stop.* But, honestly, he

kinda hoped Gertie had gotten some. "Did you deliver her something extra special?"

Getzel watched the smoke curl into the sky. "Nah. I let the client lead, and I expected she would come on to me, but..." He chuckled and met Petrosky's eyes. "She kept calling me Richard. Told me to come back later to fix the oven too."

29

THE RIDE back to the precinct was blessedly short, Jackson casting him sidelong glances as if he'd broken some unspoken covenant by snagging a smoke from a man-whore. They'd taken a little more information from Getzel on the man who had given him the knife, but the fucker hadn't even seen a vehicle—it hadn't occurred to him that the perp needed one since he'd approached him "outside his own house." *What an idiot.* A thousand bucks and you could buy an unwitting accomplice. Maybe that was the point: better to have a helper who had no idea who the fuck you were. Who had zero connections to you.

Who would never be able to turn you in.

Petrosky and Jackson spent hours alternating between the files and the phones and then met in the break room as the sun was beginning its slow western descent. His stomach was tied in knots. He couldn't remember the last time he'd eaten, and the gritty heat of sleeplessness was dragging on him, though he was certain he'd managed at least a few hours at his desk—the ache in his cheek proved that much. But it was more than his physical afflictions; every hour seemed to pass more slowly than the one before, and it was in those stretched minutes that the hollow ache of hopelessness grew, a void he was desperately trying to ignore.

What was the point? This murder spree was probably finished if past history was any indication, and they didn't know who the bastard might go after next even if he did decide to keep killing. They had no real leads outside of the truck. And though Petrosky had racked his brain, though he'd stared at the files until his eyes crossed, convinced he was missing something, he had not been able to figure out what it was. All they'd really accomplished was getting Lockhart off the street—permanently. Maybe that should be more of a relief, a victory, even, but it felt inconsequential in the face of so much death.

He finished filling his cup and passed Jackson the coffeepot. "So...Gertrude Hanover's nurse was on a strict schedule. He always took a shower at two thirty and called his girlfriend when she got off work at two forty-five." That discussion had been far more tense than necessary like it was Petrosky's fault the guy had lost his job. Like it was his fault the nurse had let a male prostitute into the house packing the blade used to slaughter a cop.

Jackson didn't look surprised. "No wonder he had Getzel go in at exactly two thirty. Our suspect did his homework, that's for sure."

He nodded. "Scott called too; he's towing Lockhart's truck in now." Likely a pointless endeavor—Lockhart had been inside his house molesting Jared Wyndham while Michael Myers was offering Getzel a thousand dollars to play hide-and-seek, but they hadn't known that when they'd gotten the warrant. It was far too coincidental that Lockhart drove a similar truck—they didn't have confirmation on the exact type—but maybe Lockhart and the killer were partners. Or maybe the killer had taken the truck, used it, and returned it. Time would tell.

Are you involved, Lockhart? Or are you as clueless as Getzel?

He jumped when Jackson slammed the coffeepot down. "It's just so fucking ridiculous," she snapped.

Petrosky raised an eyebrow. "What is?"

"Getzel. Oh, and he has alibis for almost all of Decantor's homicides: work."

Not that they'd thought he was their killer—the guy would have been sixteen at the time of Morrison's murder, and teenage impulsiveness, even young-adult arrogance, didn't fit their profile. "Alibis, huh? Weird that his clients are willing to offer themselves up to help their side piece."

"His clients didn't need to. Getzel works for a food delivery service on evenings he isn't selling his ass. Probably where some of his clients come from—Lockhart's used the service himself. Getzel might be targeting lonely folks ordering meals for one until he can make that lead pipe thing a full-time gig." She sipped at her coffee and smirked. "You going to offer him a place next door in your harem?"

Next door. Where there was now an empty bedroom. Because Billie was dead. *Dead.* "Yeah, there's room now, I guess." The void tugged at him, demanding to be acknowledged.

Her eyes widened. "I'm sorry, I shouldn't have said that."

Billie's dead. Duke is dead.

He could not breathe. His hand was on fire. He looked down—he'd smashed the Styrofoam coffee cup in his fist, soaking the floor and the cuff of his jacket. Coffee trickled down his fingers like muddy tears.

Jackson reached for the napkins, but he waved her off and wiped his smarting arm on his jeans. "I'm fine, okay? Fine."

I'm not fine. He felt like a train was suddenly barreling down on him, and there was nothing he could do to get out of the way. *They're dead, Morrison's dead, Julie's dead, they're all—*

"Petrosky, I—"

"I'm going to head home. Get some rest." Was it quitting

time? He didn't care. *You should stay here*, Morrison whispered. *Nothing good will happen if you leave. That's why you slept here last night.*

He didn't bother to put his things away; he left the pages spread on his desk, all those useless fucking files that would never make Billie's bedroom less empty, would never make his pillow wet with slobber, would never give Shannon her husband back. The void tugged harder. What was the point, what was the fucking point?

If Jackson called a goodbye on his way out, he did not hear her.

His hand burned hotter by the time he got to the stairwell, the dry kind of needling sting that meant it would blister. The breeze outside was a welcome reprieve—cool despite the mugginess that still clung to the evening. He hustled across the lot, thankful he'd driven his Caprice here from the vet; had that been only yesterday? It suddenly seemed as if he'd lost Billie and Duke years ago, that the discomfort behind his breastbone was not the fresh pain of grief, but the duller ache of wistful sorrow. But it was possible that he just couldn't fully feel his chest over the vibrations in his bones—he hadn't noticed it building, but now his skeleton was shuddering, dancing a rhythm his flesh could not match.

This is it, old man, the night your body finally gives up. And good riddance.

He forced himself unsteadily onward. Ridiculous. He was being ridiculous. The sodium lights clicked on with a staccato *bzzt*.

"Ed!"

He turned. *McCallum?* The doctor was hustling toward him across the lake of asphalt, his belly jiggling, his face red even in the twilight. "What's up, doc?"

"Ah, yes, when in doubt, turn to cartoons," McCallum huffed.

Petrosky cocked his head, but McCallum was already extending a bag—white paper. No grease stains, so it wasn't a donut. "What's this?"

"Prescription," McCallum said, his voice low. "Benzodiazepines."

Benzo... He narrowed his eyes and pushed the bag back. "I don't need this."

McCallum shoved the sack his way once more, the doctor's meaty fist hitting his chest with a thunk like an external heartbeat. "I suspect you have a little withdrawal to work through, and these should help some, though obviously, they can't ease all of it. Can you stay home for a few days?"

Petrosky tasted blood; his molars ached. "Did Jackson call you?"

McCallum's face was a mask. "You're no good to anyone if you're not sober, yourself included." He leaned in close. "Don't forget what happened with Morrison." And the meaning in his words was clear: *You were drunk then. You let him die.*

He felt something snap deep inside his hollow chest. He nodded goodbye to McCallum and let himself fall into the void.

———

YOU LET ME DIE.

All the way home, he listened to that voice. Sometimes it was Morrison's, sometimes it was Billie's, but every time it was accusatory. And every time it was *right*.

He stopped at the liquor store near his house and took his time in the parking lot, maybe waiting for something to stop him, the haze of neon red leaking into the car and staining his shaking hands a sickly pink. The stinging in his burned arm was barely noticeable over the stabbing fire in his chest.

This was bullshit; it was all bullshit. The parking lot gravel ground beneath his shoes; the fluorescents seared into his brain; the cash register binged. The bag was a cool and welcome heaviness in his arms.

I need help? Fuck them; they need help. He couldn't have saved Morrison. He couldn't have helped Billie either. Jackson had been sober when Billie was taken, so had Decantor—they hadn't been able to do a goddamn thing. Shannon had been sober both times too—she'd been *right fucking there,* and she'd let this asshole take Billie away. And with Morrison, my god, his boy had left the house to canvass, and Shannon didn't call him all damn night. Maybe if she had...

You let them die, Petrosky. Stop blaming other people.

He locked the car. He drank. He smoked. He drank more. The road was hazy on the way home, the bleat of a car horn snapping him back into his lane just in time to avoid a head-on collision. And he didn't give a shit. Even in the face of death, his heartbeat throbbed more slowly than before—steady now. His hands no longer shook.

Fuck it all.

He hit the brakes as he approached the house, easing his way up the street. The trees on either side wavered as if he were looking at the landscape from beneath the surface of a dark lake, the world undulating to grayer and dimmer hues with every breath he took. Like drowning—watching the slowly vanishing moon while sucking water into his lungs.

He swerved into the driveway and slammed the car into park. One of the flatfoots in the patrol car parked across the road got out as he stumbled from his Caprice, but he waved them off, his hand heavy. The bottle. He still had the neck of the bottle clenched tightly in his waving fist. *Fuck it.*

You let them die.

Fuck you.

He tripped up the stairs and into the house; Shannon and

the children looked up from the dining table as the front door banged open. He smiled, though he had no idea why. Shannon's eyes widened.

He vaguely heard her talking to the kids, telling them to go to their rooms, as if this were their house, as if they fucking lived here—like they'd never leave. Maybe they wouldn't. Maybe he was the invader. Was this even his house? He stumbled into his bedroom and collapsed onto his bed, eyes on the ceiling. But the sheets were all wrong—they smelled of fabric softener, not like Duke's fur. She'd changed them. Why had she changed them?

She's trying to hurt you.

He deserved that, but damn if it didn't piss him off. Tears smarted in his eyes. He blinked them back, the horrible stink of laundry soap from the pillowcase leaking into his sinuses like a toxic gas. Everything was wrong. *Everything.*

"Petrosky?"

He looked over. She stood in the doorway, her arms crossed, one shoulder against the jamb. "Why are you doing this?"

He drew his gaze back to the ceiling. "Why are you? You should be in Atlanta."

She hissed in a breath, and for a moment, he thought she'd left, but then he heard her footsteps. *Thud. Thud.* He kept his eyes on the ceiling, yellowed with age and tobacco and overlaid with a murky tint like the sky before a storm. The air felt energized, too, laced with unstable electricity—he could practically hear the thunder.

"I understand," she said, "god knows I do, but you need to get your shit together. I came all the way back here so the kids could have a grandfather. I know you love them. And I know you love me too."

"No one asked you to come back," he said. The words tripped from his mouth like he was gargling with marbles, and his chest, numb until now, spasmed with bright white pain—*there's the lightning.* "You didn't ask me if I wanted you here."

"Fuck you," she hissed. And then she was there, standing over him, her face blocking his view of the ceiling, her fists battering his shoulders, his face, his gut, her knuckles beating twice as fast as the throbbing of his heart, but it didn't hurt—it didn't hurt. He felt the bottle being torn from his hand. Heard the bright jangle of shattering glass when it hit the wall.

"I tried. I've fucking tried everything with you! Can't you see this isn't about you anymore? I deserve better. My kids, your son's kids, they fucking deserve more from you!" She was gasping, whispering, maybe so the kids couldn't hear, but like the moon above the wavering trees, her words came from afar—too distant to grasp. She hit him again, and his head jerked to the side. He tasted blood. His cheek was wet. He rested there with his face aimed toward Duke's pillow.

The pummeling stopped. "I'm done," she said. "I'm fucking done."

He let his hands rest at his sides. Where they had been.

He felt nothing.

30

Pain.

It woke him with a hot throbbing that made his eyes feel as if they might bulge from their sockets and pop out onto his cheeks. But one eyelid refused to open. The half slit he got out of the other revealed the empty pillow beside him bathed in early white light. No…not empty. It took everything in his power to close his swollen knuckles around Duke's collar.

The sheets stank of soap and the sourness leaking from his pores. But the collar still smelled like his dog.

Shannon. She'd put that there to hurt him too.

He deserved that.

He deserved worse.

Time passed.

Foggy.

Unknowable.

The quality of light was different the next time he opened

his eyes—yellower. His nose was clogged, tight with blood, but he could still taste the alcohol along with the iron on his tongue. He tried to sit; managed to heft himself onto his elbow. Shards of glass on the floor, a shattered bottle, dark stains—the liquor. He wanted to puke. He collapsed backward onto the pillow instead and let the blackness take him.

"PAPA ED?" Evie.

He heaved himself onto his side, clutched the collar against his chest, and closed his eyes, listening as Shannon's voice filtered through the door, low words meant for her daughter. Shushing her? Maybe telling her he wasn't worth her time.

He waited for Shannon to knock, to walk in like she owned the place, demand he get up, demand he be better.

Just footsteps. Walking away.

Maybe she knew he was beyond help.

SOMEONE WAS KNOCKING. He rolled over toward the wall, toward Duke's pillow. His throat burned. He swallowed the bitterness back down.

Thunk, thunk, thunk.

He rested his hand on Duke's pillow. Cold. And next door, Billie's bed was just as cold, cold like her porcelain cheek, her stiff hand, like Morrison's body, like the bloody tissue when his own fingers had slipped into the chasm across Morrison's throat. Cold like the barrel of his gun. He could taste the metal. His muscles shook—his arm was trembling. *Don't think, don't think about the gun.*

"Petrosky?" A female voice, but too low to tell who was speaking.

"I'm asleep." He squeezed his eyes closed as Henry had the week before when he was trying to convince Shannon that, no, he had not been jumping on the bed in the dark, he'd been resting *this whole time*. His heart spasmed and settled; he pushed the child from his mind.

"Petrosky… You need to come out, okay?" Shannon, definitely Shannon.

He opened his eyes. The light had changed again, gray now with the impending night. "Come back later." *Or go back to Atlanta. Forget I ever existed.*

"The chief's here to see you."

The chief? *Goddammit.* Those flatfoot patrol bitches who had watched him stumble home had probably tattled. Snitches get stitches? Fuck that. He had ditches with those assholes' names on them.

But the rage didn't reach his heart, didn't settle in his chest or tighten his lungs. They were right. He shouldn't have been driving. Shouldn't have been trashed half an hour after the precinct shrink had cornered him in a parking lot and warned him to stay off the sauce.

"Send her in here, would you?" He didn't want the kids to see him like this, like… He glanced down. Same clothes he'd worn yesterday—musky and sour. He had blisters on his hand that almost looked like burns, though he couldn't remember hurting himself, and a dark stain like coffee on his jeans. His gray T-shirt was speckled with blood….his pillow too. He flipped it over as the knob turned.

Carroll stopped short just inside the doorjamb, her onyx hair a curtain along her collarbone made deeper by her yellow blouse. Thin; she was so *thin*. "What the fuck, Petrosky?"

He shrugged, though the action slung a comma of pain up through his neck and into the base of his skull. He stayed seated lest he hurt himself worse. "You should see the other guy."

"Oh god." She pressed her fingertips against her forehead in a what-the-fuck-is-wrong-with-you gesture. "Did you get into a bar fight? Am I going to have a complaint waiting for me at the station?"

"I doubt it." Unless Shannon decided to call him up on charges of Knowing How To Take A Punch in the first degree.

Carroll dropped her hands and squared her shoulders as if deciding whether she, too, should slap him around for being a worthless sack of shit. "Do I need to call Linda?"

"Has my ex-wife ever helped me before?" She wouldn't come anyway. Linda was done with him; she'd made that clear enough last time she'd stopped by.

Carroll was still watching him, her dark eyes black in the waning light. Thank god she hadn't turned on the overheads —his brain might have literally exploded.

He cleared his throat. "Are you going to tell me why you're here, or are you just going to stare?"

Her shoulders relaxed, but it looked more like defeat. She sighed. "I came to see if you're okay."

Of course I'm not fucking okay. But was he ever? She'd gotten him clean before, and he didn't think she was up for the job a second time—nor was he. He'd stopped letting her be his sponsor when he realized the strain it was putting on her marriage.

The look in his eyes must have been response enough. "I'm still your boss. I need to know you're okay—that you'll be okay."

He pushed himself to standing, a groan ripping itself from the depths of his abdomen. His legs. His back. His heart —his head. Everything throbbed, spiked hammers bashing at his temples in time to his heartbeat. "You might be my boss, but I don't give a shit what you think about me." He stepped closer and stared her down, their noses almost touching. She smelled of coffee and gardenia, and that made his heart hurt more.

"I know you don't," she said. "I wish I didn't care, that I could turn it off, but I just…" She shook her head. "You know what? Fuck it. Maybe a dose of reality is what you need." She turned for the door.

"What's that supposed to mean?" Not a threat—surely a promise. She should have fired his ass a long time ago.

She whirled back, the air charged, her shoulders rigid. "It means that after next week, I'll be out of your hair permanently, and you can explain your bullshit to the new chief."

A pulsing, throbbing ache spread through his blood and into every muscle, every joint. "What?"

"I resigned." Her eyes spat fire, as if she were angry at him, as if it were his fault. But that made no sense—she wouldn't have resigned over him.

Oh shit. Was this about the case? Their suspect had gone after everyone Petrosky loved. First Morrison, even if they couldn't prove that yet, then Ruby, Billie, his fucking dog, and every time he upped surveillance on one place, the killer showed up somewhere else. And they sure hadn't been watching the chief.

This is my fault, too—all my fault. "Did he get to you?"

She frowned. "Did who get to me?"

I'm sorry, Steph, I'm so sorry. He advanced on Carroll, the tendons around his knees burning. "Did he kidnap someone you care about? Threaten you?"

Her eyes narrowed, confused, then widened with realization. "Oh god, you really are out of it." She shook her head. "It isn't about this case. I was kidnapped, Petrosky, just a few months ago. That's enough to give anyone pause."

"I got that motherfucker," Petrosky assured her. "He's locked up tight. Forever."

She put her hands on his face, and the warm, gentle pressure of it was so familiar that the stabbing in his chest started up anew—fresh grief and old regret. She offered him a wan smile. "I was on shaky ground before the kidnapping. I resigned for the sake of my family, for my sobriety—for my sanity. You should do the same before there's nothing left of you." She dropped her hands. Strange how it felt like goodbye.

31

SLEEP CAME QUICKLY AND EASILY, an utterly blank unconsciousness that engulfed him the moment he closed his eyes. He awoke with a headache and a more pressing urgency in the region of his bladder, the sun already brilliant against the windowpanes. Carroll was leaving the force for good. And why not? Might as well have everything in his life fall apart.

You selfish piece of shit. Carroll resigning didn't have anything to do with him; he'd seen her husband at Dr. McCallum's. Maybe she'd relapsed, maybe it was martial issues, maybe it really was the trauma of the kidnapping—that was certainly enough. Either way, she'd obviously been struggling for some time if her weight loss was any indication. She was doing the right thing; she usually did.

Unlike him.

His clothes were too sour to ignore—the stench was rank. He cranked the hot water and stood beneath the showerhead, but he did not feel the wetness on his skin, nor the cold when he emerged. He could not smell the coffee, though he watched it percolate. And his phone said it had been...

Two days. Two days since he'd hidden himself away in his

bedroom, two days since Shannon had beaten his ass. He sipped at his coffee and stared out the front window at his lawn—emerald green concealing deadly things like the tropical jungles where one wrong step meant fangs in your ankle. Poor Duke. Had the killer used cheese? Had the poison been hidden in meat? Maybe a steak. Duke deserved far more than a tenderloin as a last meal, but god, he hoped the old boy had enjoyed it. But those weren't the only questions swirling in his brain. *Was it really you, you fucker? Did you kill my partner? Or are you a cheap knockoff who somehow ended up with that knife?*

Petrosky turned at a clatter on the dining table. Shannon snatched up a rogue spoon and settled it on its spot in front of the chair Evie had deemed as hers, but no kids sat there, not yet. He hadn't even heard Shannon come out.

He nodded to her; it made his neck smart. Sweat dripped down his spine. He'd been sweating since he'd woken up, though he didn't feel hot. "There's coffee if you want some," he said, the words nasally—congested. He still couldn't breathe through his nostrils. Maybe his nose was broken, maybe not, but it didn't matter much either way.

She winced and headed around the table toward the living room. "How's your face?"

"As handsome as ever." He tried to force a smile, but all his muscles felt twitchy—painful and uncooperative. He tightened his fingers on the coffee mug, pulling the burned skin tight along the back of his hand, and let that ache steady him. The lower part of his sweatshirt sleeve was already speckled with coffee.

Shannon bent and touched the ridge of his cheekbone, hissing a sympathy breath when he flinched away. "You did a good enough job already, Shannon, you don't need to dig the knife any deeper."

"I…" She lowered her head. "I didn't mean to hit you that hard."

"I deserved it."

"Yeah, you did." But she still wouldn't meet his eyes. Shame or anger at him, he could not tell.

He raised the steaming cup to his lips and took an unsteady swallow. "Impressive how you managed to pummel me without making a sound; whispered threats and all. The kids probably had no idea."

"Well, you weren't putting up much of a fight. Struggle is what creates commotion." She finally met his gaze. "Don't give up," she said. "Please. Whatever happens, just hang on, solve this case, and ease some of that burden. Then we'll get you better—we always do."

Always. Until the time you can't. "Jackson and Decantor... they'll find this guy. They don't need me." The words tasted bitter on his tongue—the acidic burn of failure.

Her jaw dropped as if she were shocked by this, but she couldn't possibly be—could she see him? Even Evie and Henry surely knew what a fuckup he was. "He killed your son. Killed Billie. He murdered Duke, for fuck's sake." She gestured to his waist, and he followed her fingers. The metal buckle of Duke's collar poked from his sweatshirt pouch, glinting in the lamplight.

He tucked it back inside as she slid onto the couch beside him. "Please talk to me. Let me help."

"I..." *I don't know what to do.* He couldn't say it, but that didn't make it less accurate—his brain felt...mushy. For once, he should listen to Carroll and stay home; he'd just be thinking about Duke anyway. Billie. Morrison. Poor Ruby, who'd gotten sucked into this by being unfortunate enough to match the fucker's victim profile: redheaded and pregnant to mirror Norton's crimes, and maybe as importantly, associated with Petrosky. McCallum's voice echoed in his head: *There's an endgame, and if he did follow Norton's crimes, he followed you too.* He drew his gaze back to the lawn, away from Shannon. The fact that her eyes looked even a little hopeful punched him straight in the lungs.

How long would it be before the killer got bored out there? How long before he came back to terrorize what was left of Petrosky's family? Who else in Petrosky's life had this killer been watchi—

"Papa Ed!"

Petrosky turned.

Henry stood in the doorway, rubbing his blue eyes. Frowning. "Did you fall?"

"Yeah." *So hard, kid. So damn hard.* He blinked, his eyes aching as he tried to focus on the boy... His muscles froze. Not Henry, not anymore—Morrison, Morrison's face on the child, and then Henry's neck was a gushing wound, arterial blood spraying the walls. The boy hit his knees, blue eyes rolling back to the whites. Shannon was talking, but Petrosky could not hear her; his ears rang with his own shrill screams. But she did not appear alarmed. And Henry... The boy smiled. Standing once more. No blood. In his head, it was all in his head. *Fuck.*

"Petrosky?"

He glanced at Shannon, then pushed himself to his feet, slopping coffee over the arm of the couch. He frowned at it but left it there to soak into the material—to stain it forever. "I have to go." The kids shouldn't have to watch him crack.

JACKSON WAS PORING over files at her desk when he arrived in the bullpen. If she noticed his injuries, she didn't show it; she filled him in as if his face looking like a meatloaf was an everyday occurrence. Maybe it was. Maybe this was even an improvement on his normal face—it couldn't have gotten worse.

The biggest news: Scott had found one of Ruby's hairs

when he'd searched Lockhart's truck. *Fucking hell.* Was Lockhart actually the killer and had hired someone else to give Getzel that knife? Maybe. Was Getzel lying about how he'd gotten it? Jackson didn't think so. But Lockhart didn't seem smart enough or disciplined enough to pull off these crimes, and he sure wasn't strong enough to lift those men's bodies on his own, men who outweighed him by at least fifty pounds—Petrosky would have bet money on that. So who else was there? Jackson and Decantor had torn the auto repair shop apart; questioned every employee, other customers, anyone who had access to Lockhart's vehicle. Not one looked suspicious—verifiable alibis. And with Lockhart keeping the truck in the neighbor's garage, anyone could have borrowed it.

Petrosky drank coffee, processing the new information, letting the details pull him further from the misery he'd been wallowing in for the past two days—denial, distraction, who cared so long as it hurt less? Jackson and Decantor had revisited the diner angle, too, reinterviewing the staff, showing Getzel's photo, Lockhart's picture, images of the truck. Nothing. But if their killer had stalked Ruby there, he wouldn't have gone inside where he'd have to show his face; this bastard wasn't one to take risks. As McCallum had said, he'd learned from every mistake Norton had made. They had no real leads, no forensic evidence except what he'd handed them—save one of Ruby's hairs—and no useful eyewitness statements. This fucker was clearly smarter than he was; at the very least, he was more than a day sober. Probably.

Petrosky left Jackson and took the files back to his desk, inhaling more coffee, hoping that the caffeine would ease the tremble in his hands, but he wasn't especially hopeful. Maybe he should have popped one of the pills McCallum had given him; he'd stared at the paper bag all the way to the station. He had swallowed a handful of ibuprofen, but that was barely touching the ache from his fat lip and busted eye, both of which surely looked worse than they felt. Even now, Decantor was sneaking glances at him from his desk across the bullpen.

Petrosky tried a glare on for size, but it only made his head throb. "Take a picture! It'll last longer!"

Decantor raised one eyebrow but turned back to his own work. *Kardashian-loving fuckhead.* But there was no heart in the insult. No heat.

Petrosky crossed his arms and half grimaced at the files, trying to clear his brain. *Lockhart, Lockhart, Lockhart.* Getzel didn't have a reason to protect Lockhart, wouldn't have made up a mystery man—Jackson was right on that. And Getzel's story meshed with what little Jared Wyndham had told them. But Lockhart was a significant common factor between the two cases—between Norton's crimes and the more recent killing sprees. A suspect both times. The killings had stopped when he was locked up. He had the truck. But it still didn't feel *right.*

So what was missing? What was different? Norton had been more sadistic—more into torture. But their guy was improving on Norton; his killings were less prolonged but more efficient. His vehicle was more efficient. He'd never shown his face, so far as they knew—Norton had. Then there was the partner element: Norton had always had a fall guy.

He yanked Norton's case file closer. His hand vibrated harder. If their killer had followed Norton, had learned from his mistakes, he had to have a fall guy too...which they'd already considered. But was that really all Lockhart was? That would mean their suspect had stopped killing every time Lockhart got put away, which took a hell of a lot of self-control. And it would mean he'd been watching Lockhart for, what? Five years? So why hadn't anyone seen him? Why hadn't Lockhart? Was he really that good? *Fuck.*

A partner or a patsy?

Partner?

Patsy.

And that knife… Maybe they'd been looking at this all wrong.

Petrosky swallowed hard, his throat achy and hot, and opened the file to the section on Morrison's murder. The place where Norton's crimes and their killer's had converged. The place where Morrison had figured out what Norton was. Where one of these assholes—or both—had killed his boy.

The air was gone. He wheezed in a thin breath and read.

11/13 2:20pm: Block casing: Hanover, getting mail—assisted back into home. Notes no suspicious activity, notes nephew will be home tonight. To follow up.

Morrison had helped Hanover because he was a good guy. Hanover probably liked him, too, everyone did—*had*.

11/13 6:30pm: Alicia Hart not at residence. To follow up tomorrow.

11/13 7:45pm: Block casing: Caucasian male, approx. 65, walking Labrador, identified as Wendell Zurbach. Indicates suspicious activity at home on corner, party one year prior. Poss. trafficking/prostitution of underage females.

Petrosky had found Alicia Hart himself. And Zurbach, too, that nosy dickhead, grinning like he loved a good ball-freezing winter more than anything. *Zurbach. With an* H, he'd said. *It's German. Not that I've ever been out there, ha-ha.* He would be in his seventies now, but he was probably still running around with that Labrador. What was his name? Something short. A single syllable. Duke's face flashed in his brain, his heart spasmed, and he pushed all of it away.

11/13 8:50pm: E. Lockhart interviewed, allowed search of premises, nothing suspicious. To look into underage party: Lockhart denies wrongdoing, to follow up with others present in the a.m.

Then the *G. H.* In blood.

Gertrude. Hanover. The house where he'd found Margot

Nace chained to a pole—where he'd found Ava Fenderson's corpse. But still, something wasn't right. Sure, Morrison's first instinct would have been to save those girls, and they'd known by then that they were looking for Adam Norton—he wouldn't have used Norton's initials. But what if…

Petrosky straightened, his brain suddenly on fire. Pieces of memory slipped past,

—*Morrison's smiling face, holding his stainless steel coffee mug, the bookcase at Hanover's, the torture chamber beyond—*

some connecting,

—*Lockhart's flaring nostrils, glaring out the front door, pissed someone had turned him in—*

a tornado of shards of

—*the house where Morrison had died, that abandoned Crock-Pot, the dog, that little yippy shithead of a dog—*

broken glass.

The world vanished, then pulsed back into being. The pages flipped with a frantic *thip-thip-thip*, but he stopped when he found what he was looking for: the notes from one of the officers who'd canvassed those streets before Morrison. Before the night he'd died.

Prissy little writing, each house number listed along the left side of the page, but he didn't need to verify the address —he remembered it. Remembered thinking the notation was odd.

Resident reports no activity.

Wendell Zurbach. He'd claimed no activity when he'd talked to the flatfoots, but the man had told Petrosky plenty. Zurbach had reported calling about the neighbor's barking dog, bitched like the dickens about no one doing anything. And… Oh shit, Zurbach had been the one to throw suspicion on Lockhart then, too—told them about some party at the pedophile's house, made a big deal about how he didn't want that around his granddaughters. Classic good Samaritan. And when Petrosky had asked specifically about the night Morrison had been killed, Zurbach had told him he'd seen someone walking up the road toward Hanover's place—that the man headed for Gertrude's had *come from the house across the way*. From the abandoned house where he'd found Morrison's coffee mug. *Fucking hell.* He hadn't gone there for the dog; the suspicious man Zurbach had reported was what had sent him over there—that was the reason he'd found those bloody letters.

G. H.

Zurbach. With an H. *It's German.* German started with a *G.* Was it "German H"? *G.H.?* That seemed a little far-fetched— okay, more than a little. And why not use Zurbach's initials: *W.Z.?* Maybe Morrison had been trying to tell him about both leads; maybe in his final moments, he'd scrawled those two letters and hoped Petrosky would connect *all* the dots— Gertrude Hanover *and* German H. But of course, he hadn't. He'd stopped looking the moment Norton was dead.

G.

H.

His brain felt broken. He glanced at his hands—numb— and they seemed to belong to someone else entirely, some stranger who was wearing his skin. It didn't make sense. He wasn't making sense. He knew that for a fact, and yet…

G.

H.

No, Gertrude Hanover—that was right. He had found the girls there; he had found Norton there.

But that didn't mean Zurbach was innocent. And something was wrong with that guy—no one liked the cold that goddamn much, no one smiled while shoveling the walk. Unless they had no fucking feelings at all. McCallum would say he was projecting because happiness was such a foreign concept to him, but…

Fuck it. "Hey, Jackson, I got something." He slapped the folder closed as she approached from her desk. "Let's look at trucks again." Lockhart's truck, Ruby's hair…it was all too simple, and their guy was anything but simple. When Jackson's brow furrowed, he amended: "I just want to look up one guy." He was leaving them a trail of breadcrumbs. Maybe the truck was one.

"What's the name?" she asked.

"Wendell Zurbach. With an *H*."

She was still looking at him.

"It's German." He barely recognized his own voice.

32

ZURBACH DID HAVE a blue truck registered under his name: purchased five years ago, the same make and model as Lockhart's. They had checked for blue trucks in the area before—Decantor had been especially thorough, pulling all Michigan registrations from anywhere within two hours of the crimes. But Zurbach's truck was registered to an address more than seventy miles away in Maumee, Ohio. No way for them to track that unless they'd looked Zurbach up specifically.

Jackson sniffed, her fingers attacking the steering wheel with a hard rhythmic patter—Irish step dancing for the hands. "He's not anywhere close to the new crimes…to any of the crimes. He'd have to drive a long way to stalk people."

Difficult, but not impossible. And unlike Lockhart, Zurbach felt right to Petrosky deep in his marrow. His build matched what Candace had seen, albeit a little older than they'd anticipated, but ageism was bullshit too—anyone could be a homicidal maniac. And Zurbach had been in good shape during the Norton case, out walking with his dog, out shoveling his walk, grinning the whole time. And when Morrison was killed, Zurbach had been there. *He was fucking there.* Living right across the street from the home where Morrison was murdered.

According to his driver's license, Zurbach still lived in that home, but they knew that wasn't true—they'd interviewed the new owners when they'd canvassed. And he had no hope that they'd find something at that house; not one of the clues had led there. They'd all led back to Lockhart. Zurbach had even gone so far as to buy the same vehicle—no way that was a coincidence. Hopefully, Zurbach didn't know they were onto him; hopefully, they'd surprise him by showing up unannounced. They could always ask the locals for backup later, but if he wasn't here, if this was another rouse, they didn't want a statewide manhunt to alert him. Petrosky knew he could keep his mouth shut, but he didn't trust the rest of these fuckers.

Jackson eased to a stop at the curb—rolling lawns and white bricks, each enormous house a copy of the one next door. "Are you sure you want to come in on this one? You look like someone slammed you in the face with a sledgehammer."

She still hadn't asked what happened. Maybe she already knew. "Yeah, I want in. I'm good." A few scrapes, a black eye —it wasn't that bad, was it? He glanced at his reflection in the tinted windows as they got out: he looked like a prizefighter who'd lost the battle of his life and then immediately face-planted into a beehive. Weird that it barely hurt. At the moment, he could feel nothing but the zing of electricity in his blood. Justice—it was better than ibuprofen.

Unlike Zurbach's more modest home in Ash Park, the grand colonial before them was fronted with white columns that reached the second-story eaves, the verdant lawn freshly mowed, the lines like vacuum tracks. Some lake or another shone between the houses across the way, a rippling sea of blue that stretched to the horizon. Their steps echoed over the planks of the front porch, a wide wraparound like an old plantation home, but this place was far too new to have seen the atrocities of slavery.

The woman who answered the door smiled at Jackson—straight teeth, full lips, clear skin dotted lightly with age spots, probably from jogging sans sunscreen based on her calves. Her brown eyes widened when she saw Petrosky's face. *Maybe it's worse than I thought.* Not that it was relevant.

They flashed their badges. "We're looking for Wendell Zurbach."

"And you came here? That's a laugh." She chuckled as if to accentuate the point.

"His truck is registered to this address," Jackson said.

The woman frowned, deepening the lines around her eyes. Slightly older than he'd first thought. Fifty, maybe.

"You obviously know him even if he isn't home," Jackson went on. "What's your relationship to him?"

The woman shook her head. "I'm Honor, Honor Holt." She leveled her gaze at Petrosky, no longer flinching away from his battered head. "I'm Wendell's daughter. You should come in."

That was easy—too easy.

She led them through a foyer replete with modern furnishings: a circular mirror, a plastic-looking table shaped like a cube and topped with a square vase filled with lilies. The living room was more of the same. Three-dimensional shapes devoid of color and topped with padding as if that would ever be as comfortable as a squishy Lay-Z-Boy. They sat kitty-corner from one another on an L-shaped sofa that was just as hard as it appeared.

"So, what did he do?" Honor asked.

Petrosky's eyes grazed the fireplace behind her—glass block, no brick or stone. A family print hung to the side of the impersonal hearth, Honor with a taller Ken-doll looking man, one of those CrossFit types, and two teenage girls—the perfect, happy little family.

"He's a person of interest in a homicide investigation," Jackson said.

This seemed to surprise her—Honor's jaw dropped, her breath catching in her throat. "I...wow."

Jackson leaned in, her hand on the hard seat near her hip, maybe trying to take the pressure off her backbone. "Don't think he's capable?"

"Oh, he's definitely capable," she said, far too calm now, far too unruffled after her initial reaction. "I just didn't think he'd ever get caught."

It was their turn to tense; Jackson went stock-still beside him. "Has he hurt someone else?"

"Besides killing my mother? I don't think so." *Wait...what?* Zurbach had killed his wife, and he was still walking the street? She must mean metaphorically—"he killed her spirit" would make sense; psychopaths were often abusive. But you couldn't arrest someone for crushing a soul, or there'd be more people in prison than not.

Honor crossed her legs, then recrossed them—anxious. "I guess he didn't technically kill her—he wasn't even home when she took those pills—I just..."

"You blame him," Petrosky said.

"Yeah, I do." Her nostrils flared. Her fists clenched.

"Looks like you're still pretty angry," he said, but he was stalling—Zurbach had told him his wife was dead, hadn't he? So, she'd died at least five years ago. Maybe he'd lost his wife, his kids had all moved out, and he figured he'd finally follow his murderous heart. But why start going after the people Petrosky loved? Was this really about one-upping Norton? *Why me?* Fire ignited in Petrosky's belly, then sizzled out —*Focus, asshole.*

Honor released her fists and massaged one in the other. "Of course I'm still mad—I've refused to see him since she died, didn't even invite him to my youngest daughter's graduation." She dropped her hands. "My mother knew who he was. I just wish I'd been able to put it into words sooner."

"And who is he?" Jackson asked.

"A monster." She whispered it, but the word stabbed him in the chest. That's what he had always called Norton, how he'd seen him—*a monster.*

Jackson leveled her gaze at the woman. "What makes you say that? Anything you can tell us about him might help."

Honor frowned, her eyebrows meeting in the middle—a thin caterpillar with a waxer on speed dial. "It wasn't anything he did, that's the problem. He did everything right. He went to our band concerts, came home every night at six o'clock for family dinners, took us to church on Sundays." Her eyes clouded. "It was what was missing."

"Feeling?" Psychos had that weird lack of emotion that often pinged little bells of alarm in normal humans.

"Well… No, not even that. He told us he loved us. And I had friends with abusive parents—even the thought of him hitting us was ridiculous." She shook her head. "He just…he was a jerk, but not in an obvious way. Backhanded little comments, you know? And then there was his job. After he retired, they called me, asked about some money. I couldn't help them, and nothing ever came of it that I know about, but I got the impression that they thought he'd stolen from them." She sniffed, her shoulders square. "He always acted like he was this perfect guy…but I guess he wasn't perfect, after all."

"When was the last time you spoke to him?" Jackson asked.

"Last year," Honor said. "He called and asked if my daughter could stay with him, go to college up near Detroit— called *her*, not me. I told him to go to hell. She's still mad at me for refusing, for making her pay for her own apartment. She can't understand why I would avoid him."

Not many would. The man sounded like a master manipulator, so good even Honor's own family didn't put stock in her concerns. Petrosky had missed it too. But...Detroit? "Does he still live up there?" If she had an address—

"Yeah, he has a place in Ash Park. Pike Street."

"He sold that house years ago." Petrosky watched her eyes widen.

"That's not possible. I sent Christmas cards every year until this past winter."

Huh. Without a house, what would he have done if she'd agreed to let her daughter stay with him? Had he been trying to set Honor up to fight with her child? Talk about backhanded.

Jackson narrowed her eyes. "You still sent him Christmas cards, even though you thought he was responsible for your mother's death?"

She sighed. "You don't know what it's like. Everyone thinks I'm crazy for having these thoughts—these feelings. Well, except my husband, he's never liked my dad. But I can't point to a single thing that my father ever did wrong—really, patently wrong. Being around him just never felt...*right.*"

Wrongness. It was a feeling in the guts, not the product of logical reasoning, and he was willing to trust the gut of a woman who'd lived with Zurbach for eighteen years. But how could they use that to find him? Petrosky met Honor's eyes. Zurbach had managed to hide who he was from all of them except her, and he'd led them here—he'd put her address on the truck. There had to be a reason. She was the next clue.

She was the next...

He straightened. "Where's your younger daughter now?" Jackson glanced at him, her gaze worried. The girl was the last thing they'd fought about, the thing that had finally cemented their estrangement—*I told him to go to hell.* Zurbach wouldn't have reacted well to that. Was the girl the one he'd punish? Was that why he had used this address?

Was he shifting victims again, from Petrosky's family to his own?

Honor frowned. "Crystal? She's…she's at school, taking summer classes."

"Can you be more specific than that?" he snapped. If he was right, they didn't have time to screw around.

"Oh god." She reached for one of the cube tables that sat on either end of the horribly uncomfortable sofa and snatched up her cell. She put it to her ear, her face stricken, but her features relaxed within moments. "Crissy? Thank god. Where are you?"

She listened, one hand on her heart. Protecting that little spot. Making sure it didn't open wide and swallow up her soul. He rubbed at the corresponding spot on his own chest while she finished the call.

Honor hit *End* and lowered the cell. "She's at her apartment, said she and her roommate will lock the door and stay there—she won't let anyone in, including my father. I'll go pick her up, in case." She stood.

But he stayed seated, a nagging sensation tugging at his guts. No, this wasn't right. The younger daughter…she was the one who had the disagreement with her mother. The obvious one. The one Zurbach would expect them to chase—to waste time on.

His eyes drifted again to the image beside the mantel. Honor and her husband. Their daughters—two daughters.

"Where's your other kid?"

"Upstairs. She's home for the summer." She headed past the couch and through a wide arch at the back of the living room where a polished white staircase snaked into the ceiling. "Clementine!"

Footsteps, ballerina light. Then a voice: "I'm talking to Tony!"

He looked at the photo again, at the man—Honor's husband. Tall. Muscular. A little older than most of the dead men, but…he fit the profile. Their killer's ideal victim. And he'd never liked Honor's daddy.

Honor was staring at the photo too. She met his gaze.

"Where's your husband, ma'am?"

Her hands shook as she raised the phone and dialed.

33

No answer. Five times in a row. Jethro Holt, Honor's husband, had left for lunch and never returned—an accountant just like Zurbach. He could almost see Jethro's face reflected in the passenger window, smiling, standing with his children as he had in the picture by the mantel. That could have been Morrison. Should have been Morrison.

This man didn't deserve to die any more than his own boy had.

Jackson eased her foot off the gas as she tossed her cell back into the cupholder. "They found the truck in west Detroit an hour ago."

Fuck. Zurbach had another mode of transportation. "We got an APB on Jethro's ride?"

She nodded. "Yeah. Nothing on that yet. Zurbach nabbed him in Ohio, so they could be heading farther south—"

"No, Zurbach's taking him back to Ash Park." And he had a head start; they were still half an hour out.

Jackson frowned at the windshield, her fingertips drumming at a frantic pace, more a vibration than a rhythm against the wheel. "How are you so certain? I mean, it makes sense because of the connection to Norton, to you, but this is yet another deviation from the pattern. If he's trying to keep us on our toes…" She shrugged. The engine whined.

"We don't have jurisdiction in Ohio anyway, or in any state beyond, but Zurbach's face is out there now. They're looking for him, and for Jethro's car in their zones, we can look in ours." His words had come out harsher than necessary, but the ache in his chest was growing, throbbing—the hole Julie had left. The hole Morrison had bored wider. And Billie, her shirt, covered in gore, her crimson lips, the gaping slash across her throat. He could see Ruby's chipped tooth, her bloody, beaten face. He could smell Duke's fur, musty like the dirt of the backyard—

"Petrosky?"

He looked over. "Huh?"

"Did you hear me?"

"Sorry." He glanced down at the cell clutched in his hand. Ah, yes, she was waiting for an update too—she'd been calling in APBs and talking to the local cops. He'd been researching Zurbach. "I talked to the firm where Zurbach worked. Sounds like he tried to access their accounts after he retired, which piqued their interest, but they think he'd been skimming off the top for years. They started asking questions, and he responded by selling his house and vanishing. Cleaned out his bank accounts at the same time."

"And they called Honor when they lost him?" Her voice was hollow against the monotonous buzz of the tires.

He shook his head. "Nope. They called Honor because they thought he might be using her or her husband's accounts to hide the money. But they never had enough to file charges, just suspicion." Like Honor herself; suspicion of *wrongness*. "Jethro understood the scam—helped the company parse out a theory, though they had no real evidence." Even Petrosky hadn't fully understood the scam when Zurbach's boss had explained it. "But it sounds like Zurbach knew Jethro was helping them. And all this happened right before Morrison's death. I think Morrison was a stand-in for the guy he really wanted to kill." Jethro was his endgame: the man who'd taken his daughter and conspired against him. He'd been killing him by proxy for years. Over and over and over.

"And Morrison looked so much like Jethro; he was in Zurbach's crosshairs at exactly the wrong time."

His throat was tight, threatening to clamp shut. The silence stretched. The tires hummed. He coughed to open it once more and forced out: "I also think he decided to strike then because he *could* blame it on Norton. Zurbach was nosy as hell—he knew who had parties, who was out walking at night, what bullshit Lockhart was into, who had dogs to leave behind. I think he knew about Norton, not only about the case but who he was—who he *really* was." *And where he was.* Zurbach had watched Norton as carefully as he'd watched his victims in the years that followed. He'd inserted himself into the investigation. He'd even followed Petrosky into that house across the street, that stray dog yapping at him the whole time.

Jackson's fingers tap-tap-tapped on the steering wheel. "Makes sense. He figured he could pin it on Norton, and no one would be the wiser. Unfortunately, he realized he liked it. Figured he'd play a game, have some fun before it was all over."

And I missed it. I was fucked up, and I missed it. "Yeah." His voice cracked. If she heard, she had the decency not to say.

He drew his eyes back to the window, highway signs flying past in stripes of green and white. This man had been fucking with them from day one. Maybe he was just bored when he'd gone after Petrosky—maybe he'd wanted an audience. But one thing was certain: his appetite would no longer be sated by anyone except his ideal victim—the man he'd wanted to kill from day one.

And he was nothing if not efficient.

34

WHERE THE FUCK IS HE?

They'd sent patrols to every house Zurbach had a connection to—the new homeowners at his place on Pike were surprised to see Sloan, but they didn't have anything to hide. Lockhart's house was still empty. Even Gertrude Hanover's was vacant; Richard had brought her to his home out of state. Ruby's cute little bungalow: empty. The house where they'd found Billie—nothing.

Nothing. Nothing. Nothing.

Jackson slammed down her desk phone. "Holt's cell was tossed in the dumpster behind his job; they found his car about a block away, behind a Chinese restaurant. Wife said he goes there for lunch a lot. And we've got an incoming call to Holt from a burner about ten minutes before he left the office."

The asshole had lured him out. And abducted him. "Zurbach has a place somewhere, dammit—somewhere close enough to watch his victims. It's been years since he sold his house, and it isn't like he's squatting, not a guy like that." No, this was going to be a situation like the blue pickup truck. An assumed identity, or paying cash, or otherwise disguising who he was—they weren't going to find him through normal routes. He glowered at the bullpen window. Still afternoon, but waning—gray and dusky. Much too soon, it would ease into night, the last night of Jethro's life. Had Morrison watched the afternoon wane his last day? Had he felt time winding down?

Petrosky dragged his gaze from the heavy sky, his insides heavier still. Why lead them all this way just to hide now? *Zurbach told me how to find him. He had to. He's ready to end this, or he wouldn't have involved me, wouldn't have given us the knife.* So what clue was he missing?

Bzzzz!

He jumped—the phone. *Maybe it's Zurbach calling to say he stole someone else you love. Or that he killed the only guy you might have a chance of saving.* Honor's stricken face bubbled to the surface of his brain, her cheeks streaked with tears. He'd let the Ohio PD deliver that death notification. But it was not an unknown number on the caller ID—Shannon.

"Hey, I brought you dinner. Want to run down and let me in?"

He re-pocketed the cell and hustled for the stairs, but just hearing her voice had made that hole in his chest tear open again—his abdomen was a ball of white-hot pain from his collarbone to his bellybutton. His bones vibrated. *Dammit, I was fine! I was holding it together!* He needed a drink. He needed a fucking drink. The air in the stairwell felt thinner than usual; it burned in the back of his throat as if it were laced with some caustic gas.

At the base of the steps, he paused with his hand on the door, finally realizing what she'd said. Wait…dinner? He'd treated her like dirt, gotten her husband killed, put her in danger again and again, and she'd brought him food?

He grabbed the handle and pulled, then stepped back when she pushed two bags his way.

"Thai," she announced. "I got those peanut noodles you like."

He stared, momentarily dumbfounded. *What is happening here? She should be at home; she should be with the kids.* But he obediently took the plastic sacks and headed up the steps on autopilot, his tongue numb and heavy, his ribs on fire.

"The kids are with your neighbors and two uniformed police officers, just so you know. But I needed to be here. With you."

With him? No, he was the problem. She was supposed to be in Atlanta, working a fulfilling job, watching her kids grow up while he shouldered the burden of all the people who'd died because of him. She should be moving on while he walked the streets where Morrison had taken his last breaths. Where he'd bled his life into the earth.

He couldn't breathe. His heart was a panicked animal in a cage of gnashing teeth. "Why are you doing this?"

She glanced over, one eyebrow raised. "Doing—"

"I'm sorry."

She sniffed, and it cracked against the stairwell like a gunshot—was that just his ears? Why was everything suddenly so loud? She kept walking. One step. Another. "You should be sorry. But if you feel bad, that should help you do better."

"My better isn't good enough." His legs were too heavy. "It'll never be...good enough." The words panted from his lips, and his chest... He couldn't take another step. The air was far too thin, and the world was already hazy at the corners of his vision. He lowered the bags to the stairs and collapsed beside them.

Shannon leaned over him, her brow furrowed. "Are you okay? Is it your heart? I'll get help." She tried to step past him, and he grabbed her arm.

"Wait. No, it's not my heart." Not a heart attack—was it? But his heart was fucking broken, and he couldn't watch her walk away from him, not in this moment, not now. "It's just me. I'm not who you need me to be. I can't… I can't be…" He hissed a breath through clenched teeth. "When you're here, I can't fucking breathe!" The words exploded out of him—his throat burned.

"Because I remind you. Of him." She put her hands on his face, much the way Carroll had, but Shannon's grip was firm —sure. "You remind me of him too. But you're my family. Don't you understand that? My brother was all I had besides Morrison, and when he died…" She released him and lowered herself to sit beside him on the steps. "You and I are in this together whether you want us to be or not. I can't lose you too. And I don't give a shit whether you want to be needed—I'll never give up on you. So you can either step the fuck up, or you can disappoint me forever and feel worse every goddamn day. But I'm going to keep kicking your ass; I'm not that forgiving."

He laughed, but it didn't sound right even to him, and then there were tears dripping onto his hands, and he was shaking, choking—there was no air, but he somehow managed: "I'm sorry, Taylor."

Her maiden name. He used to call her that back when it was just them, when he'd smiled a little more; he had felt more than pain once, hadn't he? But the pain was familiar— the pain he deserved. "I killed them," he said. "I killed all of them."

"What?" She reared back, eyebrows at her hairline. "No, this wasn't your—"

"I'm sorry. I'm so…fucking…*sorry*."

The hole in his chest expanded, eating his lungs, twisting his intestines, the stairwell red at the edges, and then she was pulling him to her, his head on her shoulder, his bruised cheek tender and raw. His shoulder was wet, too—was she crying?

"No one blames you but you," she said into his hair. "And

Duke... I was the one watching him; that was all me. You weren't even there."

The heat—god, it hurt. Everything hurt. But he could suddenly *breathe*. He inhaled deeply, letting the cool rush of air soothe his flaming insides; her hair smelled like his shampoo.

"No one blames you, Petrosky."

His heart slowed.

"No one blames you," she said again.

He finally pulled his swollen face from her neck. Her eyes were glassy—her face wet. He cleared his throat.

"Sorry about that, Taylor. I'm just emotional. Withdrawal, you know?"

She pushed herself to standing, wiping at her cheeks, and picked up the take-out bags. "Better this than the alternative."

He disagreed wholeheartedly with that, but he said nothing, just wiped his sleeve across his face, wincing when he hit his bruised nose. His knees creaked as he started up the stairs once more, Shannon at his heels. The air felt better, at least. More substantial—oxygenated.

"You want to wait a minute?" she said to his back. "I have tissues if you want to clean your face."

"You think watery eyes are worse than Decantor's pansy-ass Kardashian obsession? He's like a fucking schoolgirl." He coughed, trying to clear the snot from his throat. "And for the record, you weren't responsible for Duke. You couldn't have kept him inside all day, and no one expected this asshole to...do what he did."

"I know. It's his fault—only his. And I think Duke would want us to find him and take a bite out of his ass."

"I'll leave that one to you, Taylor." Weird how that name rolled so easily off his tongue.

She laughed—it even sounded genuine. "With pleasure."

He listened to the thunk of his shoe on the last stair. Poor sweet Duke. No one had seen that coming. Zurbach had never touched an animal that they knew of, and Norton hadn't either. It was so far outside the MO...

"Petrosky?" Shannon's voice came at a distance.

Oh fuck. Duke. Even the dog had been a sign. Not just another way to hurt Petrosky—a clue. "I'll find him for you, boy."

"What?"

"Nothing." He plowed through the door to the bullpen, leaving a bewildered Shannon in his wake.

35

JACKSON LOOKED up with wide eyes as he barged into the bullpen. She stood so quickly the chair fell over backward. "What happened? Are you—"

"He had a dog."

Jackson stopped in her tracks. "Did she beat you up again?"

"No, I..." He cocked his head. She did know that Shannon had kicked his ass. But he didn't give a shit how she knew—his brain was burning as much as his chest, and that somehow made him feel more balanced, though in the way of someone walking over a not-quite-frozen pond.

He slid into his chair while Shannon set the food on Jackson's desk. He heard a chorus of "thank yous" from somewhere over in that general vicinity, but he was already pulling his keyboard closer and booting up the computer. Zurbach had a Labrador retriever named...Mac. He'd met him the first time they'd spoken. Even homicidal maniacs loved their dogs.

Jackson slipped into the seat beside him, a plastic fork in one hand, a take-out container in the other. "What are we looking for?"

"Labrador named Mac. It's been a few years, but the thing looked healthy—if he's keeping up on shots, maybe he has a vet somewhere nearby." But when he said it out loud, it sounded crazy. Was he crazy? Definitely a little, but—

"How the hell do you remember that?" Jackson asked around a mouthful of noodles.

"I remember more than I want to," he said. *Drunk or not.* He racked his brain, trying to visualize the dog, trying to recall if it had been wearing rabies tags. For the life of him, he couldn't. But this guy had done it all by the book until the very end. His boss had admitted to liking him before the theft, and even his daughter had not a single identifiable complaint about her childhood outside of a gut feeling. And he wouldn't have complained to the police about the neighbor's little dog if his own wasn't licensed.

Decantor wandered by with his own container of noodles to peer over Petrosky's shoulder, and for once, Petrosky didn't mind. He typed but quickly realized the databases wouldn't help. He didn't have the number for the rabies tag, so he couldn't look the animal up that way. All he had was the dog's name, which wasn't listed anywhere...and the owner's name. The only thing they could do was call the vets directly.

He, Jackson, Decantor, and Shannon split the list—three each. Twelve vets in the immediate area, any of which Zurbach might have gone to; hopefully, they'd be able to catch the docs at the office. It was only four o'clock, but it felt much later.

Jackson got a hit right away. Mac had been licensed and had a rabies registration linked to Zurbach. The address was the place on Pike; no forwarding address. And Mac had died soon after Zurbach sold his house. Petrosky zoned out as Jackson hung up the phone, the ache in his chest blossoming then easing—it felt like he had water in his ears.

Goddammit it to hell. All that just to hit a wall now? He

frowned at his desktop. What was he missing? Was there even anything to miss? Duke didn't have to be a clue—maybe he was just a victim.

He closed his eyes and thought back to the day he'd spoken to Zurbach in his driveway. Mac had been all too happy at Zurbach's heel, wagging his giant tail against the snow. Quiet. And then there had been...Gigi. The little yappy-bitey something-or-another that Zurbach had called the police about; he'd said the neighbors had abandoned it when they left. Zurbach had complained to Petrosky about her, too, and... He'd used her as an excuse to follow Petrosky into the house across the street. But Zurbach had no problem picking her up, even if the little bitch had bitten him for his trouble. His eyes snapped open. Maybe she'd never belonged to the neighbors at all.

He swiveled back to Jackson. "Were there other animals registered to Zurbach with that vet?"

"Not with Dr. Wilson—I asked her to email everything she had, but it doesn't sound like there's much. Why?"

"Let's try..." He wasn't sure what kind of dog Gigi was, so it would mean asking vets about the name only. "Gigi." How many assholes out there would name their dog after a letter of the alphabet? Maybe an English teacher. Or some lame writer.

Hopefully, a killer.

They went back to their lists of veterinarians. Shannon got a hit this time, but it only took a moment to rule that one out; Gigi was most definitely not a poodle.

He pressed the phone to his ear so hard his head ached. One vet. Two. Three.

"Got him!" Decantor slapped the page onto Petrosky's desk—not even a page. A sticky note.

They all leaned in and squinted at the paper. Zurbach's name, his real name, was on it—ballsy as fuck. And this listing did not contain Honor's address where the truck was registered or the address that was in Mac's file. Petrosky stared at it, his spine a rigid piece of steel and just as cold.

"Kitesus?" Jackson frowned. "There aren't any houses over there that I know of. There's no apartment number?" Shannon straightened, her hand on the back of his chair. Decantor shook his head.

But Petrosky knew the building. He knew why Zurbach had chosen it too. "He's there for the alley." He met Jackson's eyes. "What do you want to bet his window looks directly over the alley where I found Morrison?" And that was as close to an admission of guilt as he'd ever need.

Zurbach had watched; he'd watched him find Morrison's body. Watched Petrosky put his gun to his own head. Watched Decantor drag him away.

And he'd decided this shit was too much fun.

Shannon moved her hand to his shoulder, her eyes hard. Determined. Furious.

He nodded her way—*I'll get him.* But he didn't have to say it; she already knew.

36

GIGI. And Zurbach with his German *H*. Gertrude Hanover. *G. H. G. H. G. H.* Maybe Morrison had been trying to point him at Zurbach all along, but he'd never know, not for sure. That was the problem with obscure bloody letters—they could stand for so many things.

Decantor, Sloan, he knew the other cars were out there, surrounding the building, covering every entrance, but all he saw was the blackness outside the windshield. They'd taken Shannon's car, thinking Zurbach might be on the lookout for Petrosky's Caprice, or for Jackson's SUV—that he might not recognize Shannon's ride. But that was probably nonsense. This guy had watched them all. And no matter what they drove, he'd be ready for them.

The building loomed out of the darkness like an abandoned hotel in the middle of some unreal dystopian landscape. The streetlights on the road out front were dark, but the ones near the back alley appeared intact, and in the sodium glow, the cobbles glistened like the tips of undulating waves on a stormy sea. The black puddles were not actually moving, he was sure they weren't, but...his eyes. It had to be his eyes.

Jackson parked out front in the shadow of the building and pulled out her weapon.

The main door was paneled over, the front windows covered in boards, each secured by corroded nails—rusted right into the wood. No one had gone in that way.

They edged up the crumbling sidewalk, the light of the moon turning the brick and mortar walls into a sea of amorphous gray shapes that faded to black as they crept skyward. All the windows were the same: boarded, blocked, and ultimately settled. He stopped and pulled on the corner of the board nearest him—the nail snapped. No one had touched these either, not recently.

Were they wrong? Had the guy used this address and then taken Jethro to another building, one they weren't aware of? It was certainly possible. He lowered his weapon. Jackson was still slinking forward, headed for the corner, but he backed off the walk, off the curb, and let his eyes drift. Above the second floor, the windows were gaping holes—no boards. No lights. Zurbach wasn't here; he was better than Norton, right? He wasn't going to stoop to hiding out in some abandoned building, skulking around in the dark.

"Jackson, wait," he hissed. She turned and headed for him, but he was already marching back the way they'd come, weapon at his side. Past the front doors. Past another wall of boarded windows. He paused at the mouth of the alley. He could see the dumpster near the middle, but no one in the building they'd just looked at had use for it—the address Zurbach had entered on his veterinarian forms was utterly abandoned. But that was not the only building with a clear view of the alley.

He took one step, then another, deeper into the alley, his breath tight—stuck in his throat. He paused. The dumpster. From this side, he could see the spot where Morrison's car had been, the spot where he'd found his boy, where he'd touched his face for the last time. His cold, bloody face. His gaping throat. But he had to go on, had to keep moving, or someone else was going to die just as terribly.

Thunk, thunk, thunk, went his shoes.

Something skittered in the shadows, and again, Petrosky stopped. *I've done this before. I've been here before—exactly here.* He turned his back to the abandoned building, facing the bricks on the other side. And drew his eyes up. Second story. Third.

His heart shuddered to a stop.

White hair, stocky frame, silhouetted by the light in the room behind him. He was thinner than Petrosky remembered, but he'd been wearing a coat before—the ultimate waistline disguise. A long blade glittered in his right hand.

But that wasn't what made Petrosky's muscles seize.

At Zurbach's side, Morrison stumbled forward and pressed his face against the window. He opened his mouth. He looked like he was screaming.

37

MORRISON—HE'S *got Morrison.*

But that was ridiculous. *Morrison's dead, he's dead, he's dead.*

His sense of déjà vu increased as they hit the stairs, the security officer at the front desk shouting after them, and even that man's voice sounded familiar—a hollow memory without color or substance, but familiar all the same. He vaguely heard Jackson calling orders to Decantor, or maybe to the desk jockey; he wasn't sure. His elbow caught a gold sconce and sent it tumbling to the carpet—it shattered, but dully like it didn't have the energy to scream.

To scream. Like Morrison. *He has Morrison.*

He doesn't. He doesn't.

But he didn't believe that. He'd *seen him.* The world was unfamiliar and strange, but it wasn't his surroundings that were wrong. It was the time.

Before. He'd done this before, looked for his boy, his chest electric with panic. *But this time, I can save him.*

He climbed faster over stairs with short fibers and fussy patterns. A historic building, lots of them out there, but he'd never understand the drive to put money into something so close to ruin. There were probably plans to revamp the building next door, too, but right now, Zurbach surely appreciated the privacy; the only thing looking in his windows were dark holes and crumbling bricks, the occasional rusted nail.

Petrosky's thigh muscles ached. His breath hissed, wheezing from too-small lungs. God, he hated stairs. But if Zurbach could do it, so could he.

I'm coming for you, fuckface. Even that thought felt like a dream, something he had said earlier, at some other point in the past. But maybe it didn't matter if he'd done it before, so long as he did it right this time.

Jackson yanked at the third story door and sent it crashing into the wall. Green carpet here, and shimmery wallpaper like a hotel in a horror movie where there were monsters hiding around every corner.

But behind which door?

Jackson seemed to know. He followed her around the first corner toward another hallway, this one presumably holding the units that faced the alley. Halfway up the hall, an insistent tugging like a barbed fish hook took root near his heart—*stitches, that's the stitches from your heart attack, don't you remember? You just got out of the hospital.* Sweat trickled down his back. Jackson shoved past an elderly woman with a miniature fluffy something, like a yappy teddy bear, and he suddenly hated the dog, hated the woman, hated this entire fucking building because they were keeping Morrison, they were responsible for killing his partner, where the fuck was his boy?

Jackson slowed, then stopped, her back against the wall across from a closed door. She nodded to him to cover the other side. Should they announce their presence? Zurbach knew, the asshole already knew, they were here. And Morrison…he was still alive, wasn't he? Were they already too late? Had Zurbach slit his throat while they were huffing up the steps?

Yap! Yap-yap-yapyapyap! No, they didn't need to announce themselves. That little bitch would do it for them.

The door splintered far too easily beneath his shoulder; he didn't even feel it.

"Police!" Jackson yelled behind him. "Show me your hands!"

Petrosky skidded to a stop.

Zurbach smiled. Brilliant white hair, round face, skin sagging pleasantly, the ultimate grandfather had his feet not been nestled on a sheet of Visqueen, a blond man kneeling in front of him, hands bound at his back, his blue button-down soaked with blood. *Shit.* Deep lacerations ran the length of each of the man's upper arms; his chest was sliced up too. Defensive wounds, not the kill shot, but he'd die from them soon if they didn't get him help. Zurbach pressed the blade harder into Morrison's throat, a trickle of blood oozing around the metal to collect at his collarbone. And behind Morrison's foot… Was there a rat in here? But then he heard it again, the incessant yapping of the dog. The man kneeling on the floor did not appear to hear the animal—he stared at Petrosky, his blue eyes pleading. *Help me.*

Petrosky frowned, the gun slick against his palms. Jethro? No, Morrison.

Jethro.

Morrison.

His eyes weren't working right; his heart wasn't either, pain radiating sharp and hot through his abdomen. The room pulsed, and suddenly they weren't there, they were in the basement across the street from Zurbach's place on Pike, the air thick with wet cement and the stink of iron—his mouth tasted like he was sucking on a penny.

He's going to kill him, he's going to kill my boy.

Jackson stepped closer. "Let him go, Zurbach. There's no other way out of this."

"Oh, there's always a way out." Zurbach's gaze dropped to

the man at his feet, then landed on Petrosky. *Jethro—it's Jethro.* "You just have to use your imagination. People who have a pattern…it gets predictable."

Smug fucker. "You have a pattern," Petrosky said.

"Perhaps, for a time. But it's good to be flexible." He shrugged, and the blade dug into the man's throat—so much blood. "Your partner was an experiment to see if I had it in me to get rid of my son-in-law, but I knew that night I'd do it again and again until I got tired—I wouldn't get caught like that Norton fellow. But then, with his last breath, he begged for *your* life. Can you *imagine?*" Zurbach met Petrosky's eyes, his gaze bright and hot and sharp with vicious fury. "You, reeking of liquor when you came to interview me, and he wanted *you* to live? You don't deserve that kind of loyalty." The man at his feet whimpered, cringing, and Zurbach tightened the sharp edge against his Adam's apple.

He hates you like Morrison should have. Like Billie should. Duke. But it was more than hatred—this guy thought he deserved better. Zurbach's son-in-law and his daughter had both screwed him over; Petrosky was a fuckup, and he still had people who cared about him. And when Zurbach was done killing his son-in-law by proxy, he had punished Petrosky's loved ones as he wanted to punish his own family. Billie, Ruby, they were nothing but collateral damage, a part of his game, reminders of the case Petrosky had been too drunk to solve in time…and Petrosky's punishment for having it better than he deserved.

Petrosky's blood boiled, vibrating in his veins, but the sensation was muted, distant. *He's trying to get to you. He's counting on you to screw this up like you did with Morrison—with all of them.* Petrosky kept his eyes locked on Zurbach, and he was suddenly filled with certainty that so long as he held Zurbach's gaze, the man could not press the dagger any deeper. Zurbach smiled, but it didn't appear icy or hard or even unfeeling; he looked like he'd just told the best dad joke of all time and was grinning while everyone else groaned.

"Drop it, Zurbach." Jackson's voice was shockingly quiet. Or perhaps he couldn't hear her over the whoosh of blood in his head. "You don't want to do this. Think of your daughter —your granddaughters."

Petrosky stared at Zurbach's face, the rest of the room fading to gray, the whites of Jethro's—*Morrison's*—eyes, the black of his blood, none of it so vibrant as the shocking white of Zurbach's hair, the pink of his flesh standing out in stark contrast to the bleak surroundings. It was like staring at an altered photograph where only one central piece had been washed in color. Zurbach's eyes glittered—wild. He shifted his feet, the plastic hissing. And the man on the floor…

This was how he did it. This was exactly what he'd done in that basement.

This is how he killed your son, and you're going to watch him do it again.

Color rushed back into the room. Morrison blinked his big blue eyes, his blond hair glistening in the light. Petrosky aimed his weapon. It did not shake.

Zurbach glanced at the gun and grinned again. "You wouldn't dare, Detective. Just off the sauce, still a little shaky, and if you shoot now, you might hit—"

The first bullet grazed the man's cheek, and when he staggered back, Petrosky shot again, hit again, and the blade clattered to the floor behind Zurbach's heel. Zurbach grimaced, snarled, howled, and for once, the grandfatherly bastard looked like the monster he was. Zurbach fell to his knees and pulled his hand to his chest, two fingers shy of a high five.

Yap-yap-yapyapyap!

The little shithead was barking at them.

Jethro slumped forward, his hands still tied behind his

back, and landed hard on his shoulder. Jackson rushed his way, and then Decantor—he hadn't heard anyone come in, but now Sloan was there, too, surrounding Zurbach, handcuffs clanking into place. But quietly. Too quiet.

"Petrosky." He startled at Jackson's voice, his ears suddenly working again—she was kneeling on the floor beside Jethro. She nodded to his hands.

He still had the weapon pointed at Zurbach's face. He lowered it as Decantor dragged the bastard to his feet.

"Kill me! Why didn't you just kill me?" Zurbach roared.

Petrosky leveled his gaze at the fucker who'd murdered his partner, a partner who might as well have been his son. "It's good to be flexible."

He wasn't going to let Zurbach off that easily. To live was to be in pain. And they both deserved it.

Gigi had stopped barking. He squinted. The dog wagged her tail at him, one of Zurbach's severed fingers in her mouth, her muzzle red with blood.

38

THE TREES around the perimeter of Whispering Willows Cemetery rustled in the afternoon breeze, a gentle shhing that encouraged silence. Jackson and Chief Carroll stood across the grave from him, Decantor and Sloan behind them at even distances, their hands folded at their waists as if they were in military formation. Even Linda was there. Everyone clean and pressed, in suits and sunglasses. Most wearing gray.

He'd told them no black. It wouldn't have been right.

The headstone was simple but shiny, a gray granite that would have matched the shine in her hair. He didn't imagine Billie would want anything extravagant. He was ashamed that he didn't know precisely what she would want, but Jane and Candace had agreed that this seemed better—felt better —than any other alternative. No service. No speeches. No priest. Billie had been a woman of few words unless they really mattered, and here...nothing they could say would make a difference.

He bowed his head, and when he closed his eyes, he saw her face, not as it was in that basement, her cheeks stained by the pallor of death, but as it had been the last time they'd eaten dinner together, her eyebrow ring twinkling, her smile as she'd tucked her gray hair behind her ear—hair that he'd always joked about. But she'd known it was good-natured. She'd seen more than her share of really bad men, and she'd never believed him to be one of them.

She should have. Too late now.

He raised his head and let his gaze drift to the road beyond the wrought iron gates. So much blood here. But there was goodness out there, too, a heady peace you had to seek out. Had she felt it on the days they'd walked these blocks together, Duke panting happily between them? Perhaps at the dog park mere miles from here. Or the college. She'd had so much promise. Zurbach had stolen that away.

But Candace and Jane were still here, standing to his right. He'd told them they were better off moving on, finding another place—he'd even offered them start-up funds. Being associated with him seemed to be the nail in a great many coffins.

As if on cue, Candace squeezed his arm. They'd refused to move out. He'd signed the house over to them this morning, and they'd refused that too; said they were going to buy it from him. He could get behind that. Maybe people would still know they were associated, maybe not, but he could hope not. The risk to their lives might not be high, but it'd never be zero as long as he was around.

Yip! Yip!

Gigi wriggled in the crook of his left arm. Not an angry sound; her little tail beat frantically against his ribs. Why he'd chosen to take the old girl in he wasn't entirely sure, but then again, Duke had also been a surprise. And Gigi needed a home now that Zurbach was gone—the man would never see the light of day again, especially if someone accidentally let it slip that he'd taken a woman's child from her guts and left it to die.

Convicts had kids too. It was old news, an old creed, but that didn't make it any less accurate.

Yip! Yip!

Candace leaned across Petrosky and scratched Gigi's ears. "She needs a bath."

"I'll give her one later." She usually just sat on the floor of the shower while he shampooed his hair. She'd been skittish as fuck for the longest time, but not anymore, not since the day he'd laid on the floor for hours until she'd finally come to him. She'd been up his ass every day since, but he didn't really mind. She was a sweet little thing; she had probably just been scared of Zurbach. Without a logical reason to hate someone, humans rationalized those feelings away, as Zurbach's own daughter had for most of her life. But dogs knew. Dogs always knew.

His back went cold. He turned.

Shannon had been a silent presence at his side all morning, steadfast and warm, her arm around his waist or threaded through his elbow beneath Gigi's wagging ass. Now she stepped past him toward the grave. She kissed her fingers and knelt to press her fingertips to the stone.

Her suit was the color of Billie's eyes.

Shannon straightened, blocking his view of the gravesite for a moment, then returned to her position at his elbow. But in that span of seconds, the world had changed.

They were no longer alone.

Behind Decantor and Sloan, another group had arrived, spaced farther apart, but he could see all their features clearly. Ruby held a cup of coffee in her hand, her bright red lips a beacon in the dull afternoon. Billie stood beside her, silver hair gleaming, Duke panting happily at her heel.

The trees hissed. Heather smiled, the first woman he'd ever wanted to marry, but her head was intact once more, her purple jacket unmarred by blood and bone. And Julie, oh Julie; his daughter was spinning, her arms out at her sides, her face flushed and joyful—laughing. God, he'd missed her laugh, and…

His breath caught. Morrison. Taller than all of them, his muscular shoulders rising above the rest, his blue eyes sparkling in true surfer-boy style. Like the ocean. And in the space between Morrison and the gates of the cemetery, more, so many more. Women, children. People he'd fought for. People he'd lost. People he'd let die.

People he'd killed.

But Morrison held his gaze—*Don't look at them. Stay with me.*

Across the way, Jackson lowered her sunglasses for a beat and narrowed her eyes at him. She looked over her shoulder, then turned back with an eyebrow raised.

He nodded to her, and she replaced her glasses. Behind Jackson, Billie smiled and scratched Duke's ears.

"Petrosky? I think it's time." Shannon's hand was warm on his wrist.

He knelt by the gravesite, cradling Gigi against his chest. The headstone was cold, but not unpleasant, like a glass of water on a hot day. Across the cemetery, Billie waved at him. Duke wagged his tail. He dropped his gaze to the stone. "Goodbye, honey."

He pushed himself upright, and for once, his knees didn't hurt—for the moment, there was no pain. He looked beyond Jackson again as Morrison laid one hand on Julie's shoulder and the other on Billie's as if to say *I'll take care of them. Until you can.*

But Julie…she was crooking a finger at him. *Come on, Daddy!*

The world receded, all of it gray except those little pinpoints of color from his past. His chest—*fuck.* It squeezed, a bright heat radiating into his shoulders.

He cleared his throat and hugged Gigi tighter against him. *Time to go, girl.*

He kept his gaze on Morrison. And walked past Billie's grave, past his coworkers, until he was in their midst—beside his son. Morrison smiled. Petrosky blinked.

They vanished.

Calm washed over him all the same.

He didn't need to see them; each and every one was as much a part of him as his own flesh. He clutched Gigi and headed for the gates, the grass whispering against his jeans, and he could almost imagine it was all those he'd loved and lost, saying hello.

He smiled. No, they wouldn't leave him, not like the living. The dead stayed exactly as you remembered them, the way they made you feel imprinting on your soul over and over every time you let them surface. The pain that came with it was inconsequential.

Misery meant he was alive.

**Can't get enough Petrosky?
Find out where it all began! GET *SALVATION* AT
MEGHANOFLYNN.COM.**

**If you're looking for a new killer series to dive into,
check out Meghan's other killer thrillers and
bestselling standalone novels on
MEGHANOFLYNN.COM.**

Savage

"Dark, gritty, and raw, O'Flynn's work will take your
mind prisoner and keep you awake
far into the morning hours."
~*Bestselling Author Kristen Mae*

"From the feverishly surreal to the downright demented,
O'Flynn takes you on a twisted journey through the
deepest and darkest corners of the human mind."
~*Bestselling Author Mary Widdicks*

"With unbearable tension and gripping, thought-
provoking storytelling, O'Flynn explores fear in all the
best—and creepiest—ways. Masterful psychological
thrillers replete with staggering, unpredictable twists."
~*Bestselling Author Wendy Heard*

"Nobody writes with such compelling and entrancing
prose as O'Flynn. The perfectly executed twists and
expertly crafted web woven into this serial killer series
will captivate you. Born Bad is chilling, twisted, heart-
pounding suspense that kept me guessing all the way up to
the jaw-dropping conclusion. This is my new
favorite thriller series."
~*Bestselling Author Emerald O'Brien*

LEARN MORE AT MEGHANOFLYNN.COM

SALVATION

AN ASH PARK NOVEL

THE ASH PARK SERIES STARTS HERE.

Edward Petrosky joined the Ash Park police force with two goals in mind: escape the military and silence the demons that followed him home from the war. And no one soothes those traumas better than his fiancé, Heather—he doesn't even mind that she has a checkered past of her own.

But his dreams are obliterated when one night, on a routine call, Ed stumbles upon a scene as horrifying as any he's seen in combat: Heather's bloody body, half-buried in the snow. Though his superiors order him to stay away from the investigation, Ed can't help but notice the inconsistencies in Heather's case—her supposed cause of death doesn't mesh with what she's told him about her past.

When another body turns up, Ed realizes that Heather's murder wasn't an isolated act of violence; this new victim was connected to the same shelter where Heather volunteered and attended the same church where a kindly priest seems to know more about the murders than he should. And the detectives working the case seem indifferent to these links despite being no closer to finding Heather's killer.

Now Ed must choose whether to play by the rules or sacrifice his career to seek justice for the woman he was supposed to spend his life with. One thing's for certain: Ed can't go down without a fight, because Ed isn't the only one seeking vengeance.

And in Ash Park, the innocents aren't always who they appear to be.

THE FUCK you want to be, boy?

The drill sergeant's voice rang in Edward Petrosky's head, though it had been two years since he'd left the army, and six years since he'd had the question barked at him. Back then, the answer had been different. Even a year ago, he would have said "a cop," but that was more because it felt like an escape from the military, just like the Gulf War had been an escape from the loaded silence of his parents' house. But the urge to escape had passed. Now he would have said "Happy, sir," without a trace of irony. The future was shaping up to be good; better than the early nineties or the eighties, that was for damn sure.

Because of *her.*

Ed had met Heather six months before, in the spring before his twenty-fifth birthday, when the air in Ash Park still smelled like earthen death. Now he rolled over on the purple sheets she'd called "plum" and wrapped an arm over her shoulders, his gaze on the popcorn ceiling. A tiny half-smile played on her face with a strange twitch at one corner, almost a spasm, like her lips weren't sure whether to smile or frown. But the corners of her still-closed eyes were crinkled —definitely a smile. *Screw going out running.* The night he met her, she'd smiled like that. Barely forty degrees outside and she'd been taking off her leather coat, and by the time he rolled to a stop, she'd had the jacket wrapped around the homeless woman sitting on the walk. His last girlfriend used to stuff extra garlic bread in her purse when they went out to eat but refused to give even a quarter to the hungry, citing the degenerates' "lack of willpower." As if anyone would choose to starve.

Heather would never say something like that. Her breath was hot against his shoulder. Would his parents like her? He imagined driving the thirty minutes to Grosse Pointe for Thanksgiving next week, imagined sitting at their antique dining table, the one with the lace tablecloth that covered all the scars. "This is Heather," he'd say, and his father would nod, impassive, while his mother stiffly offered coffee, her steel-blue eyes silently judging, her lips pressed into a tight, bloodless line. His parents would ask thinly veiled questions, hoping Heather came from money—she didn't—hoping she'd make a good housewife or that she had dreams of becoming a teacher; of course, only until she bore his children. Dark ages shit. His parents didn't even like Hendrix, and that was saying something. You could get a read on anyone by asking their opinion on Jimi.

Ed planned to tell his folks Heather was self-employed and leave it at that. He'd not mention that he met her during a prostitution sting, or that the first bracelet he put on her wrist was made of steel. Some might argue that the start of a great love story couldn't possibly involve prostitution and near-hypothermia, but they'd be wrong.

Besides, if he hadn't put Heather in his squad car, one of the other units would have. Another time, another girl, he might have responded differently, but she'd been sniffling, crying so hard he could hear her teeth chattering. "You okay?" he had asked. "Do you need a drink of water or a tissue?" But when he glanced in the rearview of the squad car, her cheeks had been wet, her hands frantically rubbing her arms, and he'd realized her shaking was more from the cold.

Heather stretched now with a noise that was half groan, half meow, and snuggled farther under the covers. Ed smiled, letting his gaze drift past her shoulder and to his uniform on the chair in the corner. He still couldn't believe he'd uncuffed her in the supercenter parking lot and then left her sitting in the heated car while he headed into the store alone. When he came back with a thick yellow coat, her eyes had filled, and she'd smiled at him again in a way that made his heart feel four sizes bigger, made him feel taller like he was a hero and not the man who'd just tried to arrest her. They'd talked for hours after that, her whispering at first and looking out the windows like she could get in trouble just for speaking. She hadn't told him then that she hated yellow—he'd found out later. Not like there'd been a ton of options at that off-the-freeway supercenter anyway.

Ed let his vision relax, his black uniform blurring against the chair. Heather had told him she'd never talked to anyone that way before, so open, so easily, like they'd known each other forever. Then again, she'd also said it was the first time she'd ever walked the streets; the odds of that were slim, but Ed didn't care. If a person's past defined them, then he was a murderer; killing someone during wartime didn't make them any less dead. He and Heather were both starting over.

Heather moaned gently again and shifted closer to him, her light eyes hooded in the dimness. He brushed away the single mahogany tendril plastered to her forehead, accidentally snagging his calloused finger on the corner of the notebook under her pillow—she must have stayed up writing notes about the wedding again.

"Thanks for going with me yesterday," she whispered, her voice husky with sleep.

"No problem." They'd taken her father, Donald, to the grocery store, Donald's gnarled fingers shaking every time

Ed looked down at the wheelchair. Congestive heart failure, arthritis—the man was a mess, hadn't been able to walk more than a few feet for over a decade, and by all accounts, shouldn't be alive now; usually, congestive heart failure took out its victims within five years. One more reason to get out of the house and enjoy each day, Heather always said. And they'd tried, even taken her father to the dog park, where the old man's miniature Doberman pinscher had yapped and run around Ed's ankles until Ed picked him up and scratched his fuzzy head.

He lowered himself to the pillow beside her, and she trailed her fingers over the hard muscles of his arm and across his chest, then nestled her head into his neck. Her hair still smelled like incense from church last night: spicy and sweet with the bitter hint of char over the gardenia shampoo she used. The church services and Donald's weekly bingo game were the only outings that Petrosky begged off. Something about that church bothered Ed. His own family wasn't particularly religious, but he didn't think that was the problem; maybe it was how the pope wore fancy hats and golden briefs, while less fortunate folks starved. At least Father Norman, Heather's priest, gave as well as he got. Two weeks before, Petrosky and Heather had taken three garbage bags of clothes and shoes the father had collected to the homeless shelter where Heather volunteered. Then they'd made love in the newly empty back seat of his car. What woman could resist an old Grand Am with squealing brakes and an interior that stank of exhaust?

Heather kissed his neck just below his ear and sighed. "Daddy loves you, you know," she said. Her voice had the same raspy quality as the frigid autumn air that rustled the branches outside.

"Eh, he just thinks I'm a good guy because I volunteer at the shelter." Which Ed didn't. But weeks before Ed met the man, Heather told her dad that she and Ed worked at the shelter together, and even after he and Donald were introduced, she hadn't told her father they were dating. He could understand that though—the man was strict, especially about his only daughter, another parent from the "spare the rod, spoil the child" era. Like Ed's own father.

A curl fell into her eye, and she blew it away. "He thinks you guys have a lot in common."

Donald and Ed spent most of their time together talking about their posts in Vietnam and Kuwait, respectively, but they'd never discussed exactly what they'd done. Ed assumed this was another reason Donald liked Father Norman; the priest had been a soldier before he joined up with the church, and nothing turned men into brothers like the horrors of the battlefield. "I like your father too. And the offer is still open: if he needs a place to stay, we can take care of him here."

She shifted her weight, and gardenia and incense wafted into his nostrils again. "I know, and you're sweet for offering, but we don't need to do that."

But they would, eventually. Unease prickled deep in the back of Ed's brain, a little icicle of frost that spread down into the marrow of his spine. Donald had worked at the post office after the war, through Heather's early childhood, and through his wife's suicide, but his heart had put him out of commission when Heather was a teenager. The man had squirreled some money away, but if Heather had been desperate enough to sell her body, Donald's carefully laid nest egg must have been running out. "Heather, we might—"

"He'll be fine. I've been saving since my mom died, just in case. He has more than enough to support him until he…goes."

If she has all this money, why go out on the street? "But—"

She covered his mouth with hers, and he put his hand on her lower back and pulled her tighter against him. Was living in his own place her father's way to maintain independence? Or was it Heather's? Either way, intuition told him not to push it, and the military had taught him to listen to his gut. Her father was one subject Heather rarely broached. Probably why Ed hadn't known his relationship with Heather was a secret...until he'd let it slip. And the next day, he'd come home from work, and Heather's things were in his bedroom. *It's perfect for us, Ed. Can I stay?*

Forever, he'd said. *Forever.*

Were they moving too fast? He wasn't complaining, didn't want some long, drawn-out courtship, but it had only been six months, and he never wanted Heather to give him the same look his mother always gave his father: *God, why are you still alive? Go ahead and die already so I can have a few happy years alone before I kick off.*

"Are you happy here?" he asked her. "With me?" Maybe they should slow things down just a little. But Heather smiled in that twitchy, spastic way of hers, and his chest warmed, the icicle in his spine melting. He was sure. His gut said, "For god's sake, marry her already."

"Happier than I've ever been," she said.

Ed kissed the top of her head, and as she arched against him, he smiled in the subtle gray of the dawn. Everything smelled sweeter when you were twenty-five and done with active duty in the sand, when every path was still yours for the taking. He'd seen some shit, god knew he had, and it still came to him at night: the horror of comrades shot dead beside him, the burning smog of gunpowder in the air, the tang of blood. But all that seemed so damn far away these days, as if coming home had turned him into someone else, someone who'd never been a soldier at all—all that military shit was someone else's baggage.

He traced the gentle curve of Heather's spine and let the porcelain sheen of her skin in the dusky morning erase the last remnants of memory. Even with the streets covered in slush that froze your toes the moment you stepped outside, her smile—that quirky little smile—always warmed him up.

Yes, this year was going to be the best of Ed's life. He could feel it.

GET *SALVATION* AT MEGHANOFLYNN.COM.

"WICKEDLY ENTERTAINING . . . A PERFECT ADDITION TO THE ASH PARK SERIES, AND EVERY BIT AS SHOCKING."
~*BESTSELLING AUTHOR KRISTEN MAE*

DEADLY WORDS

A BORN BAD NOVEL (#1)

CHAPTER 1

THE NAME'S POPPY, Poppy Pratt, and I'm at your service, though I'll be the first to admit that I'm not always so agreeable.

It's in my nature I suppose, and always has been—that fire I keep hidden within me is in my blood. Dad says it's like air, like water, anything that sits there unnoticed until you don't have it anymore. I don't have a single reason to disbelieve him.

I think we're all one step from a storm if we don't get what we need, but I guess that makes it sound more intense than it is. You won't find maniacs here, frothing at the mouth —we aren't those people.

Maniac adjacent, maybe, but only if you believe the gossip around town. The gossip is not about us, though; it's never about us. It's about the "deserters"—the folks who leave this or any of the other nearby towns looking for something better. This is the kind of place people move on from—they find a job, they find love, they drive away as fast as they can. It's not a shock that anyone might up and disappear, so most of the gossips cluck their tongues, but they don't worry about the deserters. They don't know they should.

I know more than most people. I can read the high school books, even if I'm not allowed to in my elementary classes, and the education I get at home…well, that's a different kind of smart.

I rest my elbows on the railing of our narrow back porch, the wood already wet, little slivers embedding themselves in my forearms. I like the way it feels, damp and prickly—like *something*. *Thrashy*. I made that word up when I was smaller to describe the way some things get through your defenses against your will, stabbing at your soft spots. I don't think my father likes the word much. That's why he bought me a dictionary, then a thesaurus. He doesn't like anything he's on the outside of, and here, in this house, the things you don't know can be dangerous.

I press my arms harder against the wood, letting the slivers prick, letting them stab—*thrashy, thrashy, thrashy*. Acres of glistening grass stare back at me. Beyond the green, the sky cuts the horizon with a wound of deep indigo that looks like a mark left by a good whipping. I wouldn't know from personal experience—my father would *never* hit me— but almost every other child I know bears the scars of their parents' rage. It's no wonder people leave here.

The wood of the shed is damp, too, I can tell by the darker color along the slab. What little remains of twilight glows against the west-facing boards and paints the roses that bloom around the building with a grayed blush of color. The single window is a hazy black.

The wind brushes silky fingers through my hair, but there's electricity in the clouds tonight—not just rain. We're going to get a storm. Just as well—it happens all the time down here in Alabama, one hurricane after another some years—but this'll be a soupy wet trek toward a flood, and that's worse than the wind. Torrential rains took out our shed one year, the water rising over the concrete slab, picking up the lower boards like it was going to lift the thing clean off like a newfangled Noah's Ark. I stood in the door-way, Dad's arm warm at my side, and imagined myself climbing aboard, my blond curls like corkscrews in the breeze, setting sail for somewhere else. Anywhere else.

That was a bad year. Until we rebuilt the shed. That's the thing about life, about all things that fall apart, that crumble under pressure: they can't stay crumbled. Not when they're up against me. Nature gave me glue, too, and I don't break easy.

I blink. The light in the shed goes on, and the glass of the single window glares at me from the other side of the yard, the path to the shed glowing a hazy reddish-orange. Tepid. Watered-down.

It still looks like blood.

GET *DEADLY WORDS* AT MEGHANOFLYNN.COM!

"Brilliant, dark, and impossible to put down. O'Flynn masterfully crafts a twisted tale of buried secrets in *Deadly Words*. Poppy is unforgettable—unlike any character you've read before. This is storytelling at its finest, and will sit with you long after you've turned the final page. Get this on your must-read list now!"

~*Bestselling author Emerald O'Brien*

THE FLOOD

**Seven people. A locked storm shelter.
Inevitable starvation.
WHAT COULD YOU DO TO SURVIVE?**

VICTORIA LARSON AND HER HUSBAND, Chad, are sitting on their rooftop, waiting for the end. For three days, they've watched their coastal Louisiana town turn into a lake, battered by an unprecedented series of hurricanes. With the levees obliterated, the waters rise higher and higher—the next storm is sure to swallow their house whole.

Just when all hope seems lost, a rescue boat emerges through the driving rain; a woman named Windy plucks them from their roof and motors them to a waterproof bunker—to safety. There, with a ragtag group of other evacuees, Victoria and Chad bed down and prepare to wait out the storms.

But it isn't long before Victoria notices a few things seem...off. The cement bunker has a door that locks from the outside. Many of the boxes of food don't contain food at all.

The bottles of water smell like rubbing alcohol. And everyone in the group has a secret; even Victoria's own estranged husband seems to have known their captor prior to making the trek to the shelter. And some of her fellow evacuees are far too intent on defending the woman who locked them in this dungeon. Are they really storm victims like Victoria? Or are they accomplices in a sick game?

One thing is certain: none of them will survive if they can't find something to eat. And if the stories the others tell about Windy are any indication, Victoria suspects their captor's plans are far more evil than simply watching them die of malnourishment.

The blade Windy gave her is proof enough of that.

And it won't be long until starvation devours the last of Victoria's sanity.

GET *THE FLOOD* AT MEGHANOFLYNN.COM!

CHAPTER 1

VICTORIA COULD ALMOST SEE IT: the way the cotton pillow would pucker around her fists as she clamped it over his face, how the misshapen lump beneath would wriggle as he tried to force air through the goose feathers, how everything would lapse into silence, nothing to break the stillness but her hushed exhale of relief. On any normal evening, at least. Now, the night breathed wetly, almost as loudly as he did, a thick swooshing against her eardrums. Viscous. Raindrops *plink*, *plink*, *plink*-ed against her soaked hair. The shingles caught the skin on the backs of her legs sharply no matter how she tried not to move, like being slowly ground to dust by sandpaper, and water stung in every scrape. Victoria inhaled in the soupy night, stifling her gag reflex when the musky, acidic stench of shit hit her. Her muscles cramped harder. The sound of the rain against the lake of sewage around them was a constant reminder: they were going to die.

Three days they'd been stranded so far, sitting on top of Chad's family home, separated from the nearest dwelling by a mile of farmland and animal pastures. Three days of not eating, of her belly twisting and angry. Three days of filling her hands with rainwater to avoid dying of thirst.

Three days on the roof with the husband she'd been planning to leave.

The forecasters had said it was a long shot, the storm hitting here, and an even longer shot that the enormous storm systems out in the Atlantic would build in strength and aim themselves at their little low-flood-plain section of Louisiana. *That would be ridiculous*, they'd insisted, *unprecedented*. And they'd all been wrong, especially that twit on the news with his gray hair, his eyes an odd purple-blue that didn't exist in nature—"Probably won't be more than a category two, and a little rain the week after," he'd said. Bullshit. And now all the people who'd stayed were fucked. Totally, one hundred percent fucked. *We should have left.* That would have been the rational thing to do, *honey*, the logical thing.

Her heart seized, her stomach cramping too, a burning knot of hunger. Her lungs were far too small. But panicking made you stop thinking clearly—it could only make things worse. She forced air through her mouth as loudly as possible, drowning out the sound of the storm and Chad's equally labored breath. But not his words.

"Are you okay, Vicky?" He said it in a high voice, almost sing-song, the kind of voice he'd use to ask one of his students about a skinned knee.

Victoria wiped her wet hair from her forehead and tried

to relax the painful knot in her guts. Raindrops tapped against her flesh, incessant, like a petulant child. The gray of Chad's irises seemed darker than usual in a world haunted by yesterday's storms and pregnant with electricity and anticipation of the second hurricane. She wished they had a radio, a cell phone to check the status of the upcoming storm, but their electronics had been impossible to keep dry. Their phones were sitting on the roof somewhere near the chimney, useless. *Why the fuck did I listen to you?* She turned away from Chad. Couldn't stand to see the guilt in his eyes, like she was supposed to make him feel better.

Chad always felt awful if he gave someone bad advice—he'd once teared up when he realized he'd given a stranger the wrong directions—but he had this way of convincing people not to bitch at him by making them feel guilty or sorry for him. That wasn't going to last. If they stayed on this roof much longer, he was going to get an earful.

In her peripheral vision, off the edge of the roof, the shitty, brackish water rippled like the skin of an enormous serpent, oily scales shivering with the anticipation of finishing them off. Half a block down, the broken post that used to hold their street sign stabbed through the surface of the filth. And to her other side loomed the muscly bulk of the chimney, topped with the grate she'd installed to keep the animals out, now ripped open like snapped metal ribs—some creature had been at it. Maybe whatever had clawed it apart was still there, lurking in the brick tunnel, drowned and bloated, tenderizing in the sea of bacteria.

Her throat closed. She forced it open. Her black leather work boot tap-tap-tapped against the soggy shingles. She tugged on her cut-off shorts, then the hem of her favorite black T-shirt, so dark she couldn't see the film of dirt and wet. The water was still rising, the red of the shingled roof so dark it looked like drying blood, and some of it probably was—Chad had a gash across his shin from a torn aluminum gutter. Behind Chad, the expanse of sky darkened, threatening, and the rush of rain on water seemed suddenly louder; she felt sure he wouldn't be able to hear her unless she yelled. But she said nothing. There was nothing to say.

If only they lived somewhere else, somewhere higher, somewhere the earth wasn't perpetually soggy from April to August, somewhere with some semblance of civilization. All they had in this section of Fossé, Louisiana was the community college, but that was over an hour away by car—and the levees had failed, leaving the paved roads leading to the college impassable by car or truck. The college itself would be underwater too before the week was out, especially if this storm didn't move on, or the second hurricane hit as hard as they'd been saying. And if the next storm hit while the citizens of Fossé were on their roofs... The winds would rip over the flooded streets, tearing shingles and people alike from the tops of their homes, flinging them against the treetops, impaling them on the remains of fences or drowning them in the sewage from overflowing septic tanks. Even if it did pass quickly, the water table was so high that people would be stuck for weeks. No power. No food. No drinkable water once the rain stopped. These might be her last days on this earth, and she and Chad should not be living their final hours together.

They'd been inhabiting their own little worlds for months now, independent planets merely circling the same sun. Even now he was staring out over the water, waiting passively for someone else to come to their rescue, though for once, she had no other ideas herself. They weren't going to swim twenty miles, and the waste products from the farmland—pig and chicken shit—were rife with E. coli and salmonella and other antibiotic-resistant bacteria that would spread through their injuries into their blood before they got to safety. Sepsis. That'd be a fun way to go out. Better than drowning though—she'd done that once, and once was enough.

The rain spit, water on water. The wind howled, an angry beast bellowing from the sky. The expanse of water pulled her gaze, but she refused to look at it, like it was a monster that could only exist if she let herself notice. Victoria shivered.

"Is there more peroxide?" Chad said.

"It's gone."

She sat back on the gritty shingles and turned away from him, squeezing her eyes closed, forcing the sound of the rain and the image of the storm from her mind. But in the blind starbursts of light behind her eyelids, she saw her parents' Chicago apartment and the square of afternoon sunlight that hit the living room floor when the sun snuck between the neighboring buildings. She and her twin brother Phillip used to sit on that little spot whenever they could, which wasn't often—usually the room was occupied, her father out there screaming at her mother, or screaming at Phillip for stealing money, and later for taking their mother's painkillers. Once she'd tried to help and ended up in the emergency room with a broken rib. Phillip had held her hand the whole way there, sung her songs, refused to let go even when the nurses came to ask her questions about her "fall."

Why the fuck am I thinking about this now? But she always thought about Phillip when she was stressed. He was like…a teddy bear, the memory of his voice somehow comforting. Illogical, sure, but everyone was entitled to one foolish, illogical thing. Better than Chad's foolishness—his was going to get them killed.

She leaned back, resting her head against the sandpapery shingles.

You're going to be okay, Victoria, you know that.

Her brother had said that just before he left Chicago for good. That was why she'd come to Louisiana in the first place, Phillip's last known address—she'd hoped their twin connection would help her do what a PI couldn't. She'd been wrong, yet she'd stayed—too long. Ten years now, fourteen since she'd seen her brother. She did get occasional postcards from him, pictures of historical spots around Louisiana, little notes on the back like "I hope you're doing well. I'm still working on 'well'. See you when I manage to get there." Those cards ripped her wounds open every time, kept her up hearing the words in her brain, his voice whispering to her while she tried to sleep. She could help him. If he'd just fucking *call*.

"Hey!"

Her eyes snapped open. Chad scuttled to his feet, the grating sound ringing through the night as he slid on the gritty roof tiles. The sky was pitch as tar, not even a glimmer of haze on the horizon. Oh god, how long had she been out? Was the next storm here? She'd slept through the last dregs of light leaving the sky. But she didn't feel the harsh gusts of wind, didn't see flying debris, only Chad's silhouette, and she'd not have seen him at all were it not for...

The light.

Far out over the water, a hazy circle swept first one way, then the other, the rippling muck glittering like yellow diamonds in its wake.

Victoria pushed herself to standing, but the roof was slick despite the grit; her foot slid from beneath her and she went down hard on her knees, scrabbling at the tile with her fingernails, cursing under her breath at the wretched shingles.

"Hey!" Chad cried, waving his arms. "Over here!"

The light glided back and forth, back and forth, and only then did she realize the whoosh of rain was muddling the noises around them. She'd become so accustomed to the patter and slap of rain that it had all but vanished from her awareness, but now, looking over the water...the night was *loud,* the wind screaming, the rain hissing into the muck around their little island of house. They'd disappear into the landscape if they couldn't overcome it, and...the water was higher than it had been just hours ago, the ripples licking at the base of the gutters. A few more hours and the nasty water would creep over the shingles, and then—

"Help!" she yelled, still on her hands and knees. The roof and the water went black again as the light swept away off to her left, then to the far side of the boat—the opposite direction. *They can't hear us.* She planted her feet. *Stand up, stand up! Yell louder!* She inhaled once through her nose, put her hands on her thighs, and heaved herself to standing. "We're out here!"

"This way! Hey, help us!"

"Over here!" Her throat ached, her eyes stinging with rain and unshed tears, but the light swept toward them once more. The beam hovered—and stayed. The sound of a motor cut the night.

They were coming to help. Hopefully, they had a place to ride out the storm.

GET *THE FLOOD* AT MEGHANOFLYNN.COM!

"Intense. Feral. Deliciously unhinged."
~Bestselling Author Kristen Mae

Want more from Meghan?
https://meghanoflynn.com

ABOUT THE AUTHOR

With books deemed "visceral, haunting, and fully immersive" (*New York Times bestseller, Andra Watkins*), Meghan O'Flynn has made her mark on the thriller genre. Meghan is a clinical therapist who draws her character inspiration from her knowledge of the human psyche. She is the bestselling author of gritty crime novels and serial killer thrillers, all of which take readers on the dark, gripping, and unputdown-able journey for which Meghan is notorious. Learn more at https://meghanoflynn.com! While you're there, join Meghan's reader group, and get a **FREE SHORT STORY** just for signing up.

Want to connect with Meghan?
https://meghanoflynn.com